WISH YOU WERE ITALIAN

The  line

Wish You Were Italian
by Kristin Rae

Fool Me Twice
by Mandy Hubbard

Not in the Script
by Amy Finnegan
(coming soon)

WISH YOU WERE ITALIAN

An IF ONLY *novel*

Kristin Rae

BLOOMSBURY
NEW YORK LONDON NEW DELHI SYDNEY

First published in the United States of America in May 2014
by Bloomsbury Children's Books
www.bloomsbury.com

Bloomsbury is a registered trademark of Bloomsbury Publishing Plc

For information about permission to reproduce selections from this book, write to Permissions, Bloomsbury Children's Books, 1385 Broadway, New York, New York 10018
Bloomsbury books may be purchased for business or promotional use. For information on bulk purchases please contact Macmillan Corporate and Premium Sales Department at specialmarkets@macmillan.com

Library of Congress Cataloging-in-Publication Data
Rae, Kristin.
Wish you were Italian : an If only novel / Kristin Rae.
pages cm
Summary: Seventeen-year-old Pippa Preston, sent to Italy for a three-month art history program, decides instead to see the country on her own, armed with a list of such goals as eating an entire pizza and falling in love with an Italian, but soon finds herself attracted both to a dangerous local boy and an American archaeology student.
ISBN 978-1-61963-286-8 (paperback) • ISBN 978-1-61963-285-1 (hardcover)
ISBN 978-1-61963-287-5 (e-book)
[1. Voyages and travels—Fiction. 2. Love—Fiction. 3. Italy—Fiction.] I. Title.
PZ7.R12313Wis 2014 [Fic]—dc23 2013044591

Book design by Amanda Bartlett
Typeset by Westchester Book Composition
Printed and bound in the U.S.A. by Thomson-Shore Inc., Dexter, Michigan
2 4 6 8 10 9 7 5 3 1 (paperback)
2 4 6 8 10 9 7 5 3 1 (hardcover)

All papers used by Bloomsbury Publishing, Inc., are natural, recyclable products made from wood grown in well-managed forests. The manufacturing processes conform to the environmental regulations of the country of origin.

For Mom and Grandma Rosie

WISH YOU WERE ITALIAN

CHAPTER ONE

You can do this. You want *to go to Italy.*

By yourself.

Outside the terminal window, the plane that will take me to my connection in Newark taxis up to the gate. Thirty minutes until they board first class. As if a big reclining seat and hot towels could make me forgive Mom any faster.

My hand cramps from white-knuckling the journal my best friend gave me when she dropped me off. I untie the string and flip open the front cover, smiling as I take in the first page decorated with red and green doodles and Pippa's Italian Summer in bubble letters nestled in the center. The next page is a note in her handwriting:

I know you're still angry this was all forced on you without much warning, but you really are going to have fun. YOU'RE

GOING TO ITALY! Think of all the fantabulous pictures you'll take! Of the food you'll eat! Of the hot Italian boys you'll see! All I ask is that you bring back a calendar for my locker this year (and maybe one of those hot Italian boys).

Since I can't be with you on your fab jaunt across the Pond (that's not sarcasm, it's jealousy), I've constructed a book of activities for you, all geared toward the documentation of your summer. I might ask you to write, draw, smear dirt on the page. You never know! The important thing is that you have to do EVERYTHING I tell you to because I spent all freaking week making this for you.

Love you, and I'll miss you!

—Morgan

My eyes sting. Looks like I won't have to be without her on this trip after all. I take a sip of Sprite and swipe my eyes with the back of my hand before turning the page to face my first task.

ASSIGNMENT NUMERO UNO: THE LIST

Write out a list of 10 goals for your summer while in Italy. Each of these goals must be accomplished IN FULL before you even think about setting foot back home. And . . . GO!

Ten goals? The only things coming to mind are fears. Accidentally doing something illegal . . . embarrassing myself in front of the locals. I shudder as I write:

* Don't get arrested
* Don't make a fool of myself in public

A worthy goal, though knowing me, it has the potential for failure. I'm not sure what I'll be allowed to do outside the snoozer of an art program I'll be attending, so I dream up things I'd like to do if given the chance.

* Get my picture taken at the Colosseum
* Find random souvenir for Morgan
* Get a makeover
* See Pompeii
* Swim in the Mediterranean Sea
* Have a conversation with someone in only Italian
* Eat a whole pizza in one sitting

I read back through the list and sigh at my lack of originality. I have to throw in something major. Something crazy.

The Italian couple behind me starts chatting and I close my eyes as the rhythm of their language washes over me. In only a handful of hours, I'll be immersed in a sea of people speaking this way. I'm not even there yet, and I already know I'll miss it when summer ends. Not the confusion of the language barrier, but the beauty of the way it sounds. If only there was a way to bottle that up and bring it back with me.

Wait.

I snicker out loud as my pen glides across the page. My final goal:

* Fall in love with an Italian

CHAPTER TWO

There are eyes on me. I can feel them. I must be a sight—a lanky seventeen-year-old with a very full and heavy backpack, a camera bag strapped across her chest, an obnoxiously feminine rolling suitcase, bloodshot eyes, and no idea where to go next. I make a point to stand up straighter and hold my head higher, but that makes me feel a bit too much like my mother, so I settle for relatively lost and observant.

A whistle rings out near me, followed by a "*Ciao, Bella!*"

A group of teenage boys waves fervently at me. Real Italians! And of course they're all gorgeous. I can't help grinning as I pass them. The potential for an extraordinary summer is definitely here, which is something I wouldn't have admitted a week ago.

As I walk through the automatic doors and step outside, I expect to see old buildings and ruins right away, confirming that

I'm actually in Rome, but it looks like every other passenger-pickup area. There's a long row of middle-aged men smoking cigarettes and chatting with one another, halfheartedly holding up little white signs with names printed or scrawled across them.

I manage to find a sign that says PIPPA PRESTON at the far right of the line. The man's light-blue polo shirt is clean, loose at his shoulders but snug around his gut. He seems awfully tan for a taxi driver.

I clear my throat and bite back my nerves, silently praying he speaks English.

"I'm Pippa Preston."

He blinks a few times, so I point to the sign.

"That's me."

He takes in my appearance and suddenly I'm self-conscious. A smile finally stretches his wrinkles and he wheels my suitcase toward the long line of taxis, stopping at a smallish red van. I climb in and quickly pull the phrase book out of my backpack and flip through it. Heat rushes to my cheeks as I imagine myself trying to speak Italian to an actual Italian and not just through the little headset that came with my Rosetta Stone software. I have no idea what to do, what to say—if he even expects me to speak to him at all.

I'm practicing *Non parlo l'Italiano*—I don't speak Italian—in my head as he pulls himself up into the driver's seat and turns to me.

"Where would you like to go, *Signorina*?"

A couple of thoughts pulse through my brain at once: *He speaks English!* and *Why doesn't he know where he's supposed to take me?*

I'm relatively sure I'm supposed to go to the train station, seeing as how I'm in Rome and the art program is in Florence, or Firenze, according to my booklet.

I hold up a finger and say, "Just a minute," as I search for the folder with all the important info. The driver faces forward, clicks on the meter, and whistles along to the radio.

I locate the folder, but as I open it, an envelope I hadn't packed slides out. On the outside is a note in Dad's chicken-scratch. For some reason, he doesn't write lowercase letters, so I always feel like I'm being yelled at even when he writes I LOVE YOU. I scan the note.

PIPPERS,

I KNOW STUDYING ART HISTORY ISN'T WHAT YOU HAD PLANNED FOR YOUR SUMMER. YOU KNOW YOUR MOTHER AND HER VISION FOR THE ART GALLERY. ONCE SHE GETS HER MIND ON SOMETHING, THAT'S THE WAY IT IS. ON THE BRIGHT SIDE, YOU FINALLY GET TO SEE ITALY!

OPEN YOUR MIND TO IT. MAKE SOME FRIENDS, TAKE LOTS OF PICTURES! I'VE ENCLOSED A LITTLE SOMETHING FOR YOU. THIS IS JUST FROM ME SO DON'T MENTION IT TO YOUR MOTHER. I DON'T WANT YOU TO HAVE TO WORRY ABOUT ANYTHING WHILE YOU'RE AWAY, SO HOPEFULLY THIS WILL HELP. EUROS ARE VERY EASY TO

USE, AND EVERYTHING IS LABELED CLEARLY. I'M PROUD OF YOU, AND I KNOW YOU'RE RESPONSIBLE ENOUGH TO HANDLE THIS (THE MONEY AND THE EXPERIENCE).

LOVE YOU,
DAD

I peek inside the envelope and my pulse pounds in my ears. He doesn't want me to worry about anything, so he gives me who-knows-how-much money, in *cash*? Someone sure was feeling guilty about this trip. I thumb through the rainbow-colored euro bills. Most of them are hundreds, but there are some smaller ones thrown in too. There must be a couple grand here.

The driver is in his own world, still whistle-humming along to Lady Gaga, the meter ticking away. As inconspicuously as possible, I pull out a hundred and a handful of the smaller bills for my wallet, then shove the envelope down to the depths of my backpack.

Looking over my itinerary for instructions, I see that I'm supposed to head straight for the train station, or *stazione*. More traveling. Awesome.

But the Colosseum is *here*.

I'm also supposed to report to an Antonia Conti upon my arrival, and classes start on Wednesday at nine in the morning. Wednesday? Today's only Saturday. Surely I have a few days to spare.

And the Trevi Fountain is *here*. And the Pantheon.

I glance at the meter, my fare climbing steadily.

The electric current of excitement radiates from my envelope full of euros. They want to be spent—it's what they were made for, after all.

I'm in Italy. Alone. With cash.

I can go anywhere I want.

CHAPTER THREE

It's summer in one of the most popular vacation destinations in the world, so I don't know why I'm surprised the hotel I randomly selected is full. My cab driver is probably halfway back to the airport by now, and I'm left to be my own translator.

The woman working behind the counter—nametag says Patrizia—looks more like a runway model than a concierge. Her rich mahogany hair even has a life of its own, while mine's pretty much the same color as dirt. I might need to meet that makeover goal ASAP.

Patrizia must be able to tell how exhausted I am, because she leads me to a couch in the lounge and brings me several chocolate pastries and a glass of orange juice. She makes sure I'm eating—like I'd say no to a chocolate pastry—and calls around to check availability for me. A few minutes and several intense-sounding phone conversations later, she points to a dot on a fancy paper map with scalloped edges.

"Room here," she says, proceeding to draw a line of the route. It doesn't look too far.

I stand, taking the map from her, and manage to get out a comprehensible "*Grazie*," which my *Rick Steves' Phrase Book* says is actually pronounced ***graht**-seeay.* Who knew? She smiles again and everything seems to be perfect until I lose my mind and give her a slight bow. I'm in *Europe*, not Asia.

I should have asked for a cab, because after about twenty minutes of dragging my overpacked suitcase behind me, my head is pounding and my legs feel like they want to give. The cobblestone street I'm navigating narrows a little and the tall, rustic buildings seem to close in around and overtop of me. A few noisy Vespas whiz past, the high-pitch squeal from their motors echoing off the nearby walls, and the crowd around me presses in to get out of the way.

Please let me be close. I really need to lie down.

I notice a line of people waiting to get into a storefront to my right. Affixed to the window is a large multicolored palm tree encircled with the best piece of news since I landed: Della Palma. *Gelato di Roma.* Customers swarm the long freezer that curves around the perimeter of the room. There must be a hundred flavors of Italian ice cream.

Mouth watering, I pull a pen out of the front pocket of my backpack and draw a big star on the map where I think I am. *I'll come back for you.*

Reluctantly, I trudge forward, now completely aware of how insanely hot it is. I'm almost there . . . I think. The hotel should be right behind—*holy crap!*

The Pantheon.

I stop in my tracks to look up, completely disrupting the flow of tourist traffic. It's directly in front of me, in all its ancient glory. Probably one of the most immense structures I've ever seen. Skyscrapers don't count—nothing modern counts. Nothing made in the last five hundred years counts against this monster, because this was built, like, two thousand years ago and it's *still* here.

With the grace of a zombie, I make my way closer to inspect it. The giant stone pillars are even taller than I expected. From a distance, the whole building looked like it was carved out of a giant rock, but now that I'm only ten feet away, I see innumerable faded red bricks. I had no idea we've been building things the same way for thousands of years.

I'm so uncultured. I know nothing about everything.

This trip is going to change that.

My room at the Albergo Santa Chiara is small but clean. And expensive. I can't stay here too many nights or I'll burn through half my money stash. I pile all my stuff on the luggage rack and let out a sigh of relief. The bathroom appears clean and, thankfully, normal. Although there are two toilets right next to each other. Wait. One is definitely a toilet, but the other contraption is trying to be. It doesn't exactly look sanitary. I'll be staying away from that.

Now that I have a minute alone with my thoughts, a wave of anxiety finally materializes. I'm not where I'm supposed to be. I need some sort of plan. How much do I tell the parental units? How many days can I get away with exploring Rome before I absolutely have to get on a train to Florence?

I decide to shower and test out the bed for half an hour before making solid decisions about contacting anyone. I put on a tank top and pajama shorts, and sprawl out as much as I can on the Barbie-size bed.

Muffled laughter from the hall forces my eyes open, and it takes me a minute to remember exactly where I am. I could have slept for seconds or hours. Unless it's hiding somewhere, the room doesn't have a clock, so I pull out my computer and let it boot up.

"Four-thirty?" I screech. I slept for six hours.

I wonder if actually calling my parents could somehow incriminate me. The caller ID probably wouldn't say Hotel in Rome, Italy, but it might say something I don't want them seeing. Clearly, I have no experience in this area. I mean, I may have stretched the truth once or twice about my whereabouts, who hasn't? But this is far beyond anything I've ever pulled.

I splurged on twenty-four hours of Internet when I checked in, ten minutes of which I wasted trying to figure out where to plug the Ethernet cable into the wall and my computer. Seriously old school.

Mom almost has OCD when it comes to checking her e-mail, so I sign into my account and send this message:

To: Mary Preston <m.preston@prestonartsource.com>
From: Pippa Preston <pippers26@gmail.com>
Subject: Ciao from Italy

Well, I'm here and I'm wiped out. Going to bed after I get something to eat. Things don't officially start until

Wednesday (as you already know), so the plan is to get acclimated and see some of the sights until then. I'll check back in later this week.

Tell Dad and Gram hi for me.

Pippa

I read back through it quickly before hitting send. No hint of excitement, which is good, because I don't want her to have any clue there's a grin plastered to my face. And I didn't lie, technically.

While I'm at it, I compose an e-mail to Morgan too.

To: Morgan Arrant <queenofdrama14@gmail.com>
From: Pippa Preston <pippers26@gmail.com>
Subject: I'm in freaking ITALY

And it's HOTTER than Ryan Reynolds over here! Seriously, sweltering. Ugh. I haven't seen much yet, but I can tell you that Italians are ALL tan and they have fashion models working in their hotels. I'm making it one of my goals this summer to get a makeover.

And about these goals, seriously, girl, I don't even know what to say. That whole journal is made of awesome. Just like you. I already miss you.

Okay, Morgs. You have to swear absolute secrecy for what I'm about to tell you. I just want someone to know where I am in case I end up missing or something (don't freak out, everything's fine!). I'm supposed to be in Florence right now, but I stayed in Rome after my plane landed. My dad gave me some play money (seriously, a lot!), so I had a stroke of genius and got a hotel right behind the Pantheon! It's called the Albergo Santa Chiara. Classes don't start until Wednesday, so I've got plenty of time to get where I need to be.

This info is for EMERGENCY USE ONLY so keep a lid on it. I just couldn't help it. The Colosseum was calling to me. Hopefully I can figure out how to get to it today. Not sure I can wait until tomorrow!

Anyway, I'm starving so I'm off to eat lasagna or pizza or something Italian.

Miss you!

Pippers

I shut down my computer and change into a sundress and ballet flats. Stylish enough to feel cute while keeping comfortable and ventilated. Morgan would be proud—of course, she did most of my packing for me. I dig out a smallish over-the-shoulder bag from my luggage and pack it with a granola bar, hand sanitizer, lip gloss, money, and my passport.

My zoom lens clicks into place on my camera and I loop it over my neck, then check myself out in the bathroom mirror. Total tourist tragedy. At least I'll blend in with everyone else.

I locate my map and start scanning it for restaurants, but I can think of only one thing. And you know what they say:

When in Rome . . . eat gelato first.

CHAPTER FOUR

There's every color of gelato you can imagine. All the little flavor signs are in Italian, but I do recognize some of the words, like "nutella" and "amaretto." Each tub of gelato is its own work of art—a swirly mound drizzled with glistening sauce or sprinkled with nuts, chocolate bits, or fruit.

The sweaty crowd impatiently nudges me to move along, and a bored server waits for me to order. Feeling the pressure to make a fast decision, I point to the one called *stracciatella* because it looks the most like cookies and cream, then pick an unlabeled green one, hoping that it's mint and not something weird like pistachio.

As I walk out to find a place to sit, a family of three—speaking what I'm pretty sure is French—abandons their table, so I slip into one of the little chairs before anyone else claims it. I set my cup on the table and take aim with my camera, zooming in nice and close with a large aperture so everything but my focal point will be blurred together. *Snap.* My first photograph in Italy.

"Nice camera."

Startled, I glance up as a scruffy-faced guy about my age pulls out a chair across the table from me.

"Thanks."

"Mind if I sit here?"

I give a slight shake of my head, looking him up and down quickly. Aside from the insane amount of curly, dark hair on the top of his head, he sort of reminds me of Morgan's older brother. Tall, same toned build, super-light-brown eyes. The crush that crushed me.

He takes a bite of his gelato. "I'd never be able to use one of those big cameras. Too many buttons."

I can't help but smile. I haven't even been in Italy a whole day, but I'm already relieved to hear English—*my* English. But . . . "How did you know I speak English?"

A dimple appears when he smirks and points at me with his little plastic spatula-like spoon. "Because you're taking pictures of your food, which means not only that you speak English, but you're also American. Probably a blogger."

I click the lens cap back on and let the camera rest safely on my lap. "Well, of course now you know I'm American because you can hear that I don't have an accent. And I'm not a blogger."

I tried blogging last year, mostly to post some of the photos I was proud of, but I never got any followers, so I took the blog down. I keep my special photos to myself now.

"Oh, you have an accent." He takes another bite and leans back in his chair. "It's *American.* And northern, by the sound of it." He points at me with his spoon again. "Gelato's melting."

I look at my cup and gasp when I see how much is being wasted, dripping all down the side and making a puddle on the table. I quickly scrape the spoon along the edge before lifting it to my mouth.

My eyes close automatically, helping to block out all other senses but taste. And the green one is mint, not pistachio, thankfully. It's the softest, creamiest, most amazing flavor I've ever experienced. My tongue is cool, not only because the gelato is cold, but because of the mint itself. It floods my whole mouth then disappears down my throat. I need more.

I dip my spoon into the other flavor. "Ohhhh, wow this is good." I sigh.

"First timer?"

I swallow and nod, looking back at my table companion. "It's amazing."

"So, you're not a blogger. Are you a photographer then?"

"Hopefully one day."

"Oh," he says as he rubs his fingers over his dark stubble. I can hear it, scratchy like sandpaper. "How old are you?"

"Seventeen."

Suddenly I feel insecure, like he'll think I'm too young to bother with now. I shake the thought away and rescue another bite of gelato from the heat.

"You seem older than that," he says, somehow finished with his monster cup. He wads his napkin into a ball before plopping it in.

I smile and watch as the melted remains saturate the entire napkin. "Yeah, I've been told that before, actually."

Mom says it's the way I handle myself, especially around adults and strangers. I've been forced into more than my share of social situations where I was often the only child, so I learned to fit in to my surroundings.

"How old are you?" I ask.

"Eighteen. Just turned."

"Really, you seem . . . younger than that."

I did *not* just flirt with him.

He smiles, revealing mostly straight teeth. One of the top ones is a little crooked, but not in a hideous way. I kind of like it actually.

"Yeah, well, I—" He stops and his eyes shift behind me, wide in amusement.

I turn my head to find a couple straight out of the 1980s at the end of the gelato line. They're both sporting mullets and faded jeans. White sneakers. When I notice the matching red fanny packs, I have to look away.

"You should take a picture of that," he says, resting his forearms on the table.

"What?" I lean in closer and speak just above a whisper. "No way."

"Do it!" he insists. "Five euros." He digs into his pocket and clanks down five coins.

I sneak a peek at the unsuspecting couple. The man is wiping sweat off his face with a hanky. They're too close. I'd never get away with it.

"I can't," I say.

"Pansy."

With a grunt, I switch my camera on and set it to automatic. I raise it to my face and start to twist my upper body.

"No, wait!" he says. "You're doing it wrong."

I drop the camera to my lap and face him. "What?"

"You're too obvious. You need stealth. Watch and learn." He retrieves a small point-and-shoot camera from his pocket and aims it toward me. "Say cheese!" he says so loudly that I'm sure everyone around us is looking.

"Uh . . . cheese?"

"Done." He hits a few buttons and shows me the display screen.

There they are. Looked right at him too. Clever. But I can't let him win.

"Wow. That's pretty pixelated. What kind of setting do you have that on?"

He frowns. "It's just zoomed in."

"Oh." I reach to zoom out, but he pulls it away too fast. "What? Why can't I see? Did you actually take a picture of me or something?"

"Stealth." He shrugs and my cheeks turn pink. "Guess these are my winnings." The coins scrape across the table as he scoops them up to put in his pocket.

"You didn't even give me a chance to redeem myself," I defend.

"Excuses, excuses. Just admit I'm the better photographer." He laughs, standing to shoot his empty cup in the trash. "Finished?"

I nod and he tosses mine too. "Braver maybe, but better? Your camera doesn't have enough buttons."

His dimples reappear as he shoves his hands into the pockets of his navy-blue cargo shorts. "Well, thanks for letting me sit with you."

"Oh, sure. No problem." I slouch into my seat and wiggle my fingers in a low wave before reaching into my bag for the map from the hotel.

He still hasn't walked away. "Where you headed?"

"Not sure." I shrug. "I want to check out the Colosseum, but I'm sort of getting hungry."

He grips the back of the chair he'd sat in and leans on it. "You ate gelato before dinner too, huh?"

I shrug again. "When in Rome."

He laughs. "It's going to get dark soon. I'm not sure you should venture halfway across the city by yourself. Unless"—he looks around—"you're with your family or something."

No. My family sent me over here. All. By. Myself.

"Oh. Well, I planned on going alone."

He moves to stand next to me and points at the map. His hand lightly brushes against mine for the tiniest fraction of a second. "We're here, and the Colosseum is over here. There's no metro close, so it'll be a bit of a walk but definitely doable. I could go with you . . . if you want."

I look up at him to gauge if he's serious and I feel a little swirl in my stomach.

"I don't even know your name," I say.

"Oh, I'm sorry!" He takes a small step back and offers me his hand.

Our fingers are just about to touch when a girl's voice calls out and startles me. "Hey, Darren!"

The guy about to shake my hand turns his head in response.

A rail-thin girl strides over to us. She's wearing jean capris with a loose, purple sundress overtop, and several brass necklaces that dangle almost to her stomach. Bulky sunglasses perch high in the messy bleached-blond hair piled on top of her head.

"I'm Darren, and this is Nina," he says to me when she stops next to him.

Nina looks me over. "Hi." Her tone is friendly with an undercurrent of protectiveness.

"Hi," I respond, with maybe a little too much *I come in peace* worked in. "I'm Pippa."

"Pippa? Isn't that a cute name?" Nina squeaks, surprisingly genuine. She looks up at Darren and smiles, and my eyes follow hers to him.

"It's a great name," he agrees. There's his little twisted tooth again.

I've always thought my name was ridiculous, but if a guy can like it . . . My cheeks flush.

Darren clears his throat. "Pippa still hasn't seen the Colosseum. How do you feel about walking over there?" he asks Nina.

"Sure!" She turns toward him and holds out her palm. "But I want some gelato first."

Without missing a beat, he pulls a few coins out of his pocket and drops them in her palm.

"Thanks, doll," she says as she scampers off.

So he has a girlfriend. My reaction to this piece of information confuses me. Part of me is relieved—I feel like if he's got a girlfriend, the chances of him being a psycho trying to lure me away are slightly less. But another part of me is disappointed.

Oh, well. He's not Italian anyway.

CHAPTER FIVE

Darren leads the way down narrow sidewalks, past street vendors and homeless beggars. Nina's quiet, busy shoveling gelato into her mouth, and Darren plays tour guide, spouting facts about various buildings and points of interest. I try to keep up with our route on my map, but there are so many tight little turns and alleys, I lose track of where we are until we reach a major intersection I recognize from my taxi ride earlier. Hard to believe that was only this morning.

On the opposite side of the street stands an enormous white building with steps and pillars all across the front and tarnished statues mounted proudly on each end of the roof. Easily one of the fanciest buildings I've ever seen. The map's key says it's the Victor Emmanuel Monument. I don't remember ever hearing about this Victor, but he must have been someone important to get a monument like this.

"It's made of marble," Darren says, after we dart across the piazza when it's clear of traffic. "Incredible, huh? They don't build 'em like that back home." I'm about to ask where *home* is, but his face turns sour and it throws me off guard. "Too bad they destroyed so much of Capitoline Hill to make it."

"Oh, would you stop with that already?" Nina says in a way only people truly close to each other can. "It's done. Get over it."

"But there would have been so much more to see. Who knows what they—"

"Done!" she says with a light punch to his shoulder. Darren grabs her fist and playfully twists her arm back until she actually cries "uncle."

I want to gag.

"So." I clear my throat as I take a few pictures. "We can't climb the steps then?"

Darren whips his head around to look at me. "No way. It's barely even a hundred years old! You need ruins," he says, gently rotating me until I've turned my back on Victor. "See that fenced-off section there?" He points out to the middle of the intersection. He's so excited about this, it's sort of precious. "They were digging around looking for a route to lay the new metro line, and they found the Athenaeum of Hadrian!"

"*Maybe* they found it." Nina doesn't even hide that she's bored.

"They found the what?" I glance between the two of them and shrug. "Sorry. I flunked Italian history."

Darren laughs and says, "Think of it like . . . the grad school of ancient Rome."

"Where do you go to school, Pippa?" Nina asks, ignoring the lecture. "Somewhere in Rome?"

"She was joking, Nina." He looks at me, one eyebrow up. "Unless your high school really does offer Italian history? In which case, you should consider studying. It generally prevents failure." A smirk tugs on his lips.

"No," I tell him with a shake of my head.

I know I'm still in high school, but to hear him make sure Nina knows makes me feel like the tagalong kid sister. I mean, he's not even a year older than me.

Just take me to the Colosseum, and you don't ever have to entertain me again. Promise.

"Are we getting close to the Colosseum yet?" I ask.

"Yeah, it's just down this street." Nina points to our right.

I turn to look, but Darren jumps in front of me, blocking my line of sight. I realize for the first time that we're almost the same height. He's not really short, I'm just that tall. It's why I never wear heels.

"You should wait to look," he says, eyes bright. "It'll be so much more impressive if you wait until you're right in front of it."

"Ooh, I like that idea." His excitement transfers to me, and my pulse races in anticipation.

It takes every ounce of self-control I possess, but I focus on the sidewalk. I can tell we're getting close because Darren picks up speed, weaving us between other pedestrians and calling out an occasional "*Permesso.*"

We stop when we reach a street of uneven cobblestones. Instinctively, I raise my head but there's a hand a few inches in front of my face. I look over and find Darren smiling at me.

"You see it for the first time only once," he says. "Are you ready?"

I take a deep breath and nod as he slowly lowers his hand, but my eyes are still locked onto his, paralyzed by his incredibly sweet effort to make this special for me. He blinks, barely tilting his head to the side as he looks at me. I take his movement as an opportunity to turn my gaze away from him.

And toward the Colosseum.

I get it now. The name fits, there's no other word to describe it *but* colossal. The Pantheon was huge, but this thing is so massive, I can't even take it all in at once. I have to sweep my eyes over it, back and forth, row by row of arched windows. Stone and bricks all set in place by workers who probably never considered even for a second that two thousand years later it would be the symbol everyone across the globe pictures when they think of Rome.

Will it still be here two thousand years from now?

I shudder at the realization that for countless people throughout history, this building was the last thing they saw. To them, it was hideous. It was death. But I feel more alive, and somehow connected to the people who built everything around me and laid the stones on the street beneath my feet.

My breath catches in my throat and my eyes sting. I hadn't anticipated this reaction, but I think for the first time today it's hitting me how far away from home I am.

The click of a camera's shutter pulls me out of my thoughts, and I look over at Darren just as he lowers the silver point-and-shoot from his face. My years of experience in drama club fail me as fire creeps up my neck and settles in my cheeks. I can't even imagine the level of nerd on my face right now.

"You did not just take a picture of me."

"Pretty sure I did." He turns the display side of the camera around long enough for me to recognize my pointy nose.

I reach for it, but he holds it above his head. "Let me delete—I mean, see it!"

He hides it behind his back, then brings both hands in front of him, empty. I refrain from reaching into his pocket for it, but bite my lip at the thought.

"I'd ask you what you think," Nina says to me, "but I can see it in your eyes. You're in l-o-v-e."

I'm glad my cheeks are already red, because for a second I'm not sure what she's talking about. I nod before turning to the Colosseum again.

"It's incredible."

I glance at the people all around us, every second person with a camera, snapping away, looking as happy as I am to finally see the Colosseum in person. I join in the picture-taking, zooming in close to explore the detail of the stone. White and gray, crevices darkened with the grime age has exposed it to.

An Australian couple near us asks Darren to take a picture of them with the Colosseum as the backdrop, and when he's done, they offer to take one of the three of us. I hesitate for a moment, fingers gripping my baby firmly, but I would like to document my trip thoroughly. And I'm sure I'll want to remember what Darren and Nina look like. Darren passes his camera over to the man, so I suck it up and turn the dial to automatic before handing mine to the woman. Even if they did steal it now, they'd only be getting the twenty photos I just took. And a freaking nice camera.

I wonder how far into my trip it'll be before I stop thinking of everyone as a potential thief.

Darren and Nina stand on either side of me, one of them touching a hand on my back so lightly, I almost think I'm imagining it. I shift to make sure I'm standing closer to Nina than I am to Darren—out of respect for her, of course—and I feel her hand down at her side between us and not on my back. Which means the hand that's there belongs to . . .

Darren leans his head toward me and says, "Say 'pizza.' "

The three of us laugh and I check out the picture on the preview screen. Shoulder to shoulder, mouths open in the laughter of a shared joke. Students studying abroad. Dropouts backpacking our way across Europe, one historical monument at a time. Best friends. The couple who took our picture has no idea I met them only an hour ago. That soon, we'll continue on our own ways. They'll go on to do whatever it is they're in Italy for, and I'll go on to Florence to learn about Michelangelo and Leonardo. The artists, not the Ninja Turtles.

Looking back at the Colosseum, I notice for the first time that the bottom row of arched windows is equipped with metal fencing, and there are people milling about on the other side of it.

"Can we go in?" I ask hopefully.

"I think they close at seven," Darren says. "Probably best to come back tomorrow when you can spend a couple of hours in there. And now you know how to get here."

Of course. Because they won't be with me tomorrow. I'll be alone. Again.

Off to our right stands a massive white structure with three arched openings. I wonder if people used to be able to walk under them or if it was always fenced off like a statue. Through my zoom lens, the detailed carvings of ancient Romans and their steeds come to life.

"That's the Arch of Constantine," Nina says.

"I was about to tell her that," Darren says with a hint of disappointment.

She throws her head back and pokes his arm again. "I know you were, dweebs, that's why I said it first."

Doll. Dweebs. Aren't they just so cute?

Not.

"And all this area behind us is the Roman Forum," Darren says quickly before Nina can say more.

I turn around, but all I see is a creepy stone building that makes me think of abandoned prison cells.

"The entrance is down that way," he says, pointing past the Arch. "Add that to your list of things to see tomorrow. Used to be *the* center of Roman civilization. It's all crumbled bits now, but there's nothing like it."

He talks about the history here with such reverence and awe. It's refreshing to listen to someone passionate about something other than the newest video game.

Darren's stomach growls, even though I can't imagine there's room for anything else after that gelato trough he inhaled. He throws a hand over his middle as if it will hide the noise. "Anyone else hungry? I'm feeling like . . . mmm, Italian?"

"My treat," I offer.

"What?" they say at the same time.

"No way," Darren adds.

"Yes!" I insist. "It's the least I can do for my own personal tour guides." And I'm not ready to say good-bye yet.

"Well," Darren says with a laugh, "we won't hold you to it after you see the bill."

We all turn to go, but something holds me back. I steal another look at the Colosseum, glowing in the rich evening light, trying to comprehend that I'm actually standing in front of the real deal. My fingers twitch at the thought of touching it.

"I'll be right back," I tell them as I nearly skip down the crowded path to the outer wall, slowing only just before placing my palm on a section of original stone. Stone once touched by the ancients who first set it in place. I feel so connected already.

And it's still my first day here, in just one city in Italy. Just Rome. There's also Pompeii, Ostia Antica, Sienna, Venice, Milan, Assisi, Verona. . . . There's so much to see and take pictures of. So much to learn.

You're in Italy for three months, Pippa.

Three months. That's a nice chunk of time. Maybe even long enough to see everything I want to see.

But I couldn't. Could I?

My eyes widen, staring at the wall but not really focusing on a particular spot. It's possible . . . with enough planning.

Three months.

But *this* was the adventure, staying in Rome a few extra days. It's enough.

Right?

I slide my fingers along the cool stone once more, unable to help the smile on my face despite the logical fear that this could all end very badly.

CHAPTER SIX

We decide on a little restaurant closer to the Pantheon, and though it's still pretty toasty outside, Darren insists we sit at a table along the street so my first official meal in Italy is everything it's supposed to be. With the light from the setting sun slipping between the buildings, and the gentle glow from the candle centerpiece, I feel like I'm inside that café painting by Van Gogh, even though that was probably supposed to be Paris.

Our ridiculously attractive waiter with jet-black hair speaks comprehensible English, but Nina shows off by ordering for us in pristine Italian. Somewhere in all the flowing mumbo jumbo was a request for pizzas and lemon sodas with extra ice—apparently ice isn't as popular over here as it is back in the States, or *gli Stati Uniti*.

I gape at her. "That was amazing."

"It better be. I've taken enough classes."

"I got a language program for my computer, but I've tried it only a couple times," I tell them. "It kept honking at me when I said things wrong. Gave me a complex."

They laugh, and warmth that has nothing to do with the temperature grows inside me.

"You should keep at it," Nina says. "It's a rush to be able to communicate with someone in a different language."

"Are you fluent too?" I ask Darren, my tone laced with a little more jealousy than I intended.

He shakes his head. "I'm far from fluent, but I get by. Nina's definitely had more formal training."

Formal training. There's a polite smile on my lips, but inside I'm frowning at my lack of worldly experience.

The waiter whistles back to our table and holds out each pizza for display before setting them in front of us. They're the furthest I've ever seen from the deep dishes in Chicago. The crust is as thin as paper and the bright red sauce peeks between patches of perfectly melted mozzarella. My mouth waters as the salty aroma reaches my nose.

Darren stabs one with a knife to slice it.

"Wait!" I blurt out before he does any real damage.

He freezes until I take a picture of it, then proceeds to snatch a slice. Head tilted back, he opens his mouth wide and dangles the pizza in the air, but he doesn't bite. "Are you taking my picture, or what, Pipperoni?"

I smile as I lift my camera to my eye again. "Like I haven't heard that one before."

The pizza is unreal. So many flavors, cheese that is melt-in-your-mouth good, sauce with a touch of sweet, and just enough crunch. I may never be able to eat at a pizza chain again.

Accordion music floods the air. An elderly man dressed in

black slacks and a plaid button-down ambles down the street, working out a slow song on a worn instrument. I relax in my chair and let the soft melody wash over me. I'm officially smitten with Rome.

Something brushes across my cheek, and I jerk my head around to find Darren swiping at my face with his napkin.

"Sorry." He hands it to me so I can finish the job. "You have sauce . . . all over you."

Embarrassed, I glance at Nina for an instant and see her staring at Darren, eyebrows arched. She opens her mouth like she's about to say something, but her cell phone buzzes, shaking the table, and she turns her attention to the text message.

"Gotta go," she announces, popping up from her seat.

My pulse quickens as I realize I'm about to be alone again. I force a smile and look at Darren, expecting him to join her, but he's still chewing away, elbows propped casually on the table.

"Pippa, it was so great to meet you. I hope you enjoy your time in Italy." She stands and wraps an arm around my shoulders, giving me a quick squeeze before turning to Darren. "You've got this one, right, doll?" She motions toward her empty plate and he nods, waving her away.

The bill, or *il conto*, comes and it's not nearly as bad as I expected for a tourist area. It's probably even cheaper than eating at Disney World.

"I was serious when I said I was paying," I say, stealing the ticket from Darren. He opens his mouth to respond, but I stop him. "Don't even try. It's happening." I count out some cash and leave it on the tray.

"Well, thank you." He smiles, scratching that sandpaper chin of his again. "So what's next on the agenda?"

"Honestly?"

"No. I want you to lie."

"Smart aleck." If it weren't beyond the boundaries of our three-hour friendship, I'd give him a playful shove. "I was actually considering more gelato."

He grins. "So it's not a rule that you can only eat it before your meals?"

Is this considered flirting? Doesn't he have a girlfriend? Or am I really so desperate that I'll take any attention from boys way too seriously?

"The rule was just amended to include after-meal gelato consumption too."

"Well, in that case," he says, stepping aside so I can exit the patio first. "Feel like company? My treat."

We walk until we spot a handful of people coming out of a doorway, licking on cones piled high with gelato in all different colors. The *gelateria* is literally an open door to a room not much bigger than a closet. I get a scoop of pomegranate and chocolate. Darren picks out mango and pistachio.

"Pistachio?" Sure, this place doesn't have as many options as Della Palma, but there are at least twenty, the rest of them all a better choice. "You can't be serious."

"Hey, don't knock it till you've tried it."

"What are you? Eighty?"

He pushes his cup toward me. "Taste it."

I scrunch my brows together and stare at the bright green mound.

"I haven't licked it yet or anything," he says. "Try it."

Reluctantly, I scoop at it with my tiny spoon and my eyes widen as the flavor surprises my tongue. It tastes exactly like a creamy, cold, sweet pistachio nut. "Okay, you win. That's actually really good."

"Told you," he says, taking a bite. "It's always good to try new things. Especially if it scares you a little bit."

I turn to look at him, expecting him to elaborate, but he keeps his eyes forward.

He pays for our cups and we stroll along the crowded street until we're in front of the Pantheon. Sitting along the base of a big water fountain in the middle of the piazza, we have a full view of the monstrous building glowing an eerie yellow in the streetlights against an indigo sky. Tourists speaking languages I can and can't identify mill about, pointing, chatting, and posing for pictures. A similar scene plays out right here every single day, and tonight I get to be part of it.

Darren is quiet for a few minutes before he asks, "So what brings you to Italy?"

I savor the taste of the rich chocolate, choosing my words carefully. "My parents sent me."

"Sent you? For what, like a learning experience?"

"Something like that," I mutter.

"I'm listening."

I hesitate, but then realize how anxious I am to talk it out with someone. "I'm supposed to go to this summer program in Florence."

"Supposed to go, huh? Now this is getting interesting."

"Yeah, I'm supposed to be there by Wednesday," I say. "But it's going to be so lame, studying art, like the old stuff people go to see just to say they've seen it. Not my thing." I look up at the Latin words across the top of the Pantheon. "So I decided today that I'm not going."

"Rebellion. I like it." The twisty tooth again. "And how did your parents take the news?"

I bite my lip, fiddling with my camera.

"They don't know?" He snickers. "How do you plan on pulling that off?"

I stare at the ground between our feet. "I haven't figured out the logistics yet."

Deciding that I'm skipping out on Florence in favor of touring the country for the summer is as far as I've gotten. But there's so much more to it than that if I plan to accomplish it all undetected. There's a school that's expecting me and parents that are paying for me to go to said school. Then there's the issue of making a budget and sticking to it so I don't starve.

Darren waves a hand in front of my face. "Anyone in there?"

I blink.

"You didn't hear anything I just said?"

"Oh. No, I'm sorry," I say. "I was trying to—"

"Come up with a plan?" I nod and he continues, "I was saying I can help."

"How?"

He sits up straighter and polishes his nails on the front of his shirt. "Because I'm the king of subterfuge."

"That's a pretty big claim."

"Well, I'm kind of a big deal."

"Ha! Okay." I snort. "Let's hear how you came to be so qualified in subterfugery."

"Well, I can't even count how many times my brother, Tate, and I said we were spending the night at a friend's house, but we really just pitched a tent at the park, pretending to be explorers or something."

"Hmmm." I scratch my chin like Darren does. "That's child's play. What else you got?"

"Hard to please. Okay." He pauses. "For a while we lived down the street from this church. We weren't even Catholic, but my parents had it in their heads that I needed to go to catechism classes. Once I figured out I wouldn't be learning about actual cats, every week I'd ride my bike toward the church, then turn off and just keep riding until I thought it was time to go home."

I groan. "Are you a cat lover?"

"She asks, disdainfully." He puts his hands up in surrender. "Look, I was ten years old. And why do you have such animosity toward cats?"

"Because of the creep factor. They're unpredictable and always have the same facial expression so you can never tell what they're thinking. Are they going to rub against your leg or slash your face open?"

"Wow." Darren rests a hand on my shoulder. "Do you need a support group? They say talking about traumatic experiences is the only way to move on."

"Wait a minute." I ignore him, holding up a finger. "Did you do anything sneaky *after* the age of twelve?"

He removes his hand and runs it through his hair, laughing halfheartedly.

"I thought you were actually going to be able to help me. You know, bring some real experience to the table here." I drop my head into my hands. "I'm in a foreign country and I'm planning to lie to my parents about my whereabouts for almost three months. It's a little more serious than skipping catechism class and camping at the park."

I take in slow, deep breaths, trying to decide if I'd rather laugh at him or cry at the situation I'm digging myself into. "This was a bad idea, wasn't it? Maybe I should just suck it up and go to Florence."

Darren's voice is calm. "Look, I don't know what kind of relationship you have with your parents, so I can't tell you what you should do. You'll be the one answering to them if—"

"Honestly, I'm not sure they'd even catch on," I confess. "They're so busy with work right now. That's the real reason I got shipped off."

I'd suspected it ever since the moment they sprung my summer plans on me last week, but admitting it to someone proves I actually believe it. It's the perfect setup for my parents—send me away for a few months to get schooled on art galleries and come back just in time for the opening of their own.

"They wanted me out of the way," I say. "Who knows what they did with Gram after I left."

"Gram?"

"My grandma—my mom's mom. She lives with us." My insides flutter as I remember saying good-bye to her at the airport. Gram and Morgan were the only ones I let see me off.

"You'll do just fine," she cooed, fingertips stroking my hair as I buried my head against her neck. "You'll get to eat carbs every day without anyone telling you not to. You'll be required *to look at sculptures of naked men! You'll say* 'grazie' *and* 'prego!'*"*

Gram always did have that magical calming effect on me. As she spoke, the tears stopped and my breathing steadied.

"Tell me I'm going to have a good time," I mumbled, taking in the scent of lavender perfume one last time.

"Pippa." She sighed, laughing in her sweet, grandmotherly way. "It will change your life."

Darren clears his throat, bringing me back to the present. "I've got two questions for you." He pulls his knees toward his chest and folds his arms over them, looking at me intently. "First, what do you have to lose if you go through with skipping out on school?"

"Well, I—"

"Don't answer out loud! The less I know, the better. I don't want you blaming me if this thing backfires."

What do I have to lose?

They could ban my phone, my computer, the TV. Hopefully they aren't cruel enough to take my camera. I'd be grounded for some unspecified amount of time, and I'd probably be forced to work in their stupid gallery every day.

Well, the gallery's my future no matter what. Doomed to a life of living out my parents' dream. I thought parents were supposed to dive headfirst into supporting what their kids wanted to do. But Gram gave me the fancy camera, not my parents. And how many of my plays have they come to together? Dad usually caught at least one showing of each run, but it wasn't uncommon for Mom to have something better to do—at the beck and call of some client with bottomless pockets looking to hang a dead artist's work on all his walls.

But it's not like I won't learn about art if I don't go to the program. I mean, real life education is better than the classroom, right? I'd still be doing what my parents want, just in a different way.

I look at Darren, feeling a little more determined to take control of my summer.

He smiles before asking, "And what do you have to gain?"

Within ten minutes, we have a plan that might actually work. All I have to do is open an e-mail account using my mother's name, compose a message to the school telling them I'm not going, and continue sending e-mails to my family periodically throughout the summer so they know I'm alive. It all hinges on the supposition that both my mom and the school's person-in-charge are such busy people that communicating exclusively through e-mail is acceptable. And that I'll consistently be able to find Internet service. Yeah, it's risky, and potentially the most idiotic thing I've ever tried, but now that the idea is in my head, I can't *not* do it.

I'm torn between wanting to sit here with Darren until all hours of the night and rushing back to the hotel to put my plan into action. I'm afraid if I wait too long, I'll lose my nerve. I'm also running out of juice and my eyes are starting to burn from being awake for so long.

But I might not see Darren again . . . and I still don't really know anything about him.

I make my body relax a little so it doesn't look like I'm anxious to leave. "Well, now that we have me all figured out, what's your story? Why are you here?"

He runs a hand through his curls. "I just graduated, like, a week ago."

"Oh, lucky!" I say, unable to mask the envy. "So is this a graduation trip or something? Backpacking across Europe?"

"Not exactly. Both Nina and my brother wanted to do this private archaeology program to pad their résumés for grad school, and since I'm planning to study archaeology too, my parents offered to pay for me to go with them. We're going to work at different field schools, learning at active excavation sites and stuff." He studies my face. "I'm totally boring you."

"No, not at all!" I say quickly. "I think it's cool. And it explains why you know so much about everything here." I glance back up at the Pantheon, wishing there was some easy way to transfer all his knowledge to my brain. "I don't think I've ever met anyone interested in that before, and now there are three of you."

Darren stretches his legs out in front of him. "Well, my parents are both anthropology professors now. They met here when they were in school. Rome is, like, their place. Which is probably one of the reasons my mom was so excited about this summer. She wants it to be as special for me and Tate as it is to her."

"Is it? Special for you, I mean."

He points a finger at himself. "Future archaeology student, remember? It's impossible not to get caught up in the history and romance of this place."

Accordion music echoes across the piazza and I smile. Rome doesn't even have to try to be romantic. It just *is*.

"Nina's already thinking about grad school? Is she that much older than you?"

"A few years, yeah."

"Whoa." I refrain from making any cougar comments. "And you're spending the whole summer in Rome?" I ask. "Digging things up?"

He absentmindedly plays with a loose string at the hem of his shirt. "We'll be here a few more weeks. Then we'll move on to a dig in Tuscany. And we get weekends off, sometimes even three-day weekends, so I plan on traveling when I can. Blowing all my graduation money," he adds with a laugh.

"Where to?"

"Pompeii, for obvious reasons, but I also want to see Venice before it sinks. And everyone says the place to see at least once in your life is the Cinque Terre."

I do my best to repeat the words he just said. "Cinque Terre?"

"It means 'the five lands.' It's a section of the northern coast, the Italian Riviera. Five little fishing villages all connected by a path along the cliffs of the sea. The trail's pretty famous. It's called la Via dell'Amore." The words flow like he's a local.

I look away quickly when I realize I'm staring at his lips, silently begging for him to keep speaking in Italian. "Sounds beautiful."

"I've heard it's one of the best places to photograph in the country," he says, pointing to my camera. "You should go and check it out. I mean, since your summer's free now." He flashes a sneaky smile. My partner in crime.

I return the smile. "Maybe I will."

"Well, I guess I should get going," he says through a yawn.

I have no clue what time it is, but it's probably late and the travel exhaustion is definitely setting in. "Yeah, me too."

We stand and I observe the sea of people around us, adjusting both my camera and tote bag so they're in front of me.

"Do you have far to walk to your hotel?"

"No, it's just behind the Pantheon."

"Oh, I'll walk with you. I'm going that way, anyway."

We walk in silence, Darren's hands in his pockets and mine gripping the strap to my bag where it crosses over my chest. My mind whirls a mile a minute. Does he want to keep in touch? Would that be weird?

"Thanks for everything," I say when we reach the front door to the hotel. "You've definitely softened the blow of my first day." It's the truth, but my smile feels forced for some reason—anxious.

He shrugs. "Thanks for dinner."

"Thanks for the gelato."

I shift my camera around to my side as Darren starts opening his arms to go in for a hug, but at the last second he plunges one hand into his pocket and offers me the other to shake. His grip is firm and he holds my gaze a few seconds longer than I expect before letting go and taking a step back.

My heart sinks, but I'm not entirely sure why. I knew this was coming. I knew I'd have to face my summer alone.

His smile is genuine, like a friend's, and he says, "Good night, Pipperoni. Maybe I'll see you again sometime."

CHAPTER SEVEN

~~Get my picture taken at the Colosseum~~

ASSIGNMENT NUMERO DUE: PUBLIC TRANSPORTATION, THE ITALY EDITION
We have the L train here in Chicago, but what do they use in Italy? Find out, get on, and get off somewhere that sounds interesting. Take pictures for evidence, and write about it, leaving space for a 4x6 once you get your pictures printed.

The next morning, I wake up on my own around nine, cursing the bright light sneaking through a gap in the curtains right into my eyes. This must be what it feels like to get hit by a truck. My legs and even my arms ache, my abs hurt like I did a hundred crunches before bed, my head feels foggy, and I've never had such a strong craving for ice water. I work my way to the bathroom for the morning rituals, and gravity seems to be tugging on all my limbs with more force than usual, which means everything takes twice as long.

And I can't help being a little mopey that I made two friends I'll never see again. Thankfully, just the thought of Rome outside my window, waiting to be explored, perks me up a little bit. I have no set plans today. I have all the time in the world.

But there's still business to take care of.

I sign in to my new bogus e-mail account and check for the program director's response to the message I sent last night, telling her I'm no longer attending. I must have revised it a dozen times before I was confident it sounded like it came from an adult—and stuffy enough to come from my mother.

And there it is! I hold my breath as I open her reply, and exhale in relief when I see she's friendly and understanding about it. But she brought up the money issue, the one thing I'd forgotten to cover. I don't know what kind of arrangement Mom had with them, but I can't imagine they'd turn down the money just because there's not a student to go with it. The last thing I need is Mom investigating an unexpected refund.

I work up another professional-sounding message, apologizing again for any inconvenience and assuring her that all agreed-upon financial support would continue. Fingers crossed that's the end of all that.

I also compose a message to Gram. She doesn't get on the Internet much, but I'm hoping with me gone, she'll check her e-mail more frequently. I tell her how much I miss her already, how beautiful Italy is, and how I got whistled at in the airport. The only truths I'm able to share no matter how much I'm dying to spill everything else.

I download the photos I've taken so far onto my computer and scroll through them, stopping at the picture of me with Darren and Nina. Before I even realize I'm doing it, I zoom in on Darren so only his face takes up the screen. He really does have nice eyes. And the stubble is a good look for him. Masculine. Rugged.

I shake my head as I insert the memory card back into my camera. It's useless to think about him.

I set off for day two and study the map. Darren said something about a metro, so after spotting an *M* with a red circle around it close to the Spanish Steps, I figure that's my best shot at starting Morgan's assignment.

On my way, I spot a middle-aged couple walking out of the open doorway of a little corner shop, pulling pastries out of a paper sack. The woman takes a bite and her eyes grow wide before holding it up for the man to try. Mouth watering, I pick up the pace and turn into the modest bakery comprising several two-person tables shoved against the wall, an L-shaped display case housing the carb goodies, a couple of drink refrigerators, and a row of space-age–looking coffeemakers.

"*Giorno*," says one of the girls working behind the counter. She looks like she's around my age, maybe a year or two older.

"*Giorno*." My reply is timid, slow to dip my toes into the waters of Italian communication.

She smiles brightly. "What can I get you?"

I gape at her. “How did you know—?”

“It is a combination. Camera around your neck? Tourist. Fair skin and lighter hair? Rules out quite a few countries. Accent? Definitely American.”

“I only said one word, and it was Italian.”

She laughs. “I get a lot of practice.”

“Well, your English is perfect.” I’m amazed. And jealous.

“Thank you. My parents made sure that I learned from an early age. And my uncle’s family lives in New York, so I spend much time there. Most every summer.”

I have to force myself not to think about the Mafia.

“I’m going to school there in a few months. After I help my aunt at her restaurant in Riomaggiore. Summer is too much for her alone with my idiot cousins,” she adds with a laugh. I wonder if all Italian girls are this talkative or if she’s just been Americanized.

A few locals wander in and strike up a lively conversation with an older man behind the counter. I shift away from them to make room and stare inside the case.

She points to the pastry I’m drooling over. “This one?”

“Sure.”

She snatches a flaky rectangle drizzled with chocolate and tosses it into a paper sack.

“So where’s Rio . . . ma . . . ?” I stop before completely butchering the name.

“Riomaggiore? Very north of here, on the Italian Riviera. Cinque Terre.”

“You’re kidding?” My stomach twists. What are the odds that this place is mentioned to me two days in a row? I don’t usually look for signs, but I can't help feeling like something cosmic is going on here.

She tilts her head to the side, observing me. "You have been?"

"No," I say, then add softly, "But I think I'm supposed to go."

Her eyebrows scrunch together, but she smiles and leans closer to me, resting her elbows on the counter, hand still gripping the open paper sack. "What do you mean?"

I clear my throat, not even sure what to say exactly. "Well, it seems to keep coming up. Makes me feel like it might be important. Like I need to go."

"I've heard it's one of the best places to photograph in the country. . . . You should go. . . . Your summer's free now."

As I think about taking pictures of a sunset over the Mediterranean, I subconsciously place a hand on my camera, not even realizing it until the girl looks down and her smile spreads. I pull my hand away quickly, not so much embarrassed, but there's really no reason to pet my camera.

"It truly is beautiful," she says. "There is no other place like it. Far better than being in the city." She holds the sack out to me and I hand her a couple of coins. "It will change your life," she adds.

I suck in a startled breath. That's exactly what Gram said to me just before I left.

Cosmic? I'm thinking yes.

CHAPTER EIGHT

The sun is roasting me, already high overhead as I stand across the street from the Spanish Steps. All I see are people, people, and more people packed like sardines on the steps and swarming the fountain of a sinking boat fenced off in the center of the street. They barely shift out of the way as cars attempt to pass, even when drivers honk and yell out their windows at them. No one cares that they're standing in the middle of a functioning road.

I take a few pictures of the steps just to document the chaos, but I'd probably have to come back at the crack of dawn to get anything usable. Considering the jet lag I'm still feeling, I don't see that happening.

The station is a few blocks north, so I push my way through the sweaty tourists and soon find the entrance to the trains, disappointed to learn they're underground and I can't see the city from an L train perspective like back home. I snag a metro map when I buy my ticket and try to study the names as the solid block of people keeps me moving forward. The stop I'm at is called Spagna, obviously after the Spanish Steps. None of the other names mean anything to me, they're just a jumble of fancy words ending in -ia and -io and . . . *COLOSSEO*!

Bingo. Morgan's only rule was that I had to get off somewhere that sounded interesting, and I have yet to actually go *inside* the Colosseum. And then there's the whole Roman Forum to explore too. Win, win.

Eventually, I find my way to the correct platform and shimmy to the edge of the crowd where I'm able to fully expand my lungs. The electronic display above our heads flashes in red that the train is one minute out, and cool, humid air pushes through the tunnel ahead of it. I let it wash over me and swirl my hair around, grateful for the temporary reprieve from the heat.

The graffiti-covered train glides to a stop, and a flood of people pour out of the doorways while those on the platform try to squeeze their way in past them. I was never a cheerleader, but a cheer rings loud and clear in my mind: Be, aggressive. B-e aggressive.

I adjust my bag to hang directly in front of me and cradle the camera with my hands. Someone steps on my heel and my foot nearly comes out of my shoe, but I clench my teeth and lean forward with my shoulders until I make it inside. I keep a firm grip on my possessions through the ride and change of trains, relaxing only when I see sunlight spilling down the steps of my exit. I emerge to the surface and stop dead in my tracks at the sight of the Colosseum towering overhead. Even though I saw it yesterday, it still takes my breath away.

I wait for more than an hour in the sticky heat to get inside, and for the first time, I'm glad I'm on this trip alone because I have no words. Brick, stone, and concrete are everywhere, forming walls, paths, stairways blocked off by locked gates, arched windows to the outside. Fragments of statues and tablets depicting Latin are strewn about various rooms and along walls, former decorations from when the Colosseum functioned as more than just a tourist attraction. As it stands now, it's hard to imagine that it was ever any other way, a bustling stadium with spectators like Wrigley Field . . . except with swords and death matches instead of hot dogs and baseballs.

I circle the entire building twice, once on each level, taking several hundred photos, desperate to document everything. In the gift shop on the second floor, I buy two small calendars with pictures from all over Italy—one for Morgan and one for me. I imagine us hanging them at the start of senior year in the last lockers we'll ever have. There's an end in sight, an end to my routine.

Time is constantly moving forward, and the proof is all around me.

As much as I hate to tear myself away from the Colosseum, I've taken more pictures than I'll ever be able to edit, and there's still plenty to see elsewhere. I exit and make my way past the Arch of Constantine and the men dressed like Roman soldiers posing with tourists, to the entrance of the Roman Forum.

From what I remember about history, there was a time when Rome had control of pretty much everything. I walk the streets, trying to piece together how it all must have looked with complete walls and rooftops like a regular city in place of the now-crumbled pillars reaching in vain toward the sky.

Hunger takes over after a couple of hours roaming the Forum and Palatine Hill, and I can't ignore it anymore. I snake my way to the metro to head back to home base, missing my first attempt at boarding and nearly getting a black eye in the process. The next train thankfully has plenty of room for me, and I stand in an open spot near the door on the other side of the aisle.

I glance out the grimy window to the crowd across the tracks waiting for the train that goes the other direction.

The doors behind me slap shut the instant I see him on the platform. My breath catches.

Darren.

Nina stands next to him, her nose in a book. His red T-shirt stretches over muscles I hadn't noticed yesterday, and the bulk of a green backpack hangs in front of him and under his arm.

I will him to look up.

He casually scans the length of the train, his eyes passing right over me. But then his head turns back to me and his eyebrows pull together. The slightest hint of a smile plays at the corners of his mouth.

I raise my arm to wave, but the sudden movement of the train forces me to brace myself against the door. I press my palm onto the window, instinctively taking a step forward as if there was some way I could get to him.

But my train plunges into the dark tunnel and he's gone. Again.

CHAPTER NINE

ASSIGNMENT NUMERO TRE: FOOD, GLORIOUS FOOD

Write down everything you've eaten so far.

* Several chocolate pastries
* Lots of gelato! This stuff is ice cream to the MAX. I tried mint, some vanilla-ish flavor I don't remember how to spell, pistachio, chocolate, and pomegranate. SO good.
* The best pizza ever
* Ham and cheese *"panino"*

Temporarily forgetting the tiny bed at the hotel is anything but soft, I fling myself onto it with a thud. I unwrap a hazelnut candy I bought called *baci*—Italian for "kisses"—and turn it over with my tongue until the chocolate melts away, leaving behind little bits of nut to crunch.

I boot up my computer and after loading all my new pictures, I give the Internet a shot and find that I still have access. There are e-mails from both Morgan and my mom, but I open Mom's first, out of fear and the need to get it over with quickly like ripping off a Band-Aid. We haven't exactly gotten along since she told me I was spending my summer learning about art and the ins and outs of being an effective gallery guide.

"You've always wanted to go to Italy," Mom said, a hand on her hip.

"Yeah, as a family to do touristy things. Not to sit in a classroom while someone prattles on about old paintings that all look the same!"

"But it's such a great opportunity for you!" she said, entirely too animated like she was trying to convince us both. "Think of all the background knowledge you'll gain. You have to understand the early works to see their influence today. It's our dream to have our own ga—"

"No, it's *your* dream to run a stuffy art gallery and host parties and be the queen of Chicago's social circuit. It has nothing to do with me! I want to study something real, like photography."

"Pippa," Dad chimed in with the even tone of a mediator. "If you don't want to go—"

"Oh, she's *going*." Mom straightened as tall as she could get, towering over him with her power. "Arrangements have been set." She turned to me again, still in giantess form. "Do you have any idea what it took to make this happen?"

"Apparently your firstborn," I muttered.

She heard me.

Yeah, it all went really well. I'd definitely be grounded right now if I weren't in a foreign country.

To: Pippa Preston <pippers26@gmail.com>
From: Mary Preston <m.preston@prestonartsource.com>
Subject: Re: Ciao from Italy

Hi, Hon,

Glad to hear you made it without any problems. How's the school? Are they treating you well? I'm confident you will have a great time this summer. Please don't hesitate to let me know if you need anything.

I have to run. In the middle of a huge estate acquisition.

Love,
Mom

I roll my eyes. It's even shorter than I expected. Although she didn't mention herself in every sentence, so I should be impressed.

I formulate a quick and equally dissatisfying response, deleting the angsty parts like "Don't worry about me, just take care of your work crap" until it's even more vague than the last one I sent. I don't know why I keep hoping for her to be different, but I do.

Next I check Morgan's e-mail, which is longer than Mom's and sprinkled with exclamation points. It's just what I need to see.

To: Pippa Preston <pippers26@gmail.com>
From: Morgan Arrant <queenofdrama14@gmail.com>
Subject: Re: I'm in freaking ITALY

WHAT?! You're actually LYING to your parents? Who are you and what have you done with the real Pippa?

Not that I blame you. I'm still surprised you actually got on the plane in the first place. You should have seen yourself at the airport. You were a MESS! And I mean that in the nicest possible way.

Don't worry. Your secret is safe with me. Just tell me when you get to school so I can stop worrying.

Let's get down to business. What do the boys look like? Are they GORGEOUS?! Have any of them tried to lure you up to their apartment yet? Shove their tongue down your throat? Kidding aside, be careful out there by yourself. You may not know this, but you're kind of adorable. Remember our mantra for all things scandalous: JUST SAY NO.

I know you've taken a million pictures by now, so pick out a good one and shoot it over. I need proof that you're really in another country. I just sighed. Did you hear it? It's our last summer of youthful freedom and we're missing our Summer-o-Rama! I need my Pippa! Okay, venting over.

My jealousy knows no bounds,

—M

I sigh too. Morgan and I had planned out the summer before our last year as slaves to mandatory schooling—because college is essentially voluntary. Even though neither of us has a choice in whether we're going or not, we at least have a say in *where* we're going. As soon as we move our tassels from one side to the other, our classmates will scatter like ants on an abandoned picnic spread. Two things I know for sure: Morgan and I will be going to the same college, and it will be far, far away from

home. Far from the gallery of forced servitude, from the monotony of what my life has become.

Even just being in Rome for two days, I've gotten the itch. This is only a glimpse of what's out there. Just one tiny corner of the world. I have to get *out*. I have to see more, and take pictures of all of it.

In my reply, I tell her she's paranoid worrying about me so much, that I'm perfectly safe. I gush about the pretty boys—especially the *polizia* in their uniforms—and send along a hastily edited photo of the Colosseum. I also inform her that I'm skipping out on the art program altogether and ask that she please keep her mouth shut.

I realize only when I click send that I didn't mention Darren and Nina. I'm not sure what I would have said. *So I met this American couple who showed me around Rome for a little bit. We shared pizza, then the boyfriend bought me ice cream and walked me home. Then I randomly saw them again today but I was on the metro train—that you made me get on—and they were on the other platform so I couldn't talk to them and I'll probably never see them again.*

My wide eyes stare at the worn bedspread but focus on nothing. Morgan led me to the metro. If I hadn't gotten on it precisely when I did, I wouldn't have seen Darren, and he'd be one day further away in my memory.

But I did see him. And he saw me.

I clutch the journal in my hands. Maybe there really is something cosmic about this trip.

CHAPTER TEN

"Mommy, I want to throw another coin in the fountain," the child sitting next to me squeaks. His mother hands him one before he skips down to the edge of the Trevi Fountain, or Fontana di Trevi.

"Jude! Don't forget to turn around!" the woman hollers above the crowd. "Now throw it behind you!" She mimes throwing it over her shoulder.

Jude smiles and tosses the coin in the air, just as his mom's camera flashes, brightly illuminating the muscular Neptune sculpture and his loincloth—more than most of the sculptures around here are wearing. For the first time tonight I notice that every third person at the base of the fountain is also throwing coins into the pool behind them. Clearly this is more than the typical wish on a coin.

I lean toward the woman and ask her what it's all about.

"Oh." She laughs and waves her hand like either what I said was silly, or what she's about to tell me is. "They say if you throw a coin into the fountain, you'll return to Rome one day. You have to hold it in your right hand and throw it over your left shoulder or it won't work."

Jude climbs back up to where we sit, but leans against a railing to face us, eying me curiously.

"Hi," he says.

"Hi. I saw you throw in your coin. That was a good toss!"

His face lights up. "I'm coming back to Rome five more times!" he exclaims in all sincerity.

"I'm not sure it works like that, sweetie." His mom gathers their things and stands. "Come on, let's go find Dad and head to the hotel. I know someone who needs a bath!"

"Another coin! Another coin!" He grips the bar behind him and leans forward, butting his blond head against his mom's stomach as he chants.

She fishes a coin out of her pocket and hands it to him. "This is the last one. Make it good."

He stares at the dark circle in his open palm, then holds it out to me.

I'm not sure what he's waiting for, so I smile and say, "This will make six times."

He brings it closer. "Your turn."

His mom is beaming at him. I try to remember the last time my mom was so visibly proud of me and come up with nothing.

She nods for me to take it and Jude leads me down to the fountain, instructing me to turn around. We count to three and I toss the coin over my shoulder, with Jude next to me pretending to. Should I feel a tingle of magic work through me? Is my next foray to Rome written in the stars now?

"How long have you been here?" the woman asks.

"Just got in yesterday."

"Oh, lucky! We're headed home tomorrow already." She glances at the Trevi one more time, eyes tired but bright. It's love. She smiles at me. "Enjoy the rest of your trip."

I stuff my hands into the pockets of my shorts as I watch them disappear into the crowd. A few coins clink between my fingertips and my eyes dart to the pool of the fountain. Before I realize it, I'm back at the edge, coin resting in the center of my sweaty palm.

This wish isn't for Rome.

Looking around to make sure no one is watching, I hold my hand out over the water and turn it over slowly, but the coin doesn't fall. It's stuck to my palm.

I keep my hand steady and close my eyes.

I wish to fall in love with an Italian.

Darren's face flashes across my mind. Definitely not Italian. Definitely not available. But it's too late. I open my eyes and turn my hand over. The coin is gone.

The girl I bought my pastry from yesterday is working again this morning, wearing the same uniform—black shirt, white apron, and white cap—like she never left.

"*Giorno*," she says as I walk up to the counter. Her smile lets on that she recognizes me.

I reply with more confidence than before, "*Giorno*."

She cocks her head to the side, studying me. "Something is different."

My eyes close for a second as I laugh to myself. Oh, how I'm different, let me count the ways: I'm in Italy. I'm lying to my parents. I met a super nice yet unavailable guy I can't seem to stop thinking about, and just when I convince myself I'll never see him again, I do, all thanks to instructions I followed from a friend who isn't even here.

She shifts closer, leaning onto the counter. "You met someone."

I blink at her. "What?" I try to play dumb, but Darren is still on my mind and I bite back a smile.

She smirks and wipes a cloth across the already clean counter. "I recognize that look."

I don't like that I have *that look*. I need to make it go away. It's useless.

"I think I need a latte. And chocolate," I say, dropping a handful of euros onto the counter.

"You want a glass of milk, or you want coffee?"

"Milk?"

"*Latte* is milk, *un caffè* is coffee. *Un caffè con latte* is coffee with milk."

"How on earth do you keep all that straight?" A tired sigh escapes my lips. "I have so much to learn, I don't even know where to start. So how about *un caffè latte, per favore*."

"*Brava!* See, you are learning already," she says through an ear-to-ear grin. "I was fortunate to grow up speaking both. Much easier. I speak Spanish and some French, too, but not so good." She points across the little room. "Sit. I will bring them to you."

"*Grazie,*" I say as I shuffle over.

"*Prego!*"

I set my bag on the floor between the chair and the wall, and place my camera on the table. A small tray presenting two cups of coffee and a plate of pastries appears, and the girl sits across from me, handing me a napkin. A lovely melody flows from her mouth, but I have no clue what she's saying, if she's even talking to me. I stare at her, unsure of how I'm supposed to react.

She finally puts a hand on her chest and speaks slowly, "*Mi chiamo*—my name is—Chiara."

I turn her name over on my tongue. Key-ahr-uh. "Really? That's the name of my hotel, the Albergo Santa Chiara."

"By the Pantheon, *sì,* I know of it. *Come ti chiami?*" she asks, apparently determined to teach me Italian.

I remember enough Spanish to note the similarity to "*¿Cómo te llamas?*" "I'm Pippa."

"Pippa? This is a whole name?"

"It's short for Philippa. But—"

"Ah, *sì*! Philippa!"

"Yeah, I go by Pippa, though." I take a timid sip of coffee, the burning liquid as bitter to my mouth as my proper name is to my ears. "Chiara is a pretty name. Does it mean anything?" I ask, stuffing the pastry in my mouth to combat the coffee flavor.

She circles the rim of her cup with a finger. "Every name means something. Mine means clear or bright."

My eyebrows pinch together. "Those don't exactly mean the same thing. How can something that's clear be bright? Wouldn't it just be clear?"

The corner of her mouth twists upward. "You haven't seen the Ligurian Sea."

"Where's that?" But somehow, I already know the answer.

At the same time, we say, "Cinque Terre."

"*Sì.*" Chiara grins and props her elbows on the tiny table, cradling her chin in a hand-hammock. "So tell me, Pippa. How did you meet this someone?"

She's not Morgan, but something about her makes me spout my whole story from the beginning. At times I wonder if she's actually listening, but then she makes an exclamation I don't understand, yet somehow completely agree with. Maybe it helps that Chiara is an outside party, unattached to everyone I mention. I don't have to worry about the truth of my unfiltered words getting back to anyone important.

By the time I finish my tale, I'm practically weightless. I hadn't realized before how much I was holding in.

She leans back and exhales. "That explains why you came in by yourself."

"Yeah. Sucks, right?"

"Do you believe that it does?"

If I hadn't come over here by myself, my story over the past few days would be totally different. Darren wouldn't have been a part of it even once, and now I've seen him twice. I'll always remember my first day in Rome with him in it, and that most definitely does not suck.

"Not anymore, I guess," I finally answer.

"And now you have the whole summer to do as you please, here in Italia."

"Looks that way." I twist the cooling coffee cup on the saucer and sigh. "Have you ever done anything this crazy?"

"Crazy? I think it is brave! What fun, no?" She's nearly lifting off her seat. "Secrets and lies! Scandals and intrigue!"

"What are you talking about?" I cover my mouth with my hand to suppress my laughter.

She giggles. "Just trying to make you feel better. I can tell you have doubts."

My smile droops. "That's some insight you've got."

"Practice." She shrugs. "So what is next for the summer travels of Pippa?"

I pull out my guidebook and flip to the Rome section for reinforcement. "There are still a couple of things in Rome I want to see for sure before moving on. Catacombs, the Vatican—"

"Oh, you must see la città del Vaticano! Tomorrow! I will take you."

I snap my head up to meet her dark eyes. "What? I can't ask you to do that."

"Who is asking? I am offering." She deflates a little. "Unless you prefer to be alone?"

My heart warms and my smile spreads. A real local to show me around the Vatican.

"It sounds great."

CHAPTER ELEVEN

ASSIGNMENT NUMERO QUATTRO: FACE YOUR FEARS

I know you well enough to know that by this point, you're struggling with a few things. You're out of your comfort zone, surrounded by a language you don't understand, studying for a job you don't want. They say you should face your fears head-on. Write some things down that you're afraid of or intimidated by, then write a way you could get over each of them. Example: I am, as you know, illogically afraid of naturally occurring bodies of water. And to get over this, I could fall in love with someone who lives on a yacht. See? It doesn't even have to be realistic. And, go!

* Fear: sneezing while driving and getting in a wreck
  Remedy: learn to sneeze with eyes open (I will prove that it's not impossible)

* Fear: that I won't know when I really fall in love with someone
  Remedy: learn to be patient
* Fear: never having a good relationship with Mom
  Remedy: learn to talk to her
* Fear: going back home to listen to said mother screech about my disobedience
  Remedy: stay in Italy indefinitely

The slow-moving line wraps around the outer wall to Vatican City, but Chiara leads us past everyone to the entrance where the tour groups gather. She approaches a woman who is clutching a clipboard and a thin wooden rod with strips of colorful fabric dangling from the top, similar to what the other tour guides are sporting. Chiara and the woman smile and kiss each other's cheeks, but I can't tell if they know each other or if that's just the way things are done here.

Chiara waves me closer and we're absorbed into the tour, shuffling through the entrance ahead of the mile-long line.

"How did you do that?" I ask after we hand over money for the entrance fee. The guide wanders to the counter to buy tickets for the group.

"I simply asked if she had room for two more!"

We're given headsets so we can all hear the guide without her yelling, and it's only after I finish adjusting the volume that I realize she's speaking in French. I catch eyes with Chiara and frown.

"Oops!" She puts a hand to her mouth.

We dissolve into laughter and I return my headset. There's

no point in a French soundtrack to my Vatican experience. At least we're not still waiting to get in.

Chiara relays anything interesting that's mentioned, but for the most part, I bring up the rear and observe my surroundings. We're led through immense halls lined with tapestries and frescoes, past statues of all sizes, some missing limbs, noses, ears, breasts, or *other* parts. We climb up stairs, down stairs. My calf muscles are killing me and even my right arm is sore from lifting my mammoth of a camera up to my eye every couple of minutes.

There is one thing this place doesn't lack: art. I'm practically drowning in it. Everywhere I turn is another reminder of my lie. Another needle to the chest.

I finally remember to breathe when we get to an open courtyard.

"You are bored," Chiara says. "I am sorry it is not an English tour." She pulls the headphones off and drapes them over her shoulder.

I manage a smile so I don't appear ungrateful. "I'm trying to be interested in all this. And it is beautiful, but . . . I don't know." I fan my hand in front of my face, hoping I can pass it off on the heat. "It's miserable out here. Hard to concentrate, you know?"

The fabric-strip beacon flutters near the door to another building and our group lines up behind it. I stifle a groan, pinch my shirt at the neck and repeatedly pull it away from my body, pumping wind down my chest and stomach.

"Here," Chiara says, pressing a few buttons on her cell phone. "A picture will make you feel better." She holds the phone out in front of us, putting her head against mine like we're old friends.

We take half a dozen photos together with serious and goofy faces, but I get distracted when I spot a head of thick, dark curls about twenty feet in front of us. My heart pounds so hard, it makes me dizzy for a second. I clutch Chiara's wrist.

"Chiara. I think that's—"

The guy turns and catches eyes with me, smiling to reveal a mouthful of braces. So not Darren. And this kid might only be, like, fourteen.

Chiara clears her throat. "That is the guy you met?"

I let go of her. "No. Not even close." A long sigh morphs into laughter. When did I become such a girl, freaking out over a boy I don't even know?

"We should rest." She points to a bench that just cleared at the end of the walkway. "We can always catch up with them later, or continue without them. I know where the important parts are."

We're facing a tarnished statue of a pinecone with two peacocks standing guard. I don't get it at all. Even if someone explained the symbolism to me, why decorate with it? It's a pinecone.

Mom will never understand this about me. She could probably look at this pinecone and know what it means without anyone telling her. She's got the brain for it. I don't. She pretends this fact doesn't exist and continues pushing me into things she likes to do, all in preparation for a career she thinks she can make me want.

But I can't let that happen. I won't.

The Sistine Chapel is dim and a musty sort of cool, which is a surprise considering how many people are crammed into the space. A camera flash briefly illuminates the room and a strongly accented man at the front yells, "*No foto*!"

Chiara points to the ceiling and my eyes follow the lead. There it is. Right. Up. There. The most famous painting I've ever heard of. God giving life to Adam.

"*Incredibile*, no?" Chiara whispers.

I swallow hard and my eyes mist over. There are no adequate words. "*Sì*."

My neck struggles with the position of my head but I can't look away. Michelangelo was in this *exact* room, way up there on scaffolding, so much higher than I imagined. If he was close enough to the ceiling to paint with a little brush, how did he know it would look this perfect from down here? That's probably the sort of thing I'd be learning at that summer program.

Did I really write to them from a fake e-mail account, posing as my mother to get out of it?

My face flames and sweat dots my hairline. It itches, but my arms refuse to let me do anything about it. The crowd blurs into a dull shifting mass, pressing in on me. I look back up at the ceiling for stability, but it only makes me dizzier. Colors swirl together. God shifts his eyes from Adam to me.

Murmurs and whispers amplify, joining my accelerating pulse until there's a stampede in my ears. My heart might explode.

What have I done?

Chiara grabs my hand and supports my weakened body through a maze of people and doorways until we're outside. The brightness burns my eyes, but I welcome the awakening.

"What happened? You looked as if you might fall over."

I avoid her question and instead gaze up at the weathered, bluish dome of St. Peter's Basilica looming over us from high above all the other buildings in the city. Is the pope in there praying for liars like me?

Laughter erupts from my mouth so loud that Chiara and I both start.

"*Che cosa*?" she asks.

I tighten my lips to hold in another bout, breathing slow and steady through my nose.

"Pippa, what?"

I wave my hand at an imaginary fly.

"You worry you made the wrong decision." It's a statement. Somehow this girl already knows me. "I do not want to influence you poorly, but the decision has already been made, no?"

I nod, not exactly sure if that's the right response to her confusing question.

"Then why anger yourself about it now?"

I close my eyes and inhale deeply, pulling my shoulders up to my ears and tucking my chin to my chest. "It's the Pippa way."

Chiara pulls my shoulders down and gives them a shake. She's right up in my face. "The Pippa way might be the wrong way. You have chosen, now you must live your choice. Regret changes nothing. Only makes you sick. Keeps you awake at night."

"O, wise one," I say with a slight bow, struggling to deflect with humor. "How old are you, anyway?"

She stands straighter. "Eighteen."

"So I have another whole year to go before I see things so clearly?"

Her head shifts to the side as she searches my eyes. "I do not think it will take you quite that long."

She winks and it makes me yearn for Gram. Her presence alone would settle any nerves. She's really the only one I'm upset about deceiving.

"Why not tell them the truth then?" She presents her cell phone to me in the palm of her hand. "You can. Right now."

I stare at the tiny phone, blood pumping and stomach churning. But I shake my head. I'm not ready for that much honesty. And the punishment that's sure to follow.

Chiara continues, "Then you have to let go of what holds you back. Free yourself from it." She takes my hands in hers and spreads my arms out to shoulder level. She sings the word, "*Volare*."

"I know that song. What's it mean?"

She closes her eyes and lifts her head toward the sun, stretching her arms out even farther. "To fly."

So I fly.

I fly back to town on the metro line, leaving my worries behind on the steps of St. Peter's, the largest church in the world. The pope can deal with it all for me.

From here on out, I'm not regretting this decision. I'm going to enjoy every minute, every catcall, every gelato scoop, sunset, pizza slice, and spaghetti strand. I'll check in with everyone intermittently so they don't get suspicious, take my prize-winning photographs, and have the experience of a lifetime. The kind of summer people only dream of. I'm going to live it.

CHAPTER TWELVE

The train brakes squeak and Chiara hooks her arm through mine. "This is our stop."

I look at the display at the end of the car but don't recognize the name. "I thought I needed to get off at Spagna."

The doors glide open and she sneaks us through the mob, unharmed. She keeps her arm in mine, but I don't mind it there. It makes me feel local. Like I belong.

"Would you like to have dinner with my family?"

There's a renewed spring in my step as we walk a few blocks from the metro and turn down a narrow, vine-draped street that I would have passed by without noticing. Chiara unlocks an unmarked door and leads me to the second floor to her family's apartment.

The space is small, but clean and organized. The scent of garlic makes my mouth water. The cramped, lemon-yellow kitchen along the far wall is teeming with women, each with a utensil hovering over a different bowl or pot. First impression tells me this is Chiara's grandmother, mother, and sister.

The three women look up when the door closes behind us, utensils are abandoned and hands rise in the air. Excitedly chatting in singsong phrases, they swarm me. The shortest of the women takes my hands in hers and leads me to a chair at the dining table.

"You are Philippa?"

"Pippa, Mamma." Chiara rolls her eyes and leans toward me. "Stuck in her ways. She might not call you Pippa."

I giggle, completely overwhelmed with the warm welcome into a real Italian home. And touched that she already talked to her family about me.

My first impression was correct. My hostesses are Chiara's grandmother Anna Maria, who speaks no English; her mom, Cristina, who looks only slightly older than Chiara; her sister who might as well be her twin, Liana, already twenty but still living at home.

The front door swings open and two young boys bounce in and run to Chiara's mother, shouting, "Nonna! Nonna!" A tired-eyed woman saunters in behind them, and Chiara introduces her as Maria, her oldest sister. I'm starting to wonder if all Italian girl names end in the letter *A*.

Dizzying Italian words fly around me, and Chiara leans in to tell me that normally dinner would wait for her sister's husband—her family always tries to eat together—but he's stuck at work. I can't even remember the last time my family shared a meal.

Even with Chiara's father away in New York, the tiny apartment is bursting at the seams. It's a little overwhelming for this only child, but there's something comforting about witnessing it. Chairs of various sizes are brought in from other rooms, and somehow we all fit at a single round dining table. I tuck my elbows to my sides as I tear at a hunk of bread and guzzle a glass of water.

"Philippa," Cristina says as she sets out the first course, or *il primo piatto*. "You are young to travel Italia alone." Her tone is more curious than reprimanding, and I'm grateful. I'd hate to have to return to the Vatican and strap all my anxiety back on.

The fettuccine wraps around my fork, taking a basil leaf with it. "I'm used to being independent. I was brought up that way."

"Good. *Va bene*." She reaches across Chiara and pats the top of my hand. "You will be strong."

I can only smile in thanks and wonder what it is about this family. I already love them.

The boys fling noodles at each other and one of them lands on my arm. Maria removes it and tosses it back at them, clucking until they sit still and eat with their forks instead of their hands. I turn my head to hide my laughter and catch eyes with Chiara.

"I so needed this," I say with as much sincerity as I can muster. "You have no idea."

She beams at me, because she does know. She's got me figured out more than I do.

Our second course, *il secondo*, is sliced beef, asparagus

drizzled with olive oil, more bread, and cheeses. I'm already feeling satisfied from the pasta, but it all looks so good, I can't help but take a little bit of everything. And I hadn't even considered dessert, but Liana waltzes in with a chocolate torte. I don't ask for fear of being rude, but I'm curious if this is a special meal for company or if they eat like this every night.

After *il dolce* is finished and the plates are stowed in the kitchen for later, Maria and her boys file out with hugs and kisses to all, even me. Liana emerges from a room down the hall shortly after, dressed in a tight red skirt and matching flowy top with a glitzy, beaded strap around the neck. Her black heels rap the floor with every step, raven hair rhythmically caressing her shoulders.

"Not even dead would you see me dressed like that," Chiara says to me after Liana leaves, one hand propped on her hip. "My legs are not that nice. I want her legs," she huffs.

"I want her hair."

She clasps a section of my hair and lifts it up, letting it fall back down strands at a time. "What is wrong with your hair? It is perfectly fine."

"It's perfectly boring. I plan to get a makeover as soon as possible."

Cristina's voice beckons us to the sitting area. "What is next for Phillipa? Where do you travel to after Roma?"

"I was actually hoping to get opinions on that." I shift, and a spring in the couch squeaks. Anna Maria opens her eyes briefly but dozes off again immediately, nestled in a cushy recliner that takes up a big portion of the living room.

Chiara chimes in, "Pippa's plans changed last minute,

Mamma. She is deciding what she wants to do with her summer days here."

"Ah. Difficult to find rooms now," Cristina says, absent-mindedly running a finger along the rim of her wineglass.

"So I'm learning. My hotel told me I have to leave tomorrow because they're booked." And in reality, one of those youth hostels is probably all I can afford from now on. I shudder at the thought of sharing a tiny room with who knows how many smelly people. And sharing a bathroom.

Chiara and her mom speak to each other rapidly, leaving me to study the tattered upholstery of the armrest. I'm torn between trying to decipher what they're saying and tuning them out because they obviously don't want me to know what they're saying. Either way, it doesn't matter. The only word I pick up is "Mamma."

Cristina turns to me. "We would like to invite you to stay with us."

"Oh." I look around the humble apartment, wondering where they would fit another sleeping person. "That's so generous of you."

"We would love for you to stay," she says.

There's a flutter in my gut. They actually want me here. I want to say yes.

"*Per favore*, Pippa." Chiara leans forward, excitement radiating from her. "We insist! And remember I am helping my aunt with her restaurant in Cinque Terre?"

"Yes. What—"

"I leave the day after next." She stands and clasps my hands as if she's leaving this instant, and her face glows even more. "I want you to come with me! There will be plenty of room with my aunt."

I sit up straight on the edge of my seat as the brilliance of her idea floods through me. Free lodging in one of the most beautiful places to photograph in the country? I'd be stupid to pass up this opportunity. And even better, I won't have to spend my entire summer alone after all.

CHAPTER THIRTEEN

ASSIGNMENT NUMERO CINQUE: BE YOU

Now, I have a feeling you've been a more reserved version of yourself thus far. Am I right? But with that last assignment, you've already faced your fears, so now reap your reward and live! Be the Pippa that I know you to be for your new Italian friends so they'll love you as much as I do (but not so much that they keep you, because I totes need you back).

Make an effort today to become more of who YOU want to be.

We have a whole day to kill before we hop on a train bound for Riomaggiore. I'll miss Roma, but the pull of Cinque Terre is so strong, electricity buzzes through every part of my body.

After Chiara shuttles my luggage and me back to her apartment in a little two-person gray cube on wheels—the "car" she shares with her sister—we walk to a shop without windows and pause outside the lacquered red door.

Chiara puts a hand on each of my shoulders. "Are you ready?"

"For what?"

A dark beauty in a tight sapphire dress slinks out of the door and passes us without a glance, her voluminous hair trailing behind. The scent of cherries wafts through the air. Jealousy courses through me.

Chiara catches the door before it closes all the way and ushers me inside. The cool air breezes by us as it rushes for the opening. Goose bumps pop up all over my skin, but it's not from the chilled air.

"For this!" She waves her arms like she made everything inside the trendy hair salon appear by magic.

My stomach drops. Why am I so nervous?

I've never done anything to my hair except for the summer I wanted to be blond like Morgan, and Mom wouldn't spend money on highlights. *Too much upkeep*, she'd said. So I took matters into my own hands and tried a poolside remedy: lemon juice. Sure it was lighter, but it took weeks to get moisture back in my crunchy hair. After that, I swore I'd never try anything else.

"You are slow to make decisions," Chiara says. "You are bored with your hair, no? Mamma always says that if I complain about something, I must find a way to change it."

"But what if it's something you don't have control over?"

"Then you find a way to live with it." She grabs a fistful of my hair. "But this is only hair. And the control"—she points to a man dressed in all black approaching us with a smile—"has you for the next two hours."

Angelo's dark hair is shorter on the sides but long and spiky all down the middle to the back—a faux-hawk. He's beautifully put together, like the exotic bad boy I've always wanted to like.

Chiara takes charge and rattles off to him with over-the-top enthusiasm, but he matches it, and together they pull me to a chair stationed in front of a giant mirror with a bright red frame. Neither of them asks me anything. They stare into the mirror while Angelo gently runs his fingers through my hair and Chiara mimes what she's saying with her hands.

A head full of foil, a shampoo, cut, blow-dry, and one energetic styling later, Angelo swivels my chair toward the mirror, finally allowing me to see.

My eyes blink repeatedly. It's my face, yet it looks nothing like me. My hair . . . I thought he cut it, but it almost looks like there's *more.* It falls all around my shoulders, ends curling slightly every which way. And the color! It's the dark chocolate I've always wanted but never thought I could pull off. Bangs reach from far back on the side of my head and swoop across my forehead above my eyes and down the right side of my face. It shines, it bounces.

"It's perfect," I say through quivering lips.

Moisture pools at the edges of my eyes and drips down one of my cheeks. I stand and reach for Chiara, pulling her into a hug. I feel one of my tears soak into the shoulder of her shirt. It doesn't quite bind us by blood, but it feels close enough. I'm so grateful I walked into that bakery when I did. Somehow I know we're going to be friends even after this summer is long gone.

Darren's face comes to mind again, and I imagine his jaw

dropping in reaction to my transformation. I shake my head to clear it and look back into the mirror. I catch eyes with Angelo and tear up again.

"*Grazie*, Angelo."

He reaches for my hand and kisses it, muttering a string of phrases in Italian.

"What's he saying?" I ask Chiara.

"He says you are beautiful." She smiles, her eyes glistening too. "And that there will be a line."

"For what, the salon?" I laugh.

"For you."

I love Italian men.

CHAPTER FOURTEEN

~~Get a makeover~~

Trains are not a new thing for me. Having grown up in Chicago, I've ridden them plenty. But this is a *real* train. One that travels across a whole country, complete with semicomfortable seats clumped together in groups of four with a table between, outlets for computer and phone chargers, overhead compartments for luggage. It's more spacious than I thought it would be, and much more tolerable than a plane.

Chiara and I sit across from each other at the window. I try to take photos of the rolling hills and villas as we pass by, but all the shots come out blurred and my reflection shows in the window.

"So tell me about your family we're staying with."

She settles deeper into her seat. "*Zia* Matilde, my aunt, is my mother's sister. She married a fisherman, *Zio* Sandro, and moved to live with him in Riomaggiore. She worked in a little restaurant and eventually took it over, so now she owns it. My uncle died a year ago in an accident."

"Oh, I'm so sorry. How awful. What happened?"

"I am not certain. They never found him, just his boat. My aunt believes he went straight up into heaven."

I'm unsure how to react.

"She is the only one that thinks this way," Chiara says with a small but knowing smile. "My cousins, Bruno and Luca, live with her and they help out. After the next school year, Bruno was to go away to university, but I am not certain he will be ready even then. His father was his world. He has, ah, what you call issues now."

"What sort of issues?"

"Wrong crowd, bad choices. I am worried for him. He has great promise, though I feel he will waste it." She stares out the window.

"You're close to him," I guess, handing her a stray napkin from my backpack for her tears about to spill over.

She still doesn't look at me. "We were closer once. We spent many summers together in New York. But things are different now. We are different. My parents are alive, both of them. I am happy, planning to go away to university. He is . . . stuck."

"Is this trip going to be good? I mean, are you excited we're visiting them?" I ask.

Her eyes widen. "Oh, for certain! I love my family—*amo la mia famiglia*. And it truly is my favorite place on earth, though I have not seen many places yet." She covers a yawn with the back of her hand and peers out the window again. "This is my first summer not to go to New York in several years, so that will be strange."

I fight back a yawn too, but they're contagious. "You said you're going to school there soon, right?"

"*Sì!* Can you imagine? Me, going to university in *gli Stati Uniti*!"

It seems crazy that people back home dream of going to places like Italy, and people in Italy dream of going to the United States. Is no one happy where they live?

We finally step onto the platform in Riomaggiore as the sun starts its descent. Pulling my bag behind me, I walk over to a low brick wall and look out at the water. I've never seen a color quite like it. It's the most delicious mixture of blues and greens, shimmering in the bright sunshine.

"Clear and bright," I whisper.

"The Ligurian Sea!" Chiara exclaims, linking an arm through mine and snapping a picture of us with her cell phone.

After dragging our luggage through a crowded tunnel that cuts through a hill, we have to practically hike up the steep street—Via Colombo—toward her aunt's building. As I struggle to keep up with her fast pace, I have to remind myself I'm going to be living here for a while, and resist the urge to get out my camera to document every single market and patio restaurant we pass.

We stop at a gated entrance, and I sit on top of my rolling bag, huffing and puffing. I gulp down half a bottle of water, looking up in wonder at the apartment building.

"It's pink."

Chiara giggles. "Look around you."

I stand and turn, taking in my surroundings now that I'm done being a pack mule. Boxy buildings hulk over us on both sides of the street, nearly every third one not quite Pepto-Bismol pink, but close. Some are white, mint green, orange, bright yellow. Most of the windows have dark-green shutters, open to the world outside despite the heat. Lines of laundry stretch in front of them and across balconies. It's like I've been transported to a simpler time.

"I've never seen anyplace like this."

"Wait until you see it from the sea," Chiara says, dialing a number on her phone.

Less than a minute later, a busty woman I assume is *Zia* Matilde opens the gate and pulls Chiara close to her, tears in both of their eyes. Matilde places a hand on the back of Chiara's head and strokes her hair.

"*Zia*, this is my friend Pippa."

"*Sì!* Happy you are here!" Matilde reaches out and hugs me tight, smashing my face into her overflowing chest. "Come! I have prepared the room."

She leads us up a gazillion flights of narrow concrete steps to the very last landing. I collapse on my suitcase again and down the rest of my water. Chiara and Matilde snicker to each other, neither of them winded.

"You will get used to it soon," Chiara says, helping me stand.

The air inside is only about ten degrees cooler, but it's something. The living room consists of a cushy blue couch, several chairs, a shockingly large flat-screen television on the wall, a compact spiral staircase leading up to a mystery door, a dining table, and a small kitchenette.

Matilde leads us into one of the apartment's two bedrooms, obviously belonging to Bruno and Luca. Bunk beds are stacked in the corner and the walls are covered in soccer posters.

"You can have the bottom bed, Pippa," Chiara says. "You seem to have a problem with steps."

I snatch a pillow and whip it at her, but she ducks in time, the pillow knocking over a stack of sports magazines.

"Girls same as boys." Matilde laughs as she turns back to the living area.

We pull fresh clothes out of our luggage and Chiara heads to the bathroom—the only one in the apartment—closing the door behind her and leaving me to change. I shed my shirt and freshen my deodorant, then fan my skin trying to cool off. I feel wet everywhere. I can still hear Chiara shuffling around in the bathroom, so I quickly change my shorts into ones that are more breathable, and then decide to sprinkle some baby powder down my bra.

Just as a little cloud of powder hits my chest, a voice that is neither Chiara's nor her aunt's announces its presence in the now open doorway.

"You are the American girl who is taking my bed."

CHAPTER FIFTEEN

As I scramble for my shirt to cover my chest—thank God I'd decided against changing bras—I grumble, "Don't you knock?"

He crosses his arms and rests against the door frame. "It *is* my room."

My heart pounds in my ears. I should yell, kick him out, slam the door, but I can't take my eyes off him. Russet skin, solid jaw line, caramel eyes, perfectly messy black hair. Shoulders and arm muscles stretching his baby-blue shirt tight. Is this Bruno or Luca?

I adjust the shirt hiding me, equal parts embarrassed and flattered that someone so hot is checking me out. He brushes a hand over the tips of his hair before resting it up high on the doorjamb. I'm not sure I can feel my legs. I can't believe I'm sharing an apartment with him for the whole summer.

Chiara pushes past him into the room and stops, first looking me over, then frowning at him. "You did not knock?"

He smirks. "It is my room."

Chiara spouts off in Italian, waving her hands around, and soon they're pretty much yelling at each other. Then they erupt into laughter and he shoves her shoulder before pulling her in for a hug.

"Bruno, this is my friend Pippa. Pippa, my cousin Bruno."

Bruno. The in-with-the-wrong-crowd Bruno. Divinely and supernaturally gorgeous Bruno.

And he just winked at me. Not good.

He closes the distance between us in two long strides of his tight white pants and says "*Piacere!*"—which I remember from my phrase book means "pleased to meet you"—before taking ahold of my shoulders and kissing each of my cheeks. His lips are *on* my cheeks.

I catch a glimpse of myself in the mirror and want to die. It's physically impossible for a face to be any redder.

I try to say "*Piacere!*" back but only a squeaky noise escapes my lips. I raise my shirt just enough to hide behind and fake a coughing fit, waving with the other hand for him to leave the room. He laughs and mutters something in Italian as he walks off. Chiara closes the door.

Way to make a great first impression on the sexy Italian.

"What did you say to him?" I ask when I've recovered the ability to speak.

"I told him that he should knock on doors that are closed. That you are American and do not lie on the beach with *le tette* out. You are private."

"*Le tette?* What's that?" My face pinks again. "My boobs?"

"Sì." She sprawls across the bottom bunk. "I think it is sweet. Leaves room for the imagination."

"Um . . . thanks." I finish getting dressed. "What did he say?"

She laughs. "He said, 'She will one day.' "

My nose scrunches at the thought of baring it all on a beach towel in a foreign country, with Bruno and other guys who look like Bruno watching. I shudder. "Doubtful. There are some parts of me the sun just wasn't meant to see."

Chiara rolls to her side and looks at me. "So you have never been swimming without clothes on?"

"Skinny-dipping?" I smile as I stow my dirty clothes into my suitcase. "Well, the moon can handle those parts of me just fine."

The next day, Chiara and I start helping out at the restaurant, recently renamed Trattoria da Sandro in honor of Chiara's uncle. Since I'm not Italian, which is what tourists *want* from a waitress in Italy, my job is to bus tables, refill drinks, throw salads together, slice bread, and do anything else that doesn't involve much customer interaction. But I can't complain about being a glorified busgirl. I get to eat and sleep for free. I've basically won the tourist jackpot, suddenly part of the "in" crowd. I get an extended peek behind Italy's curtain.

And I like watching the pros up close. Chiara and Bruno both have super heavy Italian accents when dealing with English-speaking tourists, and I've noticed Bruno's is especially adorable when the table consists primarily of women.

Mostly I work alongside Luca. He's shy—the complete opposite of his brother in that category—and absolutely precious for a fourteen-year-old. I can't tell if his English is poor or if he just doesn't talk much. But it's not an uncomfortable silence and we easily fall into step together.

Bruno, on the other hand, talks constantly. It's still my first day on the job and I'm already "the best slicer of bread on the planet of earth." And apparently I don't sweat; I glisten in the sunshine, which he finds sexy. The attention is quickly making me the best eye-roller on the planet of earth too.

As I grab a water pitcher to make the rounds in the shaded outdoor section, Bruno rushes past me and beats Chiara to a table of two giggling American college girls. They're both either naturally trashy, or totally wasted. Seriously? It's only lunchtime.

I refill the water glasses at the table next to them, but I can hardly pay attention to what I'm doing. The blond girl sporting a bikini top and tight jean shorts is flirting shamelessly with Bruno. She leans toward him, elbow propped up on the table, head resting in her hand as she bats her eyelashes. The brunette holds her menu out to him and insists that she just can't make out what any of it says, and would he be so kind as to help her decide.

The blonde pulls down her friend's menu and brings the attention back to her. "So what time do you get off work?" She talks slow, overpronouncing every word as if he's a hard-of-hearing child.

I'd kind of like to pour this water over her head, but I doubt it would even cool her down.

Laughter purrs in Bruno's throat and he smiles, revealing shockingly white teeth against his tan skin. He looks right at me, eyebrows raised. What is he waiting for, my reaction?

Well, he's not going to get one.

I turn to head toward the door, but just as I pass Bruno, my arm bumps into his. The condensation is slick under my fingers and my grip on the pitcher weakens. The scene morphs into slow motion as the pitcher falls to the ground and clangs near my feet. Water sprays all around us, soaking the hem of a woman's skirt.

"Oh, no! I am *so* sorry!" Then feeling like I ripped part of the magic Italian curtain for her, I start repeating a poorly pronounced version of "*Mi dispiace!*" as I rush to hand her spare napkins from an empty table.

She glares at me as she snatches them and attends to her skirt, waving me away. Hopefully I didn't just ruin someone's chances for a tip.

I squat to retrieve the pitcher but Bruno's faster. He offers it to me and I make the mistake of looking him in the eye. My balance is thrown and I start to fall back. Bruno drops the pitcher and takes hold of both of my wrists to keep my butt from slamming into the ground. He uses my momentum, and in one swift movement, we're both standing again, face-to-face. Too close. *Way* too close.

He smells of wine. And basil.

Bruno picks up the pitcher, slowly this time, and loops my fingers through the handle.

"All right?" he asks, his smile big and hypnotizing. I nod. "You should wash this." I nod again. "And refill it." Nod. "You agree with everything I say?" Nod. "You like sleeping in my bed last night?"

My face combusts, suddenly very aware of all the customers, especially the table of American hoochies not even five feet away. I steal a glance at them. The brunette's mouth hangs open and the blond one looks me up and down, her expression simultaneously appalled and impressed. I'm mortified.

And slightly thrilled.

I run through the restaurant and into the kitchen without looking back. I blast the cold water into the sink, let it fill my cupped hands, and dip my face down into it again and again until I'm no longer on fire. When my eyes clear, I notice a hand towel dangling in front of me. Luca.

I take it and quickly pat my face dry. "I—" . . . have no idea what to say. "Your brother . . ."

Luca makes an understanding noise. "Bruno is"—he struggles for the word—"loud."

I would have said something else, but his definition is accurate too. Luca wasn't even outside but he obviously knows his brother well. Bruno barging in on me while I was changing should have told me everything I needed to know about him.

Luca goes back to chopping vegetables, and I busy myself at the sink, heart rate still accelerated.

Anxious to avoid similar impromptu performances, I spend the rest of the day in the kitchen. There's a reason I'm comfortable acting in plays; we rehearse them. Improv isn't something that comes easy to me, onstage or in real life.

I'm surprised and relieved Chiara doesn't mention it when

she waltzes in to grab her orders. She doesn't even give me a sly look from the corner of her eye—the kind I'm giving her to check and see if she's giving me one. I guess she's just being nice because it's impossible she missed me making a fool out of myself. Everyone saw.

Crap. There went that goal.

CHAPTER SIXTEEN

Don't make a fool out of myself in public—FAILED

ASSIGNMENT NUMERO SEI: COMFORT ZONE

Get out of your comfort zone today! Tell the truth to someone. More specifically, tell a gorgeous guy that he's gorgeous. Yep. You read me.

According to Google Translate, "Tu sei un uomo bellissimo," is your money phrase.

Sound it out like this: too say un whoa-mo beh-lee-see-mo.

Memorize it. Find a hunk (maybe you already know one by now?). Say it. It might even be the start of a BELLISSIMO relationship. In which case, you can thank me later.

Throughout the next week, I learn to act more composed around Bruno, but it's just that: an act. My eyes find him every chance they get. At the trattoria, from the other side of the couch while watching television, in the mirror when we're running late and have to brush our teeth at the same time. I subconsciously study and memorize everything about him.

Like how his eyes get sad sometimes when he thinks no one's watching.

Bruno is everything I dreamed an Italian boy would be, the stereotype I had in my mind before coming to Italy in the first place.

And it's really, really, really hard to resist.

I'm slicing fresh tomatoes for salads when I sense a presence behind me. I slow down my cutting and try to see who it is out of the corner of my eye without turning my head.

A breath breezes over my neck as Bruno asks, "You say toe-may-toe or toe-mah-toe?"

Goose bumps avalanche down my arm and I raise my shoulder to my ear, turning my body to block him. "You left out an option," I say, continuing my work.

"*Che cosa?*"

"Toe-may-ter."

"*Sì!* That is the way!" Bruno throws his head back and laughs, raspy with a slight squeak in the inhales. Freaking adorable.

And I made that happen. I suppress a smile so he can't see what an easy target I am.

He takes the knife from me and cuts two slices of deep red tomato, then rummages around in the kitchen, gathering items on a small plate. He returns and presents a dish of fresh mozzarella circles alternating with the tomatoes. He's even finished it off with basil. It looks as perfect as the *caprese* salads they serve the customers, but miniature.

"You try this before?" he asks.

I shake my head. I've had versions of it back home, but the sight and aroma of this one renders all others impostors. I reach for a fork, but he snatches it out from under my hand and stabs a piece, bringing it to my mouth.

I look from his eyes to the fork and back again. He can't seriously think he's feeding this to me. I reach for it but he pulls away. I check to make sure Luca and the chefs have their backs to us.

"You're insane," I say before hesitantly taking a bite.

He mutters something I don't even try to decipher because the juice from the tomato explodes in my mouth and my eyes close involuntarily as I savor it. The spice of pepper, the crunch of sea salt, the sweet, almost mint flavor of basil.

"It's amazing. I can't believe you just threw that together." Assuming he made it for me, I grab the fork from him and taste more. "Seriously," I say between bites, "*incredibile*."

Bruno watches me eat, obviously pleased. He takes a step toward me and opens his mouth, somehow still smiling. He wants me to feed him. With my fork.

I should probably put up a fight but as if in a trance, I offer him a little sliver of tomato and cheese. He leans forward to take it, eyes on mine the whole time.

Holy. Crap. I never ever thought anything about eating could be sexy. I was wrong. So very wrong.

I break my gaze first and hastily gather the dirty dish and fork, carrying them to the sink to scrub them clean. When I'm finally thinking clearly enough to turn around and continue my veggie cutting, Bruno's gone and Chiara's staring me down from the drink station with her arms crossed.

After the dinner rush, I'm eager to crash on my bed—I haven't forgotten it's actually Bruno's bed—and rest my legs. As soon as Chiara and I head back to the apartment, Bruno calls to us from the door of the trattoria.

"Chiara! Pippas! Where you go?"

"To sleep! You can handle it on your own." Chiara shouts something else to him in Italian before she links arms with me.

His eyes find mine through the dark and the corner of his mouth pulls up. I bite my lower lip and turn away, allowing Chiara to lead me up the steep hill.

We walk in silence for several minutes until she says, "You know what he is, do you not?"

Italian? *Hot?*

"You Americans call him a player."

Aside from my surprise that Chiara knows that word at all, a weight tacks itself onto my shoulders. Our conversation from the train ride replays in my mind at hyper-speed. Wrong crowd. Bad decisions. Wasting potential. But I haven't seen evidence of any of that, not really. He's been nothing but sweet to me . . . and every other girl in town, but still.

I don't respond and she shoots me a pointed look. "Do not let him get to you. It will be a mistake."

"I'm not letting him get to me," I reply too quickly. "I don't even know him."

"You would be wise to keep it that way."

I stop at the gate. "He can't really be that bad."

"Pippa, you make your own choices. I only show you what you cannot see. What I know about him that you do not." She sighs and turns the key, leading me up to the apartment. "I know that he is not right for you. You like nice boys."

Nice boys like Darren.

I shake the useless thought away and press my lips together tight. Chiara's blurring the line between friend and mother now.

"And how would you know?"

"Because you are a nice girl." She frowns, shrugging her shoulders. "*Bene*. But do not cry to me—"

"Chiara, I appreciate you looking out for me, but I get it. I know what I'm doing."

I think.

I mean, I wrote it down on paper, the goal to end all goals—fall in love with an Italian. I threw a coin in the Trevi Fountain, wishing for the same thing. And I didn't even have to look. An Italian found me! But maybe I've been making it too hard on myself, taking my goal too seriously. The idea of falling in *love* love probably isn't very realistic.

And this summer is about doing what I want. So if a gorgeous Italian wants to feed me *caprese* and whisper in my ear, then I officially want him to.

After we get ready for bed, Chiara mumbles a good night as

she creaks her way up the wooden ladder to the top bunk. I hope she's just tired and not upset with me. I hate that negative vibe in the air when I'm worried someone's mad at me. I might talk to her more about it tomorrow. I want her to know I can handle myself around her cousin. At least I hope I can . . .

My eyes are closed, mind whirling through a thousand thoughts at once. What is it about Bruno that makes him so charming? Why did Chiara have to get such an attitude about it all? I wish she'd lighten up. Why did I see Darren that second time? Why do I still find myself thinking about it? About him.

I try to get comfortable but it's so hot, my legs stick together and my face is clammy. I settle on my back, sprawled across the entire mattress, one leg out of the sheet. The hum of the ceiling fan becomes my focus. Maybe it will lull me to sleep.

Toss. Turn. Toss. Turn. Too. Hot.

I shuffle into the kitchen and get a bottle of water out of the refrigerator. I press the cool plastic against my cheek and just as I take a swig, the front door swings open.

CHAPTER SEVENTEEN

I startle, practically jumping into the air, and some of the water in my mouth sneaks down the wrong pipe. Spitting what I can into the sink, I surrender to a coughing fit.

Bruno shuts the door behind him and rushes over to pat me on the back. "All right?"

I nod, coughing a couple more times and wiping the tears out of my eyes. The springs on the couch bed in the living area squeak when Luca rolls over. My hand covers my mouth as my throat forces me to cough again. I try to make it as quiet as possible, but there's really no controlling this.

"*Andiamo*—we go," he says, hand still patting my back. "Outside."

He leads me through the living room and up the small spiral staircase to the mystery door. On the other side of the door is a terrace overlooking the main street past the trattoria to the marina. Two reclined lawn chairs are lined up next to each other, beach towels laid out across each of them. Bruno pulls out a lighter from his pocket and lights a couple of candles on the table off to the side.

Once I finally stop coughing, I lie on one of the chairs, facing the deep night sky. A thin cloud passes quickly over the moon.

He picks up a soccer ball from the floor and leans all the way back in the other chair. "Who is this tall girl who stays in my home?" I can tell he's smiling, even without looking at him.

"Ah," I say. "My height. I was wondering when someone would point that out. Does it bother you?" I always say I don't want my height to be an issue, but I end up making it one anyway.

"*Perché?*"

"It just seems like most guys don't like tall girls. I guess it intimidates them."

Bruno laughs, repeatedly tossing the ball into the air and catching it.

"What? It doesn't intimidate you?" I press. "What if I were the same height or taller than you?"

He crosses his right foot over his left. "I buy taller shoes."

We laugh together and fall silent. A cat screeches somewhere on the street below, its cry echoing several times before disappearing. It makes me think of Darren. The closet cat lover who skipped out on catechism class.

I fight a smile and close my eyes, relaxing deeper into my chair. I've often closed my eyes and pretended to be somewhere else. Exotic places, just like this. On a terrace, at night. With a gorgeous Italian. So why my mind drifts back to Illinois is beyond me.

I'm by our pool in the backyard, Gram in the chair next to me, calming me down after the Summer Abroad News Bomb. I can even smell her lavender scent wafting through the air. What's she doing right now? Is she bored out of her mind without me there? I wish I could talk to her.

"You miss home, *sì*?"

I blink a few times, talking my eyes out of welling up. "Parts of it."

"Parts?"

"My grandmother mostly, and my best friend, Morgan."

He shifts onto his side, facing me, resting an arm on the soccer ball. "Do you have parents? You do not miss them?"

I consider his question carefully before answering, aware that Bruno's father recently passed away and it wrecked him. Here I am, on the other side of the world from mine, and I haven't even been thinking about either of them, both alive and well. But that's not really my fault. Sure I miss my parents. I miss the kind of parents they *could* have been. Mom more so than Dad—he sides with me most of the time. At least he makes an effort.

"We have different . . . ideals."

He clears his throat again, harder this time. "You have boyfriend waiting for you?"

I fold my hands over my stomach. "Not for a long time."

He playfully rolls his eyes and sighs. "Boys."

A laugh escapes my lips. The boys back home seem so lame in comparison to Bruno, with their retro superhero T-shirts and baseball caps. They're trying too hard, whereas Bruno doesn't have to. He just *is* the kind of guy who demands to be noticed.

"So," I say, steering the conversation away from my lack of a love life. "Why did you think I was missing home?"

"You were quiet," he answers, a catch in his voice. "People think of home when they are quiet. Miss things. People."

I lower the back of my chair so I'm lying completely flat, and roll over onto my side, mirroring him. The warm orange light from the candles brightens his face. He looks older than seventeen in this light, with harsher angles, yet there's something vulnerable about him. Like I'm seeing a part of him no one else ever has.

"Is that what you think about when you get quiet?" I ask.

He studies me but says nothing.

"I see you," I say. "Sometimes your eyes lose focus and you sort of . . . go somewhere else." My throat tightens. The thought of the pain he works through every day breaks my heart.

Bruno looks above me, past me, anywhere but my eyes. The muscle along his jaw tightens. I have nothing to help him. No words of wisdom. No personal anecdotes. I've never been through anything close to what he has.

"I'm sorry," I say. *Sorry for asking. Sorry about your dad.*

He inhales, breath almost imperceptibly shaky. "You know?"

"Is that okay? That I know?"

He allows his eyes to meet mine again and his face softens. "*Sì.* I am glad that you know."

We stare at each other and his mouth twists into a sleepy smile. So does mine.

"Pippas," he nearly whispers. "I tell you something that you do not know."

My heart picks up speed and I nestle deeper into the chair, waiting for his revelation. I know it's not right to get hung up on appearance, but he's *so* freaking hot. It's hard not to get excited that he wants to spend time with *me.* I have no clue what it all means, but I'm going to soak it up while it lasts. Because it's very likely it won't ever happen again. According to Chiara, it isn't even really happening now.

Bruno strokes my cheek close to my ear with a couple of fingers, back and forth, back and forth. I'm tempted to think he might lean over and kiss me. I'd probably even let him. My body tingles at the thought. The anticipation.

You know what he is, do you not?

Nothing happens. His palm rests flat against my cheek, prompting me to look at him.

A player.

Shut up, Chiara.

"Everything about you is lovely," he says.

My heart leaps, bounds, springs. Floats.

Chiara has to be wrong about him. He's kind and sweet and achingly romantic.

And he thinks I'm lovely. He could have his pick of any Italian beauty he wants, and he thinks *I'm* lovely.

Overwhelmed with the need to touch him, I reach out and trace along his sharp jawline, stopping just before his lips. I swallow hard. So does he.

He clasps my hand in his and lightly kisses the tip of each finger, his eyes never breaking their gaze on mine.

There's something I'm supposed to say to him. Something in Italian.

One word. My brain remembers one word.

"*Bellissimo.*"

CHAPTER EIGHTEEN

"Wake up, *principessa*!"

My eyes fly open at the sound of Bruno's voice, but I immediately squint in the light streaming through the window.

"It is noon!" he says.

I pull the sheet over my head, but he fights me for it and wins, exposing my face in all its puffy mayhem. I groan. Then panic.

"Wait! Did you say it's noon?" I sit up, careful not to smack my head on the top bunk.

"Mamma gave us today free. *Andiamo a* la Via dell'Amore." He roots around the room and I spring out of bed, suddenly very awake. I've been in Riomaggiore this entire week, but we've been so busy with the trattoria, no one's had much of a chance to show me around farther than our little village. But I'm still not complaining. It sure beats schoolwork. Or begging for food on the street until my flight back home at the end of summer.

"What about Chiara? Is she coming too?"

"No."

She's not going to like this plan.

He finds my sneakers. "Wear these. And something . . ." He struggles for the word, grabbing the middle of his shirt and pulling it away from himself repeatedly.

"Breathable, got it." I laugh and wait for him to leave the room. He doesn't. "Um . . . I'm not changing with you watching me."

"Oh! *Sì!*" He flashes his bright teeth before darting out and closing the door behind him.

We pass the trattoria on the way to the trail. Chiara is taking orders from one table, while Luca delivers meals to another. I catch eyes with Chiara and hesitantly wave. She waves back but her narrowed eyes shift from me to Bruno, then back again. She probably thinks she should be the one to show me around, especially since she's, well, not Bruno. But he commandeered my day with promises of photo ops and food. Like I could say no to that.

I didn't expect to have to pay a fee to use the trail, but turns out it's considered a national park. It's gated with a ticket booth, business hours, and everything. I'm handed my pass and a brightly colored map of the trail between villages. The walk from Riomaggiore to Manarola is only supposed to take about twenty minutes.

Bruno winks at the attendant and she waves him on. I'm sure it's just because he's local. . . .

"*Non necessario.*" He snatches the paper from me and wads it into a ball. "I am your map!"

"Hey! I wanted to keep that! I was going to put it in my book."

He smashes his lips together in a very artificial pout and sets the crumpled ball in the palm of his hand, offering it to me. "Your book?"

I open the map again, but the wrinkles are permanent no matter how much I try to smooth them out. "Yeah, my book. Like a journal? I'm documenting my trip."

"The book under your pillow?"

Fear and anger bubble in my chest. "Were you snooping in my room? Did you read it?"

"Again, I will tell you that it is my room." A sly smile takes over half of his face and he slides his hands into the pockets of his tight plaid shorts.

I swallow hard. If he hasn't read it, I don't want to make such a huge deal out of it that he *does* read it. And if he has . . . "Just," I say, calm but firm, "tell me you didn't read it."

"Okay, okay." He weaves his fingers between mine. "I did not read it."

I stare down at our hands. A shiver climbs up my arm and pulses in my chest. This is public. This is weird. And he might have read my journal, the *idiota*. I should let go of his hand.

But I don't.

Bruno leads me to the official trail entrance and we stop underneath two golden hearts welded to the top of the gate. Padlocks and luggage locks of every size and color dangle from the hearts and from any other available hookable object.

"*Benvenuta a* la Via dell'Amore," he says, poking a bright pink lock with *Ashlee + Jake* written on it in white paint.

"What are all the locks for?"

"Do you know the history of la Via dell'Amore?" I know a little, but I'd rather hear it from him, so I shake my head and he continues. "When this path between Riomaggiore and Manarola was not here, many people did not marry outside of their own village. But with the, ah, connection to the next village, love was exciting again. Lovers walked along the seaside here to meet with one another."

I take in the view as we stroll the crowded path. High cliffs stretch up to our right, with sections of loose rock held down by wire mesh, padlocks hooked onto every wire within reaching distance. To our left, the Ligurian Sea—clear and bright, blue and green—glimmers in the afternoon sun. Fishing boats and passenger ferries race along the coast. The temptation to take pictures of every detail around me is strong, but that would require letting go of Bruno's hand, and I'm not sure I want to just yet. I'm curious to see how long he'll hold it.

"The locks are for the tourists, a symbol of love for all to see, for the eternity. Until they are cut down."

I gape at him. "Cut down?"

He laughs. "*Sì.* This path would be nothing but locks if they were not taken away."

I smile as we pass a couple hooking a tiny green lock onto an open loop of restraining cable overhead. He's well over a foot taller than she is, and she rises onto her tiptoes to meet his lips as he bends down, both of them giggling.

As we approach a tunnel, traffic gets more congested and I

feel a bit claustrophobic despite the open-air windows to the sea. Colorful graffiti covers the walls on either side—definitely not an art form my mother approves of, which makes me like it. Scattered solid patches of a neutral color suggest these walls get painted over right along with the lock cutting.

Bruno and I merge into the lazy pace of graffiti gawkers for several minutes before I realize we're all in a line. At the end of the tunnel, in front of one of the lookouts to the sea, couples take turns sitting on a concrete bench. The back of the bench rises high into a silhouette of a man and woman kissing, rods of the railing on either side packed with locks, all hooked onto one another.

Within several minutes, we're at the front of the line. I assume we're going to keep walking, but the young English couple in front of us has me take their picture, and then they offer to take ours. I open my mouth to decline, but Bruno bursts out with a "*Grazie*!" and unhooks the camera from my neck, handing it to the woman.

He leads me to the bench and we sit, the sides of our legs touching. My stomach clenches. This is the *kissing* bench. Not a single couple before us has smiled for the camera. They *kiss* for the camera.

My eyes lock on the lens like a deer in the headlights. I force a smile, a big one, with teeth. My head nearly vibrates with the strain. This is fine. We're going to break the trend and smile. Absolutely no kissing.

The woman lifts my camera to her face. "One, two—"

On two, Bruno reaches behind me and cups the back of my head in his hand, turning me to face him. His other hand is on my cheek. His lips press onto mine. The camera clicks.

"WOOOOOO!" echoes around us. One person claps. Bruno pulls away but stares into my eyes for a moment before hopping up and getting my camera back for me.

My head is spinning. *I've been kissed. In Italy. By an Italian!*

I remain seated, stupefied, until a couple shoos me away for their turn, and soon we're walking the next section of the path along with the English couple. Bruno chats with them—heavy accent enforced—but their words turn to garble. All I hear is *He kissed me. Bruno I-don't-even-know-how-to-pronounce-his-last-name kissed me!*

And it was short. Too short.

No. Too long. Shouldn't have happened. Chiara will kill us if she finds out. But she won't find out. I'll hide the picture from her. I'll delete the picture! No, I have to show Morgan. And I want proof for myself. I'll just make sure Chiara doesn't see it. It only happened because it's what you *do* at the kissing bench when you're sitting next to the hottest Italian boy you've ever seen.

I just have to stay away from that bench.

CHAPTER NINETEEN

In no time at all, we make it to Manarola. The colorful buildings are identical to those in Riomaggiore, just arranged differently. The streets are lined with shops, all of them crammed with sweaty tourists. Every visible table and bench hosts families eating slices of pizza, sandwiches, and gelato.

We wave good-bye to the English couple as they head into a store, and we decide to grab lunch at a little restaurant Bruno promises is worth the wait for a table. And of course he knows the owner.

After we order, I don't say much. Bruno just stares at me across the table with an unreadable expression. Too bad I don't know what he's thinking.

I'm so nervous, all I can do is keep shoveling food into my mouth.

"Why eat so quickly?" he asks, taking a sip of wine.

"I'm not eating fast, you're eating slow." I laugh, stabbing at another square of pesto ravioli.

He sighs and asks the waiter for more wine. "In Italia, sharing a meal is . . ." He waves his arm over the table, palm toward me, as he searches for the words. "Do not rush. Enjoy it. *Mangia*."

"I am enjoying it. I just also enjoy taking pictures, so the quicker we eat, the more I get to see." I set my fork down, finished.

He laughs and leans back in his chair. "Eat as fast as you wish, they will not bring your bill any sooner."

I cross my arms. "Well, not if you keep ordering wine, they won't."

And they don't, not for another twenty minutes. My leg bounces under the table, eyes darting around anxiously.

"Ah," he says, patting all the pockets of his shorts.

"You forgot your wallet," I mutter after a sigh. Not that I expected him to pay for me, but he should have at least made sure I had money with me before ordering anything. And two glasses of wine, no less.

A player.

No. Forgetting your wallet is an easy mistake, like locking your keys in the car. Nothing to get irritated over. Though I am a little irritated.

I pay the bill and just as we step back onto the crowded street, someone slams into my side from behind, lurching my body forward. I regain my balance and turn to see a thin local girl, possibly a few years older than I am. Before I can come up with something to say to her, she squeals and throws her arms around Bruno's neck, kissing him on each cheek. Pretty close to the mouth, I might add. They plunge into an energetic conversation and I stand nearby, waiting for an apology. Or at least an introduction.

Nothing. I'm invisible.

She offers him a cigarette and he pulls a lighter from his pocket and lights hers too. He takes a long drag and laughs at something she says, their smoke mixing together in the close space between them. I want to gag. He's definitely not kissing me again now.

I wait a few more minutes, but neither of them even looks my way. This is total crap. If he really liked me, wouldn't he be showing me off or something?

I scowl at both of them before noticing a gelato place across the street. The line's out the door but I join it anyway, eager to slip away from Bruno and his fan club. The warm smell of waffle cones tickles my nose and my mouth waters.

I'm just about to make it inside when a figure catches my attention in the street a few shops down. There's something familiar about the mop of hair . . . the cargo shorts. . . .

I hold my breath and stare at his retreating form. There's no way. It can't be.

"There you are! Come," Bruno says, tugging on my hand.

Feet firmly on the ground, I shake his hand away. "I'm getting gelato. I wasn't exactly invited into your conversation." I look up again to locate the guy with the mess of dark-brown curls. Where did he go?

"Jealous, Pippas?" His voice is bright like I've just presented him with a trophy for Player of the Year.

"Please. I know exactly what you are."

As if on cue, yet another girl greets him with a quick kiss-kiss on the cheek before she takes off.

I step out of the gelato line, no longer in the mood. "I rest my case."

Bruno's eyebrows press together as he studies me. If I didn't know any better, I'd say he almost looked offended. "We go back," he finally says.

I glance down the street toward the sea one more time, searching in vain. Oh, well. There's no way it was him anyway.

The next morning, I ask for half the day off to explore even more of the seaside trail, but on my own. I need some time away from Bruno. Need to clear my head.

I scarf down a breakfast of fruit, cheese and bread, and check my e-mail. To use the Internet, I have to plug into the wall like I did at the hotel in Rome, only the cable that Bruno has hooked up is super long. It pretty much reaches everywhere in the apartment.

I gasp when I see that Gram finally responded. My dad may write in uppercase letters, but Gram types in all caps. I guess it's easier for her old eyes to see. It makes me laugh anyway.

To: Pippa Preston <pippers26@gmail.com>
From: Lorelei Mead <lorelei@prestonartsource.com>
Subject: Re: Ciao from Italy!

PIPPERS!

SORRY IT TOOK ME SO LONG TO SEE YOUR E-MAIL. YOUR MOTHER IS CRACKING THE WHIP

AROUND HERE. I'M GLAD TO HEAR YOU ARE SAFE AND SOUND. HOW IS SCHOOL GOING? I WANT TO HEAR ALL ABOUT IT.

AND WHY DOES IT SURPRISE YOU THE BOYS ARE WHISTLING AT YOU? YOU ARE THE MOST BEAUTIFUL GIRL IN THE WORLD.

I LOVE YOU AND MISS YOU!!!

GRAM

I swallow the lump in my throat and type up a quick response. I tell her how hot the weather is, how I'm making friends with my roommate, and that I'm taking pictures of everything, getting comfortable with the area I'm staying in. Not quite lies, not quite truths. I just skip the part about school. It kills me that I can't tell her everything.

I also send a message to Mom—a shorter, less enthusiastic version of the one I sent to Gram.

I fill my backpack with bottled water, a few energy bars, extra sunscreen, money for shopping and food, my trail pass, and one very wrinkled map. The five seaside villages have paths between them and today I hope to at least make it to the third, Corniglia. And if I get tired, a five-minute train ride can take me right back where I started.

I spend a couple of hours in Manarola, exploring the shops—I'm still on the lookout for a silly souvenir for Morgan—people-watching, eavesdropping on conversations I can't understand, sampling foods so delicious I couldn't describe them to someone if I tried. Finally scoring a cone of gelato, I let it cool me as I start the path from Manarola to Corniglia.

This section of trail is not as well kept as la Via dell'Amore, which was mostly paved and relatively flat. At least it's fenced so I'm not completely terrified of falling off the ledge, but the rock-strewn terrain demands my eyes to bounce between my feet and the spectacular view that I don't want to miss a second of.

But a second is all it takes. The path makes a sharp right turn, and my eyes are focused on the hazardous stone steps ahead, not on the loose rock I step on. My ankle rolls and I cry out as I slam onto my knees, palms scraping against the gravel. I gasp as my camera dangles perilously close to the ground.

I stand as quickly as I can, afraid someone may have witnessed yet another feat of public embarrassment. Fire climbs up my faulty limb to my hip. This is not something I can walk off. I turn around and aim for a bench I remember seeing not that far back. It must take me a good ten minutes to shuffle to it.

It's occupied by a hyperventilating overweight woman and her husband, but I squeeze myself onto the end, my back to them. I examine my hands. A couple of tiny rocks still cling to my palms. I knock them off and a bead of blood appears just below my right thumb. The antibacterial hand wipes burn but they're better than nothing. I guzzle half a bottle of water and eat two granola bars before my body relaxes and the stabbing pain in my ankle reduces to a dull pulsing. The wheezing couple finally leaves and I spread out a little more.

The sun is roasting. There's not much escape from it on this cliff trail anyway, but for some reason being stationary makes the rays feel a thousand times more severe. I finish off a water bottle, then perch my sunglasses on top of my head, swiping at the sweat on my nose and forehead with my arm.

I can't sit here all day. At some point I'm going to have to tough it out and walk back. I stand on my right foot first, then slowly add weight to my left. A jolt shoots up my spine and tickles my brain, heart pounding in my ears.

I lower myself back down to the bench. No phone—not that I know who I'd call anyway. I'm going to have to hobble back to Manarola, take the train to Riomaggiore, and once I get there . . . hop on one foot up a steep hill and three flights of steps to the apartment. I can do it. I have to.

I prepare to stand, when a voice I recognize says, "Pippa?"

CHAPTER TWENTY

I turn and a warm tingle generates in my chest and spreads through me. "It *was* you!"

With one eyebrow raised, Darren—*the* Darren—walks over and sits beside me. Same thick curls fly out at all angles, framing his face, stubble still magically the same length. He's so close I can smell the musky heat radiating off his body.

"It was me? When?"

"Yesterday!" I say. "I thought I saw you. In Manarola."

"That's where I'm staying, actually. Well, until the morning anyway. Why didn't you say anything?"

"I wasn't sure it was you. You were sort of far away." *And I was with a guy I didn't want you to see me with who kept trying to hold my hand.* "And I saw you last week at the metro too. Back in Rome."

"I saw you!" He's rocking on the bench like he has so much

energy traveling through him he doesn't know what to do with it all. I know exactly how he feels. "I went to your hotel later that night when I got back to that side of the city, but the woman at the front desk wouldn't tell me anything."

My heart leaps. "You came to see me?"

"Yeah." He runs a hand through his curls and shrugs. "I wanted to see how your summer of freedom was going, but the woman practically barked at me to leave, like I was a thug or something."

I laugh. "Well, you do look a little sketchy behind all that hair."

He laughs like I just delivered the best line in the world. "Speaking of hair. You went dark."

In a panic, I attempt to smooth down all my sweaty flyaway pieces. "My new friend Chiara took me for a 'makeover' back in Rome," I say, complete with air quotes.

"Looks good."

My eyes seek out the ground. "Thanks."

He leans his back against the bench. "Man, this is so crazy, running into you here."

"What are the chances?" we say at the same time. I'm still focused on the ground, but I can feel him looking at the side of my face.

He asks what I've been up to, and I tell him about meeting Chiara, the invite to Riomaggiore, and how I got the job helping at the trattoria in exchange for room and board. I make a point to leave out Bruno.

"After you mentioned Cinque Terre, it came up again," I tell him. "And I just had this feeling. I knew I was supposed to come here."

"What, like fate?" The eyebrow rises again, but half his mouth is turned up too.

I copy his smile and allow myself to stare at him for a moment. He stares back.

"Yeah. I think so, maybe," I say.

His smile widens and he clears his throat. "Guess your summer's turning out okay after all, huh?"

I look out at the sea. "Until I go back home and get the paddle." I force a laugh, upset that I reminded myself summer isn't eternal.

"They actually *beat* you?" Darren asks, his smile gone.

"No no no." I amend, "But I doubt I'll be allowed to do anything again until I'm thirty."

He laughs. "Well, let's hope that's not true."

"Sometimes I forget what I'm getting away with, that my parents still have no idea where I really am. Then I remember and it feels like I'm having heart palpitations. Like my heart might actually explode." I wave the subject away with my hand. "Enough about me. Tell me about your summer program. Are you loving it? The digging part, I mean." I nudge him with my elbow. "Are you digging it?"

"Wow." He laughs deep. "Haven't heard that one before."

"Really?"

He cocks his head to the side, scrunching his eyebrows and biting his lip.

I join in his laughter. "Of course you have."

"It's a lot of work," he says. "Meticulous work. You have to log every little thing you find. But yeah, no matter how geeky I am admitting it, it's a pretty sweet gig."

"What's the most interesting thing you've found?"

"Like me, personally?" I nod. "A human jawbone."

I reach up to my own jaw and touch it. "Just the jawbone? Nothing else?"

"No skull or anything, just the jaw. Even had a few teeth still attached."

"That's disgusting."

"We've found lots of animal bones, especially when you get to a section that used to be a street gutter or something. But that jawbone was definitely random." He unbuttons a pocket on the leg of his shorts and buttons it back, several times over. "It sort of puts things in perspective for you."

"What do you mean?" I turn to face him once more.

A seagull lands on the railing across the path and stares us down before pecking at a black speck and taking off.

"Well," he begins slowly, "finding tools or broken pieces of pottery is one thing. They're just things people used. But finding a part of an actual person? That bone used to be covered in muscle and skin. The teeth used to chew food to fuel a body that used those tools. Makes a person think about their own life. How short it is. How temporary."

I swallow, attempting to bring moisture back to my throat. "That's—"

"Too heavy, I know. Sorry." He shakes his head and laughs at himself. Between curls I can see his ears turn red.

"No. Well, it's a serious thought, yes, but . . ." I laugh at myself.

"What?"

"Well it's just . . . when I went to the Colosseum and the Roman Forum, that's the kind of stuff I kept thinking. I wondered about the people who walked there when the city was at its height. About what it all looked like."

"Right? It's incredible the inventiveness they had so long ago. We think we're so smart now, but if it weren't for them—"

"Who knows what things would be like today?"

"Yes, exactly. It's all just so—"

"Fascinating," we say simultaneously.

We hold our gazes on each other until the button Darren's been playing with breaks away from his shorts and falls to the ground. We both lean down to pick it up and our heads smack together.

"Ugh!" I say, popping right back up, rubbing my forehead. "I'm sorry!"

Abandoning the button, Darren reaches for his head too. He parts his hair where I hit him and tilts his head down toward me. "Am I bleeding?"

For the split second I think he's serious, I lean closer and search for anything out of place. Then it registers that he's joking, so I dig my hand into his hair and gently but quickly push him away. His hair is so much softer than I expected.

"Pansy," I tease.

Once we get over the laughing fit, Darren fidgets on the bench, preparing to stand. I move too, but then remember my ankle.

"I believe I owe you dinner," he says, hooking his thumbs on the straps of his backpack. The same green one I saw him with at the metro station.

"Dinner!" I say at a near-shout, checking the angle of the descending sun. "I promised to be back in time to help with dinner at the trattoria. I was sitting here for, like, an hour before you even sat down."

"Why?" he asks, observing our surroundings with a sweep from left to right. "I mean, there are better views than this one."

I slouch, defeated. "Don't laugh. I sort of hurt my ankle."

Even though his eyes are concerned, he bites his lip, dimples in full force.

"I'd consider that laughing," I say with a hand on my chest, pretending to be offended.

"I'm not laughing! It's just—" He looks down at my feet. "How were you planning on getting back?"

"Well, I didn't *plan* on twisting my ankle!" I stand but keep the bum leg bent. "Walking. Walking is my plan."

Adrenaline pumping, I take a step forward, putting all my weight on my left leg. I let out a shriek as pain worse than before tears through me and I stumble. Darren jumps up to steady me, one hand at my elbow, the other at my waist. A sharp breath sneaks through my teeth.

"You need a crutch," he says, wedging himself alongside of me, our hips touching. He pulls my right arm over his shoulder and keeps his other hand loosely on my side. "If you weren't so tall, this would be really awkward."

I want to ask how this isn't awkward anyway, but I can't really concentrate enough to speak. The throbbing is gone for this instant, but someone let loose a flutter of butterflies in my chest and that's all I can feel.

We work our way along the path toward Manarola, most of it simple enough. But since we have to walk side by side, forming somewhat of a roadblock on such a narrow path of two-way traffic, we often have to move over to let people pass. And even though the sun is sinking lower in the sky, it's still ridiculously hot. Our clothes are damp between us, and sweat rolls down the side of Darren's face from his hairline.

He stops our momentum and looks ahead, prompting me to take my eyes off my feet. Stairs.

"What do you think, Pipperoni?"

I smile at the nickname, surprised he remembers calling me that. I urge us forward and he helps me hobble up a couple of steps. It's pathetic. We won't make it to Riomaggiore until midnight at this rate.

He rotates me and stands two steps down, back facing me. "Hop on."

I freeze, jaw dropping. No way. He turns his head and smiles wide, revealing his crooked tooth. I'd almost forgotten about it.

"Pansy," he throws at me.

"I'm too heavy for you to carry," I protest.

"My travel backpack weighs more than you do."

"Doubtful."

"Do you have a better idea?" He stands up straight and looks around, shading his eyes from the sun. "Taxi!" he shouts, letting out a whistle.

A group of old people eye us in alarm as they pass.

"I don't know him!" I call out to them before I look at Darren and sigh. "You win."

He adjusts his backpack so it's against his chest. I make it onto his back and he hooks his arms around my legs—freshly shaved, thankfully. He trudges up the steps with surprising speed and I arch my back as much as possible to keep my chest from completely smashing against his back. I can just see two round sweat marks on the front of my shirt . . . and on the back of his. No thanks.

He finally sets me down and we decide to walk la Via dell'Amore back to Riomaggiore instead of taking the train from Manarola. We would have to defeat a steep hill and a lot of steps to get to the station, then wait for the train. In all that time, we could probably three-legged race it on the trail.

We chat about all kinds of things: movies, hobbies, places he's been, places I want to go. Though I'm curious, neither of us brings up Nina. I ask him more questions about archaeology, and his face lights up when he talks about it. He says he's heading back to the dig tomorrow, and he's anxious to get his hands dirty. I try to act excited for him, but I wish we had more time together.

I have to piggyback a few more times before it's all said and done, but eventually we make it through the mosaic-tiled tunnel and we stand at the base of the familiar monster of a hill.

"Well, this is my stop. The trattoria is right up there." I swallow hard, then make myself look at him, study him. Will this be the last time I see him? "Thanks so much, Darren. I never would have made it without you, seriously. I'd probably still be sitting there waiting for who knows what. I can't believe you showed up when you did."

"Crazy, right?" He's still holding my waist and I'm delaying pulling my arm from his shoulders.

"Totally crazy." I test the weight on my foot and wince. We both look back up at the hill.

"I don't really see how you're going to be able to—"

Bruno's deep voice calls out from just up the hill, "Pippa *mia*! What happens?"

CHAPTER TWENTY-ONE

My stomach drops and Darren shifts, making me wobble.

Bruno's eyes don't even register Darren's existence. "All right?" He looks down at the foot I'm favoring.

"She's fine," Darren says before I can respond.

"Are you?" Bruno rests his hands on each of my shoulders and hunches so we're eye to eye.

"Stop," I tell him, shifting back. Of course he'd try to stake a claim on me now when there's another guy around. Why can't I get this much interest back at school?

Darren releases my arm and takes a step away. I can't look at him.

"Tell me," Bruno says, dropping to his knees to assess the damage. His skilled fingers glide all the way down my bare leg.

My face flames so quickly, my eyes water. "I stepped on a rock. My ankle fell out." In my periphery, Darren brings a fist up to his mouth to suppress a laugh.

Bruno looks up at me, puzzled. "Your ankle . . . what?"

"It twisted or something. It's no big deal." I swipe at my forehead with the back of my hand.

"You cannot walk. Look." Bruno whistles and points to my foot. "It is . . ." He makes a gesture with his hands, but I can see for myself. My ankle is swollen like a baseball.

Chiara bounds down the hill to us, spouting something frantic in Italian. Her wide eyes take in the scene and she's at my side, relieving me of my backpack within seconds.

"Pippa! What—"

"My foot. Rock. Twist. Really, it's a lot less dramatic than you're all making it seem."

Before I know what's happening, Bruno scoops me up in his arms, cradling me like a child. I have no choice but to cling to his neck. His really thick, strong neck. He smells of sweat and balsamic vinegar with a tinge of smoke.

"You don't have to carry me. We've been getting along just fine." I nod toward Darren, whom Bruno still hasn't acknowledged.

"You must put ice on it. Soon," Chiara says. "I have to go back to the trattoria; it is madness right now. But you should go home." She offers a smile to Darren just before she turns and says, "*Grazie, signore.* For helping my friend." And she's gone, taking my backpack with her.

Bruno starts up the hill after her, leaning slightly forward, which makes me feel like I'm going to roll right out of his arms. I grip his neck tighter and he smirks.

"I'm telling you, you really don't need to carry me."

He shushes me with a string of Italian phrases I can't

respond to. I look around to find Darren since I assumed he was walking along with us. He's not. He's still at the bottom of the hill, near the tunnel entrance, jaw slack.

Panic. Why isn't he following us? Then I remember Nina. I wonder where she is. Maybe he has to go back to her. Of course he does. He didn't come here for me. He didn't even know I was here.

I don't know what I was thinking. I'm one *idiota grande.*

I strain my neck over Bruno's shoulder and yell, "Darren! Thank you for your help! And tell Nina I said hello!"

He waves good-bye, his expression unreadable. I bite my lip to keep myself from saying anything else, and to keep it from trembling.

We stop at the gate to the apartment, but Bruno's still hanging on to me.

"The key," he says, swaying his hips. "Pocket on left."

"So put me down and get it out."

He lowers his lips to my ear. "You get it for me?"

Goose bumps. All over. I may have decided I want his attention, but that's a little much.

I remove my hands from his neck and push my legs down against his arm, making myself as heavy as possible. He gives in and lets me slide off, then opens the gate. I hop over to the stairs and use the railing as leverage to hoist myself up the first and second steps, blood pounding in my ears with every move. With a top floor apartment, this could take an hour.

Bruno scoops me back up without a word and trudges up the stairs. Despite the strength and precision it takes him to avoid letting any of my appendages smack into the wall, he's not even winded when we finally get to the apartment. He sets me down on the couch—the boys' temporary bed folded away inside—and carefully props my giant foot on a pillow. He rummages in the kitchen and comes back with a plastic sandwich bag filled with ice, wrapped in a hand towel.

The weight of it sends a fresh wave of pain up to my temples and I lean back, bracing myself.

"I am sorry!" he says, a deep line between his eyebrows.

"It's fine." I force a laugh. "This"—I motion to my foot—"is definitely not your fault."

"It is. I should have gone. It would not have happened."

If he had come with me, I know exactly what would have happened, and it wouldn't have involved sightseeing. It would have been The Kissing Bench Part II.

And I might not have seen Darren again.

As if reading my mind, Bruno asks, "So who is this Darren?"

My cheeks threaten to betray me. I focus on the chill of the ice numbing my foot and imagine it cooling my face, too.

"He's a—" What? A friend? Friends would have at least exchanged phone numbers or e-mail addresses, right? "He's a guy I know. Sort of." Like I owe Bruno any explanations.

"I do not like him."

"Why? You didn't even speak to him, much less look at him."

He shakes his head and kneels on the floor, pressing his upper body close to me and against the couch. "He should have carried you."

I remember the feel of Darren's arms looped around my legs, his frizzed hair brushing against my face with every step.

"He did," I say, clearing my throat. "On the stairs, when I needed the help."

He rolls his eyes and leans closer, taking my hand in his and looking straight into my eyes. "I would have carried you the entire way." He strokes the inside of my wrist.

My lips form a tight line as I try to focus on the pain rather than his touch.

"I did not know you were, ah . . . *una ragazza goffa*."

My mouth drops open. "You think I'm a goofy girl? Like stupid?"

"No! Ah—" With two of his fingers, he mimes a person walking up my arm, then crumbles his hand and says, "Oww."

"Clumsy?"

"*Sì*. Clumsy." His smirk coaxes true laughter out of me.

"I'm not. The stone moved!" I sigh and lean my head back, staring at the sloppy plaster job on the ceiling. This whole situation is so ridiculous. I just ran into Darren for a third time, hurt myself so he has to carry me halfway home, and now I'm being nursed back to health by every American girl's dream. How is this my life?

"What do you need? Are you hungry?" he asks, thankfully standing and taking a few steps back. "I go get food for you."

I nod and roll onto my side, mashing my back against the couch pillows.

Bruno's hands twist together in front of him as he anxiously glances between my foot and my face, concern worked into the crease in his brow. An idea brightens his expression just before he bounds into his room and emerges with a set of crutches.

"These were mine," he explains.

I study them as he adjusts the height. It's hard to imagine such a strong guy gimping around on crutches. "What happened? Did a rock jump out and get you, too?"

He shakes his head and leans the crutches against a chair within my reach. "*Calcio*. You say soccer."

"Of course you play soccer," I mumble as he disappears again, this time into the bathroom. He comes back with a dampened washcloth. "You're probably the best one on the team, aren't you?"

"Naturalmente." The couch creaks as he sits in front of me. Reflexively, I scoot farther back, but he adjusts to take up the extra space. One hand supports his weight on the armrest behind my head, and the other gently wipes the film of sweat from my forehead, smoothing back my damp hair. His eyes gaze into mine until they dart to my mouth. For a second I think he might kiss me. For a second I almost want him to.

But he touches his lips to my cheek, lingering briefly before standing. "I go," he says suddenly, handing the washcloth to me. "You rest."

As soon as the door clicks behind him, my body relaxes deeper into the couch, both exhausted and confused. I lay the cool cloth over my face and close my eyes.

My mind's a big swirl of Bruno heads and Darren heads, Italian accents, lips on lips, chest against back, arms around necks. These boys. . . . Bruno practically peed on me earlier, marking his territory. But he was so sweet to me tonight, especially when we were alone. Maybe all the fuss wasn't a show for Darren. Maybe he really does care for me.

And maybe deep down I wanted Darren to see it. I could've

done more to protest Bruno's help, been more vocal. Told Darren that Bruno and I aren't actually *together* and I had no idea why he was being so hands-on. But I didn't want to explain it all away. Not really.

My breathing slows as I drift into the dizzy, happy space between awake and asleep. I see Bruno, holding my hand, snuggling here on this couch, openly, for even Chiara to see. My own Italian, right here within my grasp.

I resolve to focus on Bruno, to truly *get at* the real him.

But when I sleep, I dream of Darren.

CHAPTER TWENTY-TWO

ASSIGNMENT NUMERO SETTE: WRITE A HAIKU

Hai-ku: a Japanese poem, often seventeen syllables, in three lines of five, seven, and five.

I'm sure there's a lot of creative stimulation for you in Italy. Look around you and write what you feel.

Nestled among cliffs,
my temporary home lies.
Time pulls me away.

The rest of the week, I stay confined to the apartment like I'm in quarantine as my ankle heals. Bored. Out. Of. My. Mind.

Chiara and Bruno take turns checking on me and bringing me food, and while one day I'll miss the room service, I'm itching to be outside. Building my tan from an open window isn't the same as basking on the beach with the warm breeze snaking through my hair. I could hop my way up the little spiral staircase to the terrace, but getting back down won't be as easy. Adding a broken neck to my list of injuries isn't one of my goals.

I spend a lot of time gazing out the window to the green hills lined with vineyards and dotted with houses. There's not much to this quaint valley snuggled along the coast, but it's the most magical place I've ever seen with its multicolored buildings, steep streets bordered with wooden fishing boats. It's like the postcard you stare at for hours, wishing you'd been the one to take the picture just so you could experience such a perfect place. I'm living inside that postcard. I'm taking the pictures.

Gram would love how peaceful it is here, far away from the city lights. She's always told me not to hate anything, that it's a waste of emotion. I could dislike whatever I wanted as long as I acknowledged my dislike, then moved past it. My whole life, she's lived by example in this school of thought, except for one thing: she hates the city. Moving in with us after Papa died was bittersweet. She was happy to see me, happy not to be alone, but within a month's time she'd lost her husband and given up her home.

Home. Riomaggiore is already starting to feel like home. Aside from my week holed up here in the apartment, I've got a relatively established routine, a job, friends.

But there's a problem. I'm not staying here forever. I have to give this up and go home, my real home. Back to school. Back to the city.

And I hate that. *Cosa che odio.*

Securing Morgan's journal closed with the thin leather

string, I hobble back to my room and stuff it in the bottom of my suitcase since Bruno knows the hiding spot under my pillow. I'm not completely convinced he didn't read it, but he hasn't brought it up again and I'm sure not going to.

There's still about an hour before Chiara comes home with lunch, so I plug the cord for the Internet into my computer and sprawl out on top of the bed. I send Mom another selectively worded e-mail about how busy I am, how I'm now good friends with a local girl who's helping me with my Italian, and how unique the architecture is over here. True, true, and true.

I can't believe I'm still getting away with this. Shouldn't she have noticed by now that I'm not where I'm supposed to be? Does she trust me that much? I'm probably jinxing myself even thinking this, but I'm almost disappointed neither of my parents has figured it out yet. Not that I want to be grounded for life—I just want to feel . . . wanted, I guess.

I make a mental note to be more rebellious in the future. Clearly I haven't been living up to my potential.

I'm about to start an e-mail to Morgan when my computer chimes and an instant message box pops up.

queenofdrama14: pippa? are you really online?
pippers26: OMG, MORGAN!
queenofdrama14: PIPPA! how are you?! holy crap, i have so many questions. did you really skip out on that school program? are you having the most fantabulous time?! i miss you!
pippers26: I miss you too! What time is it there? Shouldn't you be asleep?

queenofdrama14: oh psh, it's like 2 am. i'm wide awake. tell me about YOU!
pippers26: Coast is clear, right?
queenofdrama14: please. you know my parents are lightweights. been asleep for hours. and garrett's off at new student orientation this week, thank god.
queenofdrama14: he's driving me NUTSO. won't shut up about starting college.
queenofdrama14: so yeah. coast is crystal clear. no sharks in the water. spill.
pippers26: I'm spending the rest of the summer in Cinque Terre!
queenofdrama14: cinque whattie? where's this?
pippers26: On the coast. Kind of close to France, actually. It's so gorgeous here. I'm taking lots of photos to show you.
queenofdrama14: googling. hold please.
queenofdrama14: wow! you're living quite the life over there, huh? totes beautiful! speaking of beautiful. have you gotten to that assignment yet?
queenofdrama14: you know, the breaking out of your comfort zone one?
pippers26: Um . . . maybe.
queenofdrama14: MAYBE? you better not be wimping out on me, pippers.
pippers26: Hah! Yes, I got to it. I told a beautiful guy he was beautiful! Eeeep!
queenofdrama14: and?!
pippers26: . . . and he kissed me. The next day, but still.

queenofdrama14: !!!! who? details!

pippers26: His name is Bruno. I told you about Chiara, remember? Bruno's her cousin. We're staying with his family.

queenofdrama14: whoa, like in the same house? that's some serious close proximity. where does he sleep? and where do you sleep?

pippers26: Chill out there, Morgs. Chiara and I kicked the guys out of their bunk beds. They sleep in the living room.

My fingers rhythmically tap the surface of the keys, waiting for a response.

pippers26: You still there?

queenofdrama14: uh, yeah, sorry. just passed out a little. you said GUYS. that's plural. and they're italian, right?

queenofdrama14: have you died and gone to heaven, leaving me behind to navigate the dregs?

pippers26: Luca's, like, a child. Doesn't count.

queenofdrama14: whatevs. oh hey, cable's throwing rocks at my window. time for me to make like a tree.

pippers26: Cable? WAIT! You're sneaking out at two in the morning with Jeremy Cable?

queenofdrama14: maybe.

I sink down into my seat, reviewing every possible interaction between the two of them I may have witnessed since Cable joined our drama group last year. He's unarguably gorgeous, but he's so quiet, I never caught much of a personality from him. And she never once mentioned him to me apart from "Who's the new guy?" and "I sure hope he can keep up."

pippers26: No wonder you were awake. And Cable is hardly the dregs, Morgs. He's cute!
queenofdrama14: haha, i know! i miss you!
pippers26: This conversation is not over. I will get details out of you!
queenofdrama14: ditto ;) leaving now. love you!
pippers26: Love you too! Later.

I'm still smiling as I close out our conversation and crank up the music on my computer, halfheartedly sing-humming along to the songs I know and scrolling through the pictures I've taken so far this summer. I start at the beginning, my mouth watering at the rich texture of my first gelato. I'm transported back to the streets of Rome when I come to the picture of a quiet alley draped in ivy, then the Pantheon, and the Colosseum. I ache for that first day, everything about it.

And everyone . . .

I stop at the image of me between Darren and Nina, the Colosseum stretching up behind us. It's such an iconic structure, at first glance someone might think we were Photoshopped in front of it. But I know the truth. And I can feel it. The sticky heat of Rome's summer air, the chatter of languages blending together. The hand at my lower back.

My face stares back at me, only a couple of weeks younger than I am now, but the difference is shocking. There's more color and life to me now, thanks to my sun-kissed skin and my rich chocolate hair. I've gotten so used to seeing the me in the mirror that this pale, untraveled girl in the photo seems like someone else. She was still waiting.

A sigh escapes my lips and I scroll over to Darren's face until it takes up the entire screen, then zoom out to fit his mane into view. Seriously, who has hair like that? Guys don't get perms, do they?

I keep scrolling through the rest of my photos, and my breath catches at the sight of me with Bruno. The kissing bench. I zoom in. I don't remember closing my eyes. Not that I remember leaving them open either, but they're definitely closed here. My eyebrows are raised in surprise while Bruno's are scrunched together, intense. Passionate.

I pull my computer closer to me and stare at our lips. Chills run down my arms at the memory.

The music that's blaring from the computer speakers fades, and just before it transitions to the next song, Chiara shrieks behind me.

CHAPTER TWENTY-THREE

"You kissed him?"

I slam my laptop shut and roll off the bed to face her, keeping most of my weight on my stronger foot. "It's not what it looks like."

She drops the lunch she brought for me onto the dresser and crosses her arms.

"*He* kissed *me*!"

"And *you* kissed *him*. I saw you zoom in to the lips."

I swallow hard, guilt painting my face. "I didn't mean for it to happen. He really did kiss me. First."

She shakes her head and clucks her tongue.

"Yes, I know what he is, what you say he is. But you don't—"

"I do not what? *Know* him? I know him more than you do." Her nostrils are slightly flared, teeth clenched.

But when he looks at me, talks to me . . . it can't all be contrived.

"I appreciate your warnings, Chiara, I really do. But you can't expect me to want to resist the attention of a gorgeous Italian." Especially when he's taken such sweet care of me this entire week. He likes me, I know he does.

She erupts into laughter.

"Yes, I said it. Your cousin is hot. This can't be the first time you've heard it."

"Oh, I have my own pair of eyes." She pauses, choosing her next words carefully. "But you American girls always see him differently. Your vision is . . ." Chiara raises her hands to the sides of her eyes like the blinders on a horse.

"You can't seriously be stereotyping me. I am not just another *American girl*." At least I don't want to be that to him. I cross my arms, mirroring her.

"Of course you are not. You are Pippa. My friend. *Amica*." She uncrosses my arms and takes my hands in hers. "But you need to open your eyes. Get rid of these," she says, positioning my hands next to my eyes.

When she lets go, my arms drop to my sides. "I just wish you'd trust me."

"Do you truly want to allow yourself to care for him when there is no chance for it to last?"

But what if it could?

Chiara motions toward my sack lunch and goes back to work. And I'm still confined to the apartment. Alone.

Early the next morning, Chiara, Luca, and *Zia* Matilde already long gone, I scramble to get ready to go before Bruno leaves for work in hopes that he takes me with him. I can't stay trapped in here another day. My ankle will just have to deal.

I rinse the toothpaste out of my mouth and look up at the mirror one more time. Bruno's sleepy eyes meet mine and I jump forward, pulling air through my teeth as I slam my hip into the counter.

"What are you doing? Watching me brush my teeth? Creeper," I mutter as I rub my throbbing hip.

"You lied."

My heart picks up pace as I rack my brain for what I could possibly have lied about, besides the whole thing with my parents. He already knows about that.

He holds the straight face for a moment before it cracks. "You say you are not goofy."

"Clumsy," I correct. "And I'm not . . . all the time."

He laughs and it turns into a yawn as he leans his back against the wall behind me. "You are up early."

The short pieces of his black hair are spiked out every which way. The poor lighting from the singular bulb on the ceiling over the shower exaggerates the dark circles under his eyes. He looks rough.

And why I find it incredibly hot is beyond me.

"Late night?" I ask.

I'm staring. I shouldn't stare. Biting back a smirk at his disheveledness, I pull the band out of my hair, pretending that I need to redo my ponytail. Really, I just need a distraction.

"I'm going back to work today," I say, when he doesn't reply.

He snatches my hand to keep me from putting my hair back up. "It is lovely down," he says softly.

I'm frozen, watching him in the mirror as he smooths a section of my hair, grazing my bare neck with his fingers. Everything Chiara's said about him rushes to the front of my mind.

"Don't," I tell him, immediately wishing I hadn't.

His hands are at my waist in an instant and he rotates me, pinning me between him and the counter. "Why?"

Because your cousin already wants to kill me for kissing you. Because I like it too much. Because you make me feel wanted.

I clear my throat. "Because you haven't brushed your teeth yet."

I twist my upper body around and grab his toothbrush—the neon green one. I squeeze out a bead of toothpaste from my tube, get the brush wet, and hold it close to his mouth. With the tiniest hint of a smile, Bruno opens his mouth maybe half an inch and shifts his body even closer to mine. His eyes dart down to my lips and back to my eyes, down and up, down and up, leaning closer. I should dodge him but I don't—can't. All I can do is stare at his mouth, knowing full well I don't really care if he's brushed his teeth yet or not.

Our noses nearly touch. He tilts his head to his right, I tilt mine to my right. We're lined up and ready for impact. His warm breath tickles my chin as he whispers, "*Grazie*."

He turns his head, wraps his mouth around the toothbrush, taking it from me, and walks out of the bathroom.

The trattoria is buzzing with life. The smells, the sounds, the languages floating through the air. I missed it all. It's a little hotter outside than I'd prefer, but Gram always says it's useless to complain about the weather since there's nothing we can do about it.

I'm pulling eggs out of the refrigerator when Bruno shouts, "Do not drop them!"

I startle but keep the eggs steady in my hands, then turn to him and close the fridge with my hip. "I should crack one of these on your head."

"Try it. See what happens." He smirks, the circles under his eyes still there but not as noticeable.

I set all but one egg onto the butcher-block countertop, ready to tease him with it, but Chiara appears in the door to the kitchen and I lose my nerve. I may not exactly be listening to her overprotective lectures, but I don't want to deliberately make her mad in full view. I turn from Bruno quickly and scoop the eggs back up, taking them to one of the cooks hovering over the stove.

"Someone is asking for you outside," Chiara says.

Bruno rattles something off in Italian. All I catch are the names Francesca and Juliette. Something in my gut twists.

"Your girlfriends this week? How can you keep track?" she replies in pristine English, obviously a jab to both Bruno and me. "No, this is a man."

My head whips up to look at Bruno. I'm armed and ready with a joke to throw at him, but his eyes are drawn tight in thought. The unmistakable hint of fear flashes across his face.

"He is here for Pippa," Chiara says, practically bubbling over from the suspense of telling me.

A man? Now the fear spreads through me. My limbs start to

weaken and all color drains from my face. Who knows I'm here? I only told Morgan, and there's no way she'd snitch.

"Who?" I finally get out.

She shrugs, clearly pleased with the situation, and glances at Bruno. Both of their footsteps follow behind me as I limp my way through the indoor dining area and peek out the front. I scan the tables for a familiar face, but it's the hair that catches my attention first. My heart kicks into gear and blood rushes back to my cheeks in an instant.

Darren's lips are pulled in and an eyebrow is raised at a couple one table over engaged in a shameless make-out session. Honeymooners. I'm already trained to spot them. He looks away from them and catches me spying on him. His face relaxes into a smile.

I peer back at Chiara and Bruno with my best shouldn't-you-be-doing-something look. Chiara grabs a pitcher and brings it to the kitchen while Bruno heads straight for Darren's table. I snatch his arm and pull him back.

"Let me get his table," I spit out in a rush. "I already know the menu. Plus, he's here to see me, remember?"

"That is my section," he retorts, eyes slightly narrowed.

"Too bad. I'm taking it." I reach for a menu. Without waiting for a reply, I hobble as quickly as I can to meet Darren. He's still smiling.

"Hey! What are you doing here?" I ask, doing my best to tone down my inner schoolgirl.

He laughs, leaning on the back legs of his chair, hands resting just below his chest with fingers interlocked. "I'm fine, thanks, how are you?"

“I’m sorry,” I say, mentally kicking myself. “How are you?”

“Still fine.” His smile stretches to his ears tucked deep inside his curls. How did I forget those dimples?

“I’m sorry! You just sort of disappeared last time, so I’m surprised to see you. Again.”

His smile falls a little and his Adam’s apple bobs up, then back down. “Good surprise?”

Gripping the menu like a fan, I push air toward me. I open my mouth to speak, still unsure of how to answer in the least psychotic way possible, when Nina walks up, sporting a bright orange tank top and army green shorts that barely hit her thigh. She’s followed closely by a nicely tanned guy with short, wavy hair.

“I guess you really did find Pippa, didn’t you?” Nina walks up the couple of steps to the patio and wraps her arms around me. “How are you? Darren tells us he was your knight-in-shining-armor last weeke—”

“I didn’t say it like that,” he jumps in.

Nina pulls away and checks out my feet. “All healed up?”

I can’t tell if she’s genuinely concerned or if she’s about to step on my ankle to reinjure it.

“I’m a lot better now, thanks. Yeah, I—I had no idea he’d even be here,” I stammer like I’ve got something to hide. “It was a total freak accident, running into each other. And right when I’d hurt myself and needed help getting back.” Ugh. Ramble much?

Nina laughs without opening her mouth. “Lucky girl.”

She takes a seat next to Darren, and the tall guy who walked up with her holds out a hand for me to shake.

"I'm Tate."

"Pippa."

"Yes. I've heard." Tate smiles, revealing familiar dimples, and sits on the other side of Darren. He plucks a sugar packet from the container on the table and nervously tears at its edges.

Darren drops his chair on all fours and clears his throat with excessive force. "Tate's my brother."

That explains the dimples and the hair. "Oh, that's right. I remember you mentioning him."

I turn to observe Tate again. He's a little thicker than Darren, and clean shaven. Probably a few years older.

I should take their drink order, but that's not really the question I'm dying to learn the answer to. "So, what brings you guys to Cinque Terre?"

Darren steals the menu from Nina and scans it as he says, "Oh, we have a couple of weeks off. Thought it might be nice to spend most of one of them here on the coast."

I stifle a gasp. A week? Here?

"I wasn't finished with that," Nina says, taking the menu again, then looking up at me with an almost devious smile. "Darren insisted we come up here first. Wouldn't take no for an answer."

My eyes dart to Darren, expecting him to explain.

"Next week we're heading down to Pompeii," Darren says, giving Nina a pointed look.

I let out an audible gasp. "Oh, that's awesome. I'm dying to see Pompeii."

Nina sets the menu down on the table and props her chin in her hands. "You should come with us."

Her words hit me like a challenge. I look from Darren to Tate, both of them smiling like they're in on it and know my answer will be yes.

Wait a second. Is this some kind of setup?

Tate said he already knew my name, and he said it in that amused yet borderline annoyed tone as if Darren talked about me too much. Would he really try to set me up with his brother?

"You don't have to answer right away," Tate says. "We did sort of randomly spring it on you." He flings the sugar packet at Nina and she ducks behind her menu again.

"But we'd love for you to come," Darren adds, reaching to the top of his head and retrieving a pair of sunglasses I didn't even notice before buried in his hair. He folds them up and places them on the table. "You did say you wanted to see Pompeii."

"Who wouldn't?" I finally say.

Shrill laughter from across the patio demands my attention, and I find Bruno flirting shamelessly with a bleached blonde. His hand rests on the back of her chair and she's gawking up at him, her fake-baked face barely letting her natural blush shine through. Is this his way of getting back at me for wanting Darren's table, or is he like that with customers all the time no matter what? This whole week I've been trapped in the apartment, has he been here carrying on, "business" as usual?

When I turn back, Darren is glaring at Bruno, jaw set in a hard line. Nina and Tate are smirking at each other. This is all just too weird.

Another shriek of laughter comes from Bruno's table. He

catches me looking and cocks his head to the side, eyes darting between Darren and Tate before clearly checking out Nina. The blonde coughs and his attention is back on her. He's like two different people and I don't know which one to believe in.

I exhale and smile at my new friends. "I'm in."

CHAPTER TWENTY-FOUR

The next morning, I change my mind. Several times over.

Darren, Nina, and Tate are staying in Manarola—just as Darren had last weekend—so we planned to meet up for lunch at Bar dell'Amore, a tiny cliff-side restaurant between the villages. A gray wall of cloud cover looms overhead and I'm able to walk the trail without my skin melting off. I'm also able to think semi-clearly, and I teeter back and forth with my hasty decision to go with them to Pompeii. My frequent breaks allow my ankle to rest and I get a good forty-five minutes' worth of quality think time.

I shouldn't go. Even though Darren's been nothing but nice, I don't actually *know him* know him. Or Tate, or Nina, for that matter.

Besides, how can I make myself stop thinking about Darren now that he found me again? Actually sought me out this time, knowing where I'd be. Even if it was all for his brother.

I spot Darren sitting alone at a table, chewing the tip of his thumbnail, elbow propped up on the metal railing, gazing out over the sea. I can't help it. I raise my camera and snap a picture of him, then check it on my display. The perfect candid. He could be anyone, enjoying the beauty of the Italian Riviera. But he's sitting there, waiting for me.

Maybe I *should* go.

I pull out the chair opposite him and plop down, setting my camera on the table. "Hey."

The wind whirls around us, causing our hair to fly up in the air and tangle around our faces.

"Hi." He smiles, placing a hand on top of his head to control the madness.

"Windy today." I use the band on my wrist to pull my hair back in a floppy loop.

"It's supposed to rain." Darren points across the water to an ominous black cloud. "It's already storming out there."

I frown at the sky. Hiding from rain back at the apartment is the last thing I want to have to do today.

"What's wrong?" he asks. "Afraid to get wet?"

I motion to my camera. "I'm afraid to get *that* wet."

Now he frowns at the sky. "Do you want to go back?"

The distant storm flashes with fingers of lightning, probably a sign I should call it a day, but I can't make myself do it.

"I'll take my chances," I say, turning one corner of my mouth up in an attempt to look saucy.

What am I doing? He has a girlfriend.

I scan the area around us to try and spot her. "So where are Tate and Nina? I thought they'd be with you." *And I thought you were pushing Tate on me. I prepared myself for all three of you and it's just you. Again.*

"Nina had a headache."

"Okay . . . ."

"She acts tough sometimes but she's a big baby when she doesn't feel good." He gives up holding back his hair and just lets it fly where it wants. "Tate stayed with her," he adds with a roll of his eyes.

"Tate . . . ?"

"Yeah . . . ?"

"But I thought—" No. Way. "Wait a minute. Are they . . . *together*?" I manage to spit out, mouth suddenly filled with cotton.

"Tate and Nina? Yeah."

"Ohhhh." My mind is a whirlwind.

His eyes widen and the words race out. "You thought—wow, no no no no no. She's like three years older than me."

"So there's nothing between you and her?" I stare at his face but I'm unable to focus on his features.

"No. They were already dating when I met her. That sort of thing's off limits, you know?" He opens his mouth to continue, but instead bites at his bottom lip and turns his face back to study the sky.

Do I *know*? I want to tell him that's why I never asked for an e-mail address, phone number, any way to contact him. He was off limits, and I couldn't be that girl.

I fight to keep laughter from escaping my lips, my mind flipping through memories of every interaction Darren and I have had. How did I go this long thinking he was the one dating

Nina? Neither of them ever came right out and said it. They just seemed so comfortable around each other. Like . . . family.

I am one big, fat idiot—*sono un grande idiota.*

Darren crosses his arms on the table and leans toward me. My heart kicks the inside of my chest, forcing me to mirror him.

"You really thought I was with her? This whole time?"

I nod. "I guess I shouldn't assume so much."

He shrugs and studies my face intently. "Sometimes it's hard not to." He bites his lip again, obviously keeping himself from saying more.

The wind rushes around us and my face gets pelted with loose grains of sand from the edges of the nearby trail. I close my eyes tight but it's too late.

"Agh!" I shout, pressing my fingers into my eyelid reflexively—probably the absolute worst thing to do.

"Stop! You're gonna scratch your cornea or something."

I stop. A chair screeches and I sense him super close to me. My right eye is on fire, tears welling up. I bring my hand back up, but Darren snatches my wrist before I can do any more damage.

"Do you want me to see if I can get it out?" he asks.

The scent of warm spearmint reaches my nose. I try to look at him but I'm practically underwater. All I see is a flesh-colored mass with a dark halo.

I swallow. "Are your hands dirty?"

He laughs deep and my body rocks as he rotates my chair to face him better. "What do you think is in your eye, Pippa?"

"Dirt."

I catch a whiff of spearmint again. Too close.

"So am I doing this or do I have to carry you to a mirror?" he asks.

I squint and slam my fist toward where his shoulder should be. "Smart aleck." I try to relax as he pries my eyelid open.

"I see it. Look up and to the right."

My teeth clench together as a fingertip gently touches the white of my eye and pulls away. Every part of my body is tense, completely disgusted.

"Got it."

I blink a few times and try to refocus on my surroundings through the blur. "Thanks."

He observes the dark dot resting in the middle of his pointer finger. "Make a wish."

A wish. I wished on a coin at the Trevi in Rome, and I saw Darren's face in my mind just as the coin fell in. Now I'm actually looking at his face, the real one. A shiver tickles my spine and I take a shaky breath.

"You want me to wish on a grain of sand?"

"Well, yeah. It was in your eye, wasn't it?"

"It's not an eyelash."

"Oh, is that the rule? Hmmm." Darren frowns at the granule. "That's too bad. I was sure it had a wish to grant." He's just about to wipe his hands on his khaki shorts, but I stop him.

"Wait! I'll do it." If the first one worked . . . another couldn't hurt. "I've got a wish."

He raises his finger between us, a corner of his mouth turned up. I try to come up with a really compelling wish, something specific, but there is a pair of lips less than two feet away from me.

"Any day now," he teases.

I close my eyes and blow out a puff of air.

"Ow!" Darren's hands fly to his face.

"No! It did not just go in your eye!" I lean forward to try and help. "I'm so sorry!"

He shakes his head and flashes me his twisty-tooth smile, dropping his hands to the armrests of my chair.

"You are such a nerd." I laugh.

I gently rub my eye again, the fire lessening but still a bit painful. Extra tears drip down my cheeks and Darren swipes at them with the back of a couple of fingers. Our faces are level. He's on a knee in front of me, chest pressed against my legs, a pressure I hadn't noticed until now. And now I can't concentrate on anything else.

And he's not moving.

My tears dry, and I can really see him, study him. A freckle on his left cheek, one near his temple. A tiny scar makes a gap in his left eyebrow. The brown of his irises are flecked with amber that brightens the center near the pupil, the color deepening as it reaches the outer edge.

Neither of us moves. Neither of us smiles. His eyes dart to my lips for the tiniest fraction of a second.

CHAPTER TWENTY-FIVE

A fine mist slaps our faces as the wind kicks up again, forcing us to blink the moment away. The unused anticipation turns my stomach. Darren shifts backward, preparing to stand, but a nearby voice startles both of us.

"May I at least be introduced before you set the wedding date?"

Darren, still on one knee, scrambles to his feet, color spreading up his neck toward his ears.

"Chiara!" I stand and smooth back my hair. "What—"

She flashes a wicked smile. "I did not mean to interrupt. *Per favore*, carry on what you were doing."

Two girls with sandwiches quickly snatch the table we abandon, so we move closer to the building, away from the cliff side. Thunder rumbles in the darkened sky overhead.

I say, "He was just—" at the same time Darren says, "I was just—" and we're both tongue-tied.

"I had something in my eye."

Chiara moves closer to us, making room for the other trail walkers taking shelter from the imminent downpour. A low hum purrs in her throat, hands resting purposefully on her hips.

"Darren, this is Chiara, the friend I was telling you about. Chiara, this is my—this is Darren." I don't know what I was going to stick in there after *my*. Friend? Can you be friends with someone if you don't even know their last name?

Darren finally unfreezes, extending his hand, which Chiara takes in both of hers and squeezes. "Darren Ledger."

Ledger. Darren Ledger. Pippa Ledger. Darren and Pippa Ledger.

STOP!

"You helped Pippa when she was hurt," she says, and Darren nods. "You are one of those heroes we read about?" She rests her hand back on her hip, which she sticks out a little too far toward him for my taste.

Darren laughs and shifts his weight closer to me. "I don't know about that. Right place, right time. That's all."

Chiara raises an eyebrow. "But that was a week ago. You are still here?"

He shuffles his feet. "No. Well, yes, obviously I'm here now, but I left the next day. And then I came back." His eyes dart over to me a few times, but he won't completely look in my direction.

"He came back," she says to me, though not exactly softly, then looks back at him. "How lucky we are for that." She brings a section of her raven hair in front of her shoulders and combs through it with her fingers.

My pulse pounds in my ears. She cannot be flirting with him.

Rain slips through the holes in the overhang and I pull my camera closer to my body. Why didn't I think to check the weather forecast before I set out today? I would have at least brought my camera bag with me.

"I'll be right back," Darren says before approaching the order window of Bar dell'Amore.

"He is beautiful—*lui è bello*," Chiara says. "And so much hair to hold on to." She clucks her tongue as she sizes him up.

I stifle a gasp. "So you *were* flirting with him?"

"Does it bother you?" she asks, not taking her eyes off of his backside.

"Yes," I say before I can think of anything more clever.

She offers me a friendly smile without showing teeth. "Then you are welcome."

"What, I should be happy you're flirting in front of me?"

"Now you are certain that you are interested." She waves a hand, palm up, from her to me. "You are welcome."

"Uh—"

Darren returns, pulling something small from a plastic sack and holding it up. A rectangular magnet depicting a cluster of colorful buildings along the sea, with scripted font that reads Riomaggiore.

"For your fridge back home," he says, offering it to me.

He bought me a present! I reach out to take it, our fingers sweeping across each other. I swallow and try to keep from grinning like a clown.

Holding up the empty sack with his other hand, Darren says, "And for your camera."

I attempt to raise only one eyebrow but they both fly up. He takes my camera from me and wraps it up. I gape at him. Such a simple but brilliant gesture.

I stow it away safely in my tote bag, putting one more barrier between the rain and my baby. "Thanks."

Chiara's attention flits to someone at the other end of the overhang. She frowns and says, "*Solo un momento.*"

Too preoccupied with replaying the finger graze over and over in my head, I let her go without asking any questions and watch her feet disappear through the growing crowd.

"And thanks for the magnet," I add to Darren. I examine it, sliding my fingers across the smooth surface.

He pushes his hands down deep into his pockets. "Well, I didn't want your camera to get wet. And I figured the sales guy would be nicer about me asking for a big sack if I actually bought something."

Oh. Of course. Very logical. So he didn't really mean to give me a *present* present. "I can pay you for it," I say, a little too upbeat. "Or maybe you want to put it on *your* fridge."

Hurt flashes across his face, but he quickly relaxes into a smile. "No. I picked it out for you. It's the village you're staying in."

I picture this deep-blue and bright-pink souvenir stuck to the pristine stainless steel refrigerator back home. Mom freaks if there's even one fingerprint on it; there's no way this would fly.

"I'll have to find a creative use for it. My mom doesn't exactly allow magnets on our fridge."

Darren laughs as if I just told an epic joke. I smile but it's hard to find humor in my restricted reality.

"Wait." He stops laughing. "You're serious? You don't have anything on your fridge?"

"Totally serious." This can't be a new concept. "She thinks it's junky and cluttered."

"It *is* junky and cluttered! That's what's so great about it. Our fridge back home is like a montage of all the places we've been. We've even got a set or two of all those tiny words you combine to make sentences or movie quotes or whatever."

I've never seen someone's face light up talking about refrigerator magnets before. Come to think of it, I don't think I've ever had a conversation about refrigerator magnets before, period. I can't help but smile at him.

"Those are the really fun ones," he continues. "We like to be sneaky and make up stupid phrases for one another to find."

My chest tightens. "And your mom is actually, like, okay with you guys doing that?"

"Are you kidding? She's the queen of that game."

"Sounds like a fun mom." I sigh. "I wouldn't know what it's like to have one of those."

Darren's cheery expression fades. "Oh, I'm sorry. I forgot you and your mom aren't really seeing eye to eye right now."

"Right now?" I huff. "Try ever."

"That sucks." He hooks his thumbs on the straps of his backpack and shifts toward me so a family of six sporting bright-yellow rain ponchos can squeeze behind him. They look like waddling ducks.

When they pass, I catch eyes with Darren and both of us stifle a laugh. "Did your mom ever dress up your whole family in canary-colored ponchos?" I ask.

"No way. My parents are a little, I guess you'd call them free spirited. They don't see anything wrong with getting wet," he says, eyes cast out over the churning sea, lost in a memory. "It's just another side to nature."

"I don't know why, but that doesn't really surprise me."

We're laughing together when another family passes behind him. The portly father bumps into Darren's backpack, which sends Darren crashing into me. He grabs my elbows and steadies both of us. I can tell the fabric of my shirt near my hip is touching the fabric of his shirt.

And why isn't he letting go?

A woman's angry Italian shouts make us jump apart and we turn our heads in that direction. Chiara. Of course. Always ruining my perfect moments.

But she's not shouting at us, she's shouting at a man maybe in his early twenties. And he's shouting back. I know Italians sound like they're yelling eighty percent of the time even in regular conversations, but this is different. There's something off about this guy, the way he's glaring at her between strands of greasy, wet hair.

Chiara's face is flushed, which I've never seen on her, and both of them are throwing hand gesture after hand gesture, each one more animated than the last. The people nearby—tourists, mostly—scoot away to give them room, mouths hanging open, and I get a clear view of the two of them.

The thug steps closer to Chiara and towers a full head above her. His hand curls into a fist, then relaxes. He pops his fingers.

I suck in a breath. "Is he going to *hit* her?"

Darren's face scrunches in concern. He pulls away from me and begins to move in Chiara's direction.

"What are you going to do?" I ask in a quiet rush.

"No idea, but something's better than nothing." He tucks me behind him. "Stay behind me. Far enough so you don't catch any stray punches."

I nod, biting back my fear for Chiara. And Darren. It's not that Darren doesn't look like he can fend for himself, it's that this greasy guy is nearly a head above Darren. And his arms might be a little thicker.

When we approach, Chiara and Greasy Guy fall silent, eyes still locked in a staring contest. Theories are flying through my head. Ex-boyfriend? Jilted lover? Another cousin gone bad? He's not particularly attractive, so I rule out all formerly romantic possibilities quickly. Maybe they're just friends who had a falling-out. A really loud, dramatic, public falling-out.

"Chiara," Darren finally says. "Everything okay?"

Greasy Guy looks Darren up and down with narrowed eyes and spits out what I'm guessing is a question. Darren responds, calmly, in Italian. It's the most I've ever heard him say in Italian, and I can't even tell if his accent's right, but it's seriously hot.

They go back and forth a few times, Chiara chiming in once in a while. I pick out a word here and there, but I mostly make up what I think they could be talking about. My version sounds like this:

Greasy Guy: "Who the bleep are you?"

Darren: "A friend of Chiara's."

Greasy Guy: "What kind of friend?" This is when he puffs up his chest to make himself look stronger.

Chiara: "Not that kind of friend, so chill out. Besides, Pippa's got dibs on him."

Darren: "Is there a problem?"

Greasy Guy: "Yeah. You. How about you get out of my way?"

Darren: "Chiara comes with us." This is when Darren nods in my direction and I back up a hair.

Greasy Guy: "You can't have her. We're not through here."

Chiara: "I should have cut ties with you years ago! You selfish piece of bleeping ble—"

Greasy Guy: "Give me one good reason why I shouldn't put a dent in that pretty face of yours!"

Chiara backs away and links her arm with mine, pulling me over to where Darren and I had stood. I turn my head to check on him. He's right behind us. Greasy Guy takes off toward Manarola.

Okay, so my version of their conversation must not have been accurate.

Thunder cracks above us, and another round of rain sprinkles down.

"It is about to get worse," Chiara says with an edge to her voice, arms crossed. I wonder if she's really talking about the weather. "We should not be out on la Via dell'Amore when it does. Go on your way." She motions to us to continue on to Manarola.

That was my original plan—to spend the day with Darren. And his girlfriend who magically happens to be his *brother's* girlfriend. My stomach tightens. Now that I'm actually allowed to be into him, I'm freaking out.

I turn to Darren and speak so Chiara can't really hear me. "I think I should go back with Chiara. She seems a little shaken up."

"Oh," he says, shoving his hands back into the pockets of his cargo shorts.

"Plus, if it's about to storm . . . ." Lame, Pippa.

"Right, right. Yeah, you girls be careful." He takes a step back and glances at my feet. "Especially you."

Chiara studies my face with narrowed eyes. "You are certain this is what you want to do?"

I can't look at Darren because I know I'll change my mind. I need to get away. Need more time to think.

I put my arm around her shoulders and lean in close, exaggerating my concern for her situation. "Yes, I'm going back with you."

Darren pulls his hands out of his pockets and grabs on to the straps of his backpack again. "Well, I wanted to tell you . . . we're checking out Genoa for a couple of days. It's just up the coast a little."

He's leaving again. "Oh, okay," I say, unable to mask my disappointment.

"But we'll be back here by Wednesday," he adds quickly. "I'll stop by the restaurant, if that works for you."

"Sure," I say through a smile that can't be helped. For once I know exactly when I'll see him again. "See you Wednesday." I grip Chiara's shoulder harder and start to turn her toward Riomaggiore.

"And you're still coming to Pompeii, right?" he calls out after we're a few steps away.

I turn my head but keep walking. "I'll let you know."

Chiara pulls a little orange umbrella out of her bag and pops it open, linking our arms. I scoot in close, keeping my tote bag between us so it stays as dry as possible. I look back for Darren one more time, but he's gone.

Our feet scurry along the concrete path, hopping over some puddles and accidentally splashing into others. The angered sea heaves and crashes onto the rocks below, sending white sprays of water high into the air. The photographer in me yearns to risk a couple of shots, but Chiara's right. We need to get somewhere safe before things get worse.

Chiara suddenly lets out a squeal and slams against me, making me clutch the railing for support. A drenched man attempting to pass us quickly removes his hand from her bare shoulder and apologizes over and over in very poor Italian before continuing to jog. Chiara lets the umbrella go crooked and the edge drips cold water right onto my head. I take it from her to right it, and she places a hand on her chest, breathing loudly, eyes wide.

"Chiara? What just happened?"

"I thought . . ."

"You thought it was that guy?"

She nods, then shakes her head quickly. "I am all right now." She takes the umbrella back from me, holding it so hard her knuckles are white.

"What's going on? Who is he?"

She pulls in another deep breath, then bites her bottom lip. "Mauro."

"Mauro?" I ask, attempting to roll my tongue to pronounce it correctly. "Is that his name or an insult?"

Her expression turns from worry to surprise. "Listen to you! Sounding like *un vero Italiano*."

I push aside the fact that she's trying to change the subject, though I'm happy I'm finally learning something. "*Chi è Mauro?*"

She shakes her head. "No one you need to know about."

"Chiara. He could have hurt you if Darren hadn't stepped in." I'm still shocked that I walked away from him.

"I was only trying to help," she mutters. "He would not touch me."

"Well, his balled-up fist could have fooled me," I say with a bite. Sure, it might not be any of my business, but the situation seemed relatively serious at the time. And she jumped a mile in the air when she thought he caught up with us. That's not a reaction to someone you don't fear will hurt you.

"There is nothing else I can tell you," she says quietly. "So leave it be."

A hundred more questions fight to escape my mouth, but I do as she says and leave it be. No sense in me getting into a fight with her too. We walk in silence, the growling thunder urging us forward.

"This Darren," Chiara finally says as we approach Riomaggiore, still huddled under the bright umbrella. "Is he the same boy you told me about in Roma? The one you saw times two?"

"Two times," I correct, "and yes. Same guy."

She stops in her tracks. The rain's still sheeting down, so I stop with her to keep as dry as possible. I slide my hand over my tote bag to check it. It's just a little moist, not soaking wet. Yet. We really need to keep moving.

"And he happened to be there when you were hurt?" Her wide eyes stare back into mine. "And he left. And he came back."

"Yes. . . ."

She places her free hand on my shoulder, our skin clammy from the humidity. "Can you not see?"

I swallow hard. "You're scaring me."

Her tone is serious. "Pippa. This is why you are here. Why you knew you must come here."

A shiver travels down my spine. Could that be? Did I feel the pull of Cinque Terre because I'd find Darren here again?

"I know things," Chiara continues, still looking me in the eye. "And I know that Darren is for you."

But there could be another reason I was led here. "Are you just saying that because you don't want me with Bruno?"

"Run from the truth all that you want. It always has a way of finding you."

I inhale deep in a vain attempt to relax. "So you think I should go to Pompeii with them? With Darren and his brother and Nina?"

"They have invited you, *sì*?"

I exhale slowly and nod. Just the idea of seeing the ruins of Pompeii in person makes me ache deep inside. Then there's Darren, no longer off limits. When an opportunity like this falls into place, you don't hesitate. You GO. And take millions of pictures.

Chiara leaves it at that, believing I've already made my decision.

And I guess I have.

CHAPTER TWENTY-SIX

Back at the apartment, I sign in to my e-mail account to send another round of my obligatory check-in messages. My heart nearly skids to a stop when I see the subject headings from both Gram and Morgan. She spilled the beans.

To: Pippa Preston <pippers26@gmail.com>
From: Lorelei Mead <lorelei@prestonartsource.com>
Subject: OPEN THIS RIGHT NOW, YOUNG LADY

PIPPA PRESTON, WHAT ARE YOU THINKING? YOU SHOULD THANK YOUR LUCKY STARS YOUR BEST FRIEND CARES ABOUT YOU ENOUGH TO TELL ME THAT YOU SKIPPED OUT ON THE SUMMER PROGRAM. I HAVEN'T TOLD YOUR PARENTS YET, BUT IF YOU DON'T GET ME IN TOUCH WITH AN

ADULT THAT YOU'RE STAYING WITH SOON, YOU BETTER BELIEVE I WILL.

GRAM

To: Pippa Preston <pippers26@gmail.com>
From: Morgan Arrant <queenofdrama14@gmail.com>
Subject: Don't hate me!

I thought I could keep it to myself but I had to tell someone, and Gram was my best option. I'm sure you're being as safe as you possibly can, but I'm not there so I can't see what's going on day to day, you know? I'm excited for you, but honestly I've been worried out of my mind something will happen to you. I just don't want your anger at your parents to backfire on you. So I told her. At first she was really upset, but after I promised I've been in regular contact with you and everything's fine, she cooled down. Let her talk to Chiara's aunt so she knows you aren't just shacking up with some dude or whatever.

I did it because I love you. Don't be mad.

—M

I orchestrate a time for Gram and Matilde to talk on the phone on Monday, using the landline at the trattoria, and I'm a bundle of anxiety until the phone finally rings. When they actually start talking to each other, I feel so sick I have to wait in another room. What if Gram isn't satisfied with my situation and makes me come home, like, tomorrow? What if she's so mad I lied about going to art school she doesn't think I deserve this Italian vacation?

Not that it's *all* fun and games, but it's pretty amazing. I mean, who gets to do this? No one my age who I know of. I might be quite the celebrity when school starts. They'll be begging to see my pictures and to hear tales of my Italian adventures.

After what feels like forever but is probably closer to twenty minutes, Matilde pops her head into the bar area from the kitchen. "Pippas," she calls, holding out the phone to me.

I reach with a shaking hand and take it from her. "Hi, Gram."

"Hi, honey." Her familiar voice washes through me. Even though my jitters disappear immediately, tears prick my eyes.

"I miss you," I say.

"I miss you too." She sighs. "You sure know how to do a number on these old nerves, Pippa."

"I know. I'm sorry." I turn my back to the dining area and hunch over, trying to keep my conversation as private as possible.

"If you really didn't want to go to the art program, why didn't you just tell your parents?"

"Gram, I *tried* to tell them. Dad would have let me stay home, but Mom wouldn't even listen to me. I don't know how many times I can tell her I don't care about their stupid art gallery. That's not going to be my future. I have things *I'm* interested in."

"Honey, I know that, but they're your parents. And you're still in high school."

"But I—"

"I know you're almost eighteen," she continues, "and that's why I'm going to let you stay there the rest of the summer."

Get. Out. "Are you for real?"

"Matilde adores you." She chuckles and says, "I mean, I hardly understood anything she said, but I feel really good about her. And she calls you Pippas, how sweet is that?"

I can't help but laugh. "So you're sure you're okay with me staying?"

Her exhale muffles in the phone. "Well, it's not what I expected you to be doing. Working in a restaurant, living with strangers."

"I was going to be sharing a room with strangers anyway," I say.

"Oh, I know. But school is a different type of situation. Anyway, we don't need to get into that right now. I've got some conditions."

My eyebrows pinch together so hard, they throb. I rub at them, trying to get myself to relax. "Are you going to tell Mom?"

"I probably should. But I can't say I don't know why you did it. To be honest, I wish I were with you." She sighs again. "I want you to tell her yourself wh—"

"What? I can't do that. She's gonna kill me."

"I was going to say you have to tell her when you get home at the end of summer."

I drop my head on my forearm. "She's still gonna kill me."

"She's not going to be happy with either of us, but if this is your decision, you have to bear the consequences. You have to tell her face-to-face." She gasps as if she just came up with something brilliant. "Although, it would be awfully funny to watch you squirm when she starts asking about what you learned and you know absolutely nothing. That sounds like a better plan. Let's do that."

"Gram," I say, still stuck on what she said first. "I didn't even think about how angry she's going to be with you when she finds out you knew and didn't tell her."

"Oh, don't worry about me. I'm her mother, what's she going to do? Send me to my room?" She chuckles. "On a serious note, you have to check in with me consistently, or I will tell her. I also want to talk to Matilde once in a while. Make sure you're not getting in her hair." She's trying to sound stern, but the excitement creeps through her tone. She really does wish she could be here with me.

So do I.

"I've wanted to call you this whole time but I knew I couldn't keep my own secret from you. I always tell you everything."

"You do understand how much trouble you're going to be in when you get home?" Gram asks. "I hope it's worth it."

I imagine what would have happened if I'd gone straight to the train station like I was supposed to instead of staying in Rome. I wouldn't have met Chiara, wouldn't have come here, and I wouldn't have met Bruno. Wouldn't have met Darren.

"It's worth it."

CHAPTER TWENTY-SEVEN

There it is again, that mystifying *clear and bright* anomaly. The morning sky outside the bedroom window is completely cloudless, unlike my brain.

I had a dream about Bruno last night. Let's just say there was a lot of kissing involved.

I'm shaking the residual tingles out of my head when Bruno bursts in, toothbrush hanging out of his mouth and a bath towel wrapped low around his waist. *Really low.* My own stomach tightens at the sight of his. That's got to be more than a six-pack. It's, like . . . a twelve-pack.

Bruno shuffles around in his closet, intermittently brushing his teeth with one hand and pushing hangers with the other. He turns his head to me and starts to speak, but toothpaste flies out onto the tile floor.

I erupt into laughter. Even the hottest guys are *just guys.*

They brush their teeth and it spews when they try to talk at the same time. And unfortunately for me, fresh off a Bruno dream, it's adorable.

He tries to suppress a laugh and even more spit flies through the room. He clamps a hand over his mouth as he rushes to the bathroom. I hear the water run followed by an earnest chuckle deep from his gut.

I pop out of bed, careful not to bump my head on the top bunk—it's empty so Chiara must be at work already—and approach the unframed mirror hanging near the dresser. I rake my fingers through my hair, lick my lips, clear my eyes, pinch my cheeks—all that stuff girls do in the movies when they're trying to look cute in a hurry. But there's really no hope for Morning Face. It's puffy and splotchy. Lovely. Men don't wear makeup and they look perfectly fine. But not us girls, no. Splotchy zombies with big pores.

I study my appearance in the mirror one more time before abandoning the effort, disappointed that I'm not quite as tan as I thought I was.

Bruno returns, still clad in only his green towel, hair poofing out a little as it dries.

"Everything all right?" I ask, with a stupid smile. I fight my line of sight to stay above the shoulders, but despite my best efforts, my eyes dart down a few times as he strides across the room to his closet.

"Yes, clothes. Please," I say too fast. "Good idea." Shut. Up.

The corner of his mouth hitches up, and his head turns toward my open suitcase on the floor. He bends over and I realize I'm still watching, both to see what he's doing, and to see if his towel can hang on for the ride.

He pulls out a few of my shirts and flings them onto the bed, digging deeper into my suitcase until he pulls out a coral-colored sundress.

"Oh, that's going to look fabulous on you," I say.

"I do not doubt it." He laughs, turning and holding the dress up to himself, one hip jutting out, then closes the distance between us in a couple of steps.

I take the dress from him and do my best to avoid eye contact. But now I'm looking at his chest. His *bare* chest. His *tan*, bare chest. And he smells clean, like almonds and oats. A feast for all the senses.

Maybe eye contact would be better. I look up into them and immediately regret it. They're big and golden and deep, and they're looking at me. I have no clue what's happening.

"You will wear this for me today, yes?"

I nod.

"*Bene*." He walks back to the closet and pulls out a thin white button-down shirt and a pair of navy-blue shorts, then heads for the door.

"Wait," I say, shaking my head out of my daze. He stops just before he passes me. "What's so special about today? Aren't we just working?" Darren said he was coming back today and would pop by the restaurant, but we didn't set a specific time. I assumed I'd be at work all day.

"Later, yes," he says quietly, leaning in like we're co-conspirators. "First, I am taking you on my boat."

I get pulled into the conspiracy and lean in too. "Your boat?"

"My boat." He's even closer now, still shirtless. His clothes are just an afterthought of wadded-up laundry in his hands. It's probably such a chore for him to put them on every day. He's clearly in his element without them.

Chiara did say that I had to see Cinque Terre from the sea, that there's nothing else like it. The anticipation of the photo ops alone is enough to make my answer "*Sì, sì, sì,*" forget about the half-naked guy standing in front of me. Forget about his lips, inches from mine. Forget that he has his own boat in *Italy*.

"Where are we going?" I stare at his mouth, waiting for an answer. He smirks and I'm pretty sure I'll follow him anywhere.

Bruno traces my jaw with a fingertip and lightly taps the tip of my nose. "You will see."

It's early, but the marina is bustling. Small wooden boats covered in blue and green tarps line the stone wall opposite us, waiting patiently for their turn on the sea. A few are tethered and bob around in the shallow water while local men toss things down into them, chattering to one another, cigarettes loose at their lips. Robust seagulls caw from their perches on every available elevated space.

Bruno waves a hand in front of my face and it's only then I realize my mouth is hanging open as I gawk at the scene. He laughs and taps the top of the camera hanging around my neck.

I remove the lens cap, adjust the aperture and shutter speed for the morning light, and start snapping. Nothing is off limits for me. The men, the seagulls, the diners enjoying their morning coffee at the cafés behind us, the bright plastic kayaks lined up on the shore.

"*Ciao, Bruno!*" someone calls from a boat puttering slowly into the marina.

A hard line sets Bruno's jaw for a split second before he smiles and turns. "*Ciao, Mauro!*" Bruno shouts back.

Mauro? I lift my camera back up to my eye and zoom in to the white- and red-trimmed boat. It's definitely the same scumbag from a few days ago. He's glaring at me, but I click a picture anyway. Just in case I need to identify him in a lineup.

"Is that your boat?" I ask, and Bruno nods. I will not be trapped on that tiny little thing with that creeper. I inch closer to Bruno and conjure up a flirty voice. "He's not going with us, is he?"

Bruno's expression brightens. "No." He snatches my free hand and tugs me to the water's edge on the ramp to wait for Mauro, who pulls the boat up as far as it will go.

Mauro hops out into the shallow water and the two of them do this handshake-hug thing that I'd find charming if I wasn't so uncomfortable with the fact that Bruno seems to be on friendly terms with the swine.

Still gripping my hand, Bruno says, "Pippas, this is Mauro." He continues on in Italian, telling him that I'm an American.

Bruno's eyes are on me so he can't see the death stare Mauro fixes me with. I take it to say, *Don't even think about telling him you know who I am.* I do think about it. But I don't do it.

Mauro and I both fake our smiles to each other and Bruno is none the wiser. I can't wait to tell him what happened once we're out of earshot. This guy is dangerous, and I'm worried for Chiara.

My thoughts skip to Darren standing up to him. Oh no.

Darren. Surely he'll stop by later today when I'm actually at the trattoria. What if I miss him?

"Ready?" Bruno cuts into my inner panic. He squeezes my hand once, then scoops me up in a cradle.

I adjust my dress and he trudges carefully through the shallow water of the slip, placing me into the boat. It rocks a few times under my weight, but Bruno hangs on to my hands until I'm safely seated. The vessel is small but spacious enough for maybe four people. It's also either been recently painted or he does a decent job of keeping it clean. The hull is empty aside from a nest of rope and a faded red gas can near the motor in the back.

I assumed this was a fishing boat, but it's not dirty and it doesn't reek of dead fish, so I'm not sure what Mauro just used it for. Joy riding? Drug trafficking? Hopefully not for driving girls out to sea to murder them and dump their bodies. I warily eye the rope and gas can again, but dismiss my scenario as paranoia.

Bruno takes the tether rope from Mauro and they converse quietly, not that I could understand them anyway. The tone is tense, but eventually Mauro leaves without anyone swinging a punch.

Bruno doesn't come back to the boat right away. Instead he scans the marina like he's looking for someone until a young girl about twelve years old with chestnut hair flowing down to her waist runs up to hand him a small basket. A wine bottle protrudes out of the top.

Oh, *great.*

He pays the girl a couple of coins from his pocket before she skips away, clutching her riches.

And here comes Bruno with his half-buttoned white shirt, rope in one hand, picnic basket in the other, wading through the chilly water, and heading toward me. Smiling at me. The scene is just too surreal not to capture. I snap a few pictures and his smile spreads.

My stomach twists and suddenly I can't hold my camera steady. This might have been a bad idea.

He gives the boat a nudge to free it from the slip, then climbs over the side, kicking off his wet sandals. He starts the motor and steers it slowly through the shallows near the rocks.

I can't keep it in anymore. Bruno needs to know about Chiara's run-in with Mauro.

"I saw Mauro the other day."

His eyebrows pull together. "You did?"

I check the marina once more to make sure Mauro is out of sight. "He was fighting with Chiara."

His jaw tenses again. "Fighting? You are certain?"

"She was really upset about it. She seemed scared of him."

Bruno pulls in a deep breath and narrows his eyes as he navigates.

"I just thought you should know," I add since he's gone quiet, obviously not pleased with the news. "I didn't know if she was in some sort of trouble."

His expression relaxes, but it's forced.

"I am sure everything is fine," he finally says. "I will talk to Chiara. Do not worry." He offers a smile that reaches across his whole face, but he's trying too hard. Something's definitely up with this Mauro character.

I twist my hands together and keep my mouth shut. It's none

of my business, and I don't want to come across as nosey, so I leave it alone for now.

Once we're out of the cove, Bruno pushes the little motor to her limit and we fly. Water sprays up over the bow and I have to secure my camera back in the plastic sack and then inside my camera bag, which I made sure to bring this time.

Despite living so close to Lake Michigan, I haven't been out on too many boats. Compared to the occasional dinner cruise with my parents, this is heaven.

Who am I kidding? This is heaven compared to anything.

I face forward, close my eyes, and toss my head back, allowing the wind to run its fingers through my hair. The warmth of the summer sun tickles my shoulders and feet, which I prop up on a slat of wood near the front. I grip my dress tight with one hand to keep it from flying up over my head.

Bruno turns the boat so it points to the coast and cuts off the motor when we're quite a ways out. I gasp at the sight. The bright pink and yellow buildings of Riomaggiore, now small from this distance, cling to the sides of the mountain valley, tiered vineyards stretching up overhead. Giant chunks of rock jut out from the exposed cliffs along the shore and poke up through the surface of the water.

We break out the bread and cheese from the little basket and munch on them in silence, enjoying the cloudless weather and the view of Bruno's home. He takes a swig from the wine bottle and passes it to me. I pretend to sip on it, but my experience with alcohol is limited, and I need a clear head today. He either doesn't notice my deception or he doesn't mind.

A question has been burning on my mind since he

mentioned the word "boat." I've been afraid to ask, but now that we're way out here in the peace and quiet, gently swaying with the sea, I have to know.

I swallow my last bite of bread before I ask, "Is it difficult for you to be out here, since your father was a fisherman? Does it not remind you of him too much?"

After a moment he says, "That is why I like to come here. I feel he is here." A sigh escapes his lips.

"Does Luca like to come out here too?"

"No. He is not ready." He pauses. "But I will help him."

"That's good. I'm sure he needs you. I can't imagine having to become the man of the house, giving up things you want for yourself."

I hear the wine bubbling through the neck of the bottle as he takes a drink. "*Grazie*," he says, prompting me to look at him. "For asking about *il mio papa*. No one ever does. They do not know what to say."

I nod, taking in the view of the sea all around us. So open. So alone. A shudder passes through me. I hope his dad didn't drown. What a horrible way to die.

Bruno tosses the crust of his bread back into the basket. "Here," he says, removing my camera from its dry home and handing it to me to turn on. "I want to take a picture of you."

I spin all the way around to fully face him, my back to the village, and smile. He takes way more than one, zooming in and out, aiming up and down, every possible angle and frame width.

He mumbles a few things in Italian between shots, and judging by the look on his face, he's up to no good. Is this why he wanted me to wear my sundress? The temperature is suddenly roasting, my cheeks blazing. There's a reason I like being on the other side of the camera.

Finally I put my hand out in front of my face. "Okay, okay. I think you got enough."

He sets it down in his lap and cocks his head to the side, studying me. "You could belong here," he says, his tone surprisingly serious.

I turn from him and look back at the cluster of buildings, one on top of the other. A beautiful and unique place to visit, but to live long term?

"I don't know about that," I say.

"This could be your life." He spreads his arms out as if to encompass the whole of Cinque Terre. And him.

I let out an uncomfortable laugh, unsure if he's joking. "I'm not just going to move to a foreign country. I haven't even finished high school yet."

"*Sì.*" He slumps a little, but he's still observing me closely, intently. "I would like things to be different."

"What do you mean?"

"I like when you are here. Things feel, ah, *bene*. Good. Better."

I open my mouth to speak, but I'm at a complete loss how to react.

Bruno stows the camera away again and moves to sit next to me, straddling the bench. The inside of his thigh brushes against my knee, his other leg dangerously close behind me, and I shift away so we're not touching. He reaches for a section of my hair and twists it in his fingers.

"I like you," he says quietly.

I remember the girls he flirted with right in front of me and roll my eyes, making no effort to hide it from him. If anything, I exaggerate it. "What a line!"

"You would rather belong to that Darren?" he asks. His eyes actually look pained. "He is not the one you truly want."

"I don't *belong* to anyone. And who said anything about Darren?" I ask, surprised he jumped to that. "Besides, I don't even know him that well." Yet.

He drops his hand from my hair to my bare shoulder, softly touching each freckle. Despite the heat, goose bumps appear down my arm.

"Chiara says that you see him everywhere. That he is meant for you." He snorts, then meets my eyes again. "But I thought . . . maybe, you coming here meant . . . ."

Oh, he's good. *Too* good.

"Bruno," I say, turning to face him and shrugging away from his touch. "Do I really mean something to you? I *see* you with other girls, at the trattoria, out in other villages. You have girls everywhere!"

He reaches for my hands and holds them in his, stroking my wrists, which nearly renders me useless. The rising sun shimmers in his caramel eyes in such a way, I nearly forget where I am.

"Come now," he says. "That is nothing. Tourists like to be charmed by *il Italiano*."

"Please," I huff, somehow tearing my gaze from him.

"Look at me." He squeezes my hands, urging me to comply. "It truly means nothing. It is just the job." Bruno leans in, his breath warm on my face as he whispers, "Can you not see? You mean something to me."

He releases my hands and slides one of his to my waist, pulling me forward. The boat shifts under a wave, and our lips brush together for an instant, but I pull my head back just enough.

I swallow hard, mustering the courage to speak, and it comes out as a hoarse whisper. “I don’t know how to believe you.”

He sighs and the scent of wine gets pulled into my lungs.

“Pippas,” he whispers.

And I’m gone.

Bruno leans in and kisses me, hesitant at first, but then he cups the back of my head. His other hand at my waist slips down to my leg just at the hem of my skirt. He persuades my mouth open and electricity jolts through my body. Under his spell, I wrap my arms around his neck.

I don’t know what I want to believe anymore.

CHAPTER TWENTY-EIGHT

I can't believe I let him kiss me. And a *real* kiss. How weak am I? Why does he have this effect on me?

A pit forms in my gut as we walk back to the trattoria. All I can think about is how Darren would feel if he knew. It's like I cheated on him and we're not even together. And I don't even know for sure if Darren likes me like that, anyway. So what is it about him that I can't shake? He's . . . cute and funny. Smart. Driven. Sweet.

But Bruno's exciting, foreign, flirtatious, sexy. And he has a boat. All totally fling-worthy attributes.

They couldn't be more different from each other.

Once we're back, I scan the outdoor seating area. Only a couple of the tables are occupied, but I don't recognize anyone. Hopefully I haven't missed him.

Chiara pours a bottled soda into a glass for an old man before approaching me with her arms crossed.

"He came to see you. While you were . . ." Her voice trails off and her eyes dart to Bruno who's tying an apron around his waist. "While you were out."

"Darren? Did he really?" She nods and I deflate. "What did you tell him?"

"The truth." A smile plays at the corner of her mouth as she watches me squirm. "That you were out taking pictures."

I exhale the breath I didn't know I was holding. Of course she didn't mention Bruno. She thinks Darren and I are "meant to be" or whatever. She wouldn't say anything to jeopardize that.

"And what did he say?"

"That he will come back between lunch and dinner when we are not busy." She looks at her chunky yellow watch. "Which is now."

I smooth my hair back from my face. "But I'm a mess! I'm sticky and I smell like sweat and salt water." And I can still taste Bruno's kiss on my lips.

Stupida! Stupida! Stupida!

I don't wait for her to respond. Instead I take off in a brisk walk up the hill, up the stairs, and straight to the apartment bathroom. My ankle stings from the fast climb, but I push the pain aside. I freshen up as best I can—brush my teeth and hair, touch up my makeup, and hastily change into a pair of jean shorts and an aqua top. Then I grab Morgan's journal with the intention of doing the next assignment today since I keep forgetting.

I'm about to reach for the knob on the front door when an exhausted Matilde waddles inside.

She startles when she sees me so close. "Oh! Pippas!" She puts one hand on her chest and pats my cheek with the other like I'm a fat baby. "Going?"

I smile and wait for her to remove her hand before I answer. "Just meeting up with a friend." Friend. There, I said it. Must be real now. Darren and I are friends.

Her expression dampens a little. "Not with Bruno?"

"No. He already took me out on his boat this morning."

She flashes me her teeth. "He likes you."

My heart thumps like I'm standing on the edge of something very high with a long way to fall. Did he tell her that, or is this mom-talk?

"I see the way that he looks at you."

My shoulders relax. It's just mom-talk, which is completely biased and off the mark . . . half the time. It's that other half that's going to eat at me and make me analyze every look from here on out. More than I already do, I mean.

She pats my cheek again. "There is a place for you here. Always." And with that bomb, she shuffles into her bedroom and shuts the door.

For a moment, I don't move as my brain tries to figure out how to process this information. Does this mean they talked about me? Maybe she just likes having an extra pair of hands around and thinks she can talk me into believing I have a reason to stay.

No. She's not like that. She's one of the most friendly and welcoming people I've ever met. And it's genuine, not fake like my mom's famous for, always having an agenda.

Like the pain still sizzling in my ankle, I push it out of my mind. Nothing can change. I'm not even supposed to be here. I'm at a summer program in Florence.

I carefully rush down the million steps and literally run into Darren when I round the corner at the gate.

He steadies us and says, "*Permesso*," then, "Oh, hey!" once he realizes it's me. "Chiara said I might find you here. Were you headed somewhere?"

"Yes," I say, straightening my shirt. Disappointment softens his face, so I quickly add, "I was on my way to find you."

He perks up. "You were?"

"Chiara told me you were coming back soon, so I just ran up to change."

"I hope you didn't change too much."

I choke on a laugh. "Wow."

"I can't believe I just said that. Sorry. Total cheese." He palms his neck and leans his head back. "That's one of those lines that pop into your head but you don't actually say them." He looks everywhere but my eyes.

I adjust the strap on my tote bag so it doesn't cut right between my boobs. "Well, you totally did."

"Forgive me?"

I narrow my eyes in mock contemplation. "I'm not sure. It's a capital offense. It might even be illegal here in Italy."

"Ugh." He wipes his brow with the back of his hand. "Foreign prisons."

"I guess I won't report you," I say. "This time."

Darren bows. "Filter engaged. It won't happen again." He shakes his head and laughs through his nose. "Hey, where's your camera? I thought it was attached to you like one of your limbs."

"Oh." I wave my hand dismissively. "I've taken enough pictures today. Besides, I can't lug it around with me everywhere." *Translation: I didn't have time to transfer the photos from my memory card to my computer and I don't want to risk you looking through them. Too much Bruno.*

We set off down the hill and skirt past the trattoria without getting harassed. I catch eyes with Chiara, but she just winks and carries on sweeping around the tables. No sign of Bruno, and I can't decide if I'm relieved or disappointed I can't flaunt who I'm with.

"Where to?" I ask Darren once we make it to the bottom of the hill.

"I don't suppose you're hungry."

"Starving," I say, instinctively placing my hand on my stomach. "I didn't really get a chance to eat lunch."

After ordering a couple of prosciutto-and-cheese sandwiches and a bundle of grapes to go, we wander down by the marina, chatting about Genoa and my conversation with Gram, until we find a semi-shaded spot to sit and eat. A few birds hop around at our feet, but we ignore them long enough and they move on.

"Where are Nina and Tate?" I finally ask, plopping a grape into my mouth. "I'm starting to think they don't like me."

"Of course they like you!" He laughs and takes a drink from his bottled water. "Nina wanted to hunt for the best gelato in Cinque Terre." It rolls off his tongue so beautifully, like he's said it thousands of times. "And Tate follows her everywhere," he says matter-of-factly.

"What, does that bother you or something?"

"No. Not anymore. I'm happy for him."

"But . . . ?"

"No buts, really." He stares at the ground and peels the skin off a grape.

I cross my legs at my feet and tuck them under the bench. "That wasn't very convincing."

"It's just," he says slowly, as if he's not sure he wants to commit to telling me, "Tate's done with the hard part."

"What do you mean?" My eyebrows scrunch together.

"He already knows that she's it. He's done trying to figure out if she likes him or doesn't like him. If it'll work out or not." He finally chews the peeled grape and clears his throat. "I mean, it's exciting, I guess. But also infuriating because—"

"Because you still have to start from the beginning," I finish for him.

He looks me in the eye and for a moment we just stare at each other, knowing we're both in the same place. Starting from the beginning.

I sit on my hands. They shake when I'm nervous and right now I don't want to acknowledge the physical symptoms. The wind catches a curl of Darren's hair and it sticks up in the air before lying back down again.

I inhale, building my courage, then go for it. "I've got to ask you something. Don't be offended."

He laughs loudly and a couple walking by jerk their heads toward him in surprise. "I can't believe you. I'm so offended."

"Okay, now I don't want to ask you at all."

"Too bad. You have to."

I lift my shoulders toward my ears. "Well, I was just

wondering . . ." I start to reach up to his hair but pull back. "Is that a perm?"

He grins before biting his bottom lip, eyes cast to our feet. "Maybe."

"Really?"

"No."

Thank God. "Have you always kept it long?" I picture him as a toddler, his mom dressing him up like a little girl. He must have been one pretty baby with those mile-long eyelashes and ringlets.

He runs a hand through his hair and his fingers catch on a tangle. He works it out as he says, "This is actually as long as it's ever been. I let it go the start of senior year just to see what it would do."

I watch his fingers pick at the knot. "And it did that."

His eyes snap up at me. "You don't like it." It's a statement.

"No, I—"

"No?" He abandons the tangle and scans the passersby frantically, the corners of his mouth just barely turned up. "Where's a barber when you need one?"

"No, that's not what I meant!" I reach up and take over knot duty. A stray curl brushes the top of my hand. "It's . . . different."

He turns his head to look at me, but I don't let go of his hair and he yelps as it tugs. "Different like it's so weird you don't have an accurate word to describe it, or good different?"

"Darren." I shake his shoulders gently, but he exaggerates it and flops his head around. "Your hair is fine."

"Fine? That's not really making it any better."

“I like your hair, I do! Promise.” I draw an X over my heart, then cross my fingers, holding my hand up for him to see.

One of his eyebrows shoots up. “I think you just voided your promise.”

“What?” I pull my hand down to my lap. “I thought it was scout’s honor or something.”

“Um, that’s three fingers. You cross them when you say something you don’t mean. This is, like, kindergarten 101. Look,” he says, offering me his outstretched pinkie. “This is the real way to make a promise.”

He squeezes my baby finger with his and we act like we’re shaking hands. His skin is rough and dry from digging in the dirt and working with his hands, but I don’t mind.

When it should be time to let go, he doesn’t release. I meet his eyes and find him smirking.

“Your pinkie’s crooked,” he says, tracing the sides of my finger with several of his.

I stare at our joined hands. He’s got a few random cuts across a knuckle or two. I shake my head to clear it when I imagine myself kissing them. There’s a flutter in my gut. Our hands are starting to sweat where they touch.

“Yeah. It’s sort of hereditary, I guess.”

He lets go and raises his hands, palms to him, lining his pinkies up next to each other. They touch up to the top knuckle, but then the tips bend slightly in toward the rest of his fingers, creating a V-shaped gap. I mirror him. My pinkies do the same.

“Wow,” I say.

“Right? I mean, clearly your fingers aren’t normal,” he says. “I can’t believe I pinkie-promised you.”

I point a crooked pinkie at him and wiggle it closer and closer to his face.

"Get that away from me!"

We're both buckled over in laughter. He swats at me but I don't let up, and before I understand what's happening, his teeth are lightly clenched on my finger.

Darren's eyes widen but we're both frozen. His tongue is touching the tip of my littlest finger and I can't breathe. Finally he opens his mouth and I slowly retract my finger, casually wiping off the moisture on my shorts.

"I guess that'll teach me not to attack anyone with my pinkie again," I say. Silent laughter shakes my shoulders until I can't keep it in any longer.

"Man, I'm killing it today," he says. "It's just short of miraculous, how cool I am."

"You're pretty cool in my book." I give him a playful shove with my elbow, which he returns.

"So, you're still coming with us to Pompeii, right? Haven't changed your mind?"

"If you still want me to go with you guys."

He turns in his seat to face me, tucking a leg up under him. His knee rests against my thigh, but I don't move out of the way. "Of course!" he says, eyes lit up. "You'll love it. I already can't wait to see the pictures you're going to take."

I nod in agreement, trying to rein in the part of me that wants to jump up and down.

We decide to leave Monday so I won't miss the St. John's Day feast Matilde is planning. Darren says he and Tate will take care of all the arrangements.

I reach for a couple more grapes and Darren skillfully works the peel off another one. A few of the little birds come back to peck at the scraps at his feet.

"You know the peel is edible right?" I tease.

He doesn't laugh, doesn't look at me. "Do you want to hang out tomorrow?"

I hardly wait for him to finish. "Yes."

His smile reappears.

"Oh, wait." I sink into the bench. "I should probably help out at the restaurant." I hope it sounds more like truth and less like a lame excuse. "Or at least make sure they can spare me."

He nods and says, "It's not a real job though, right? Are they even paying you?"

"Well, they gave me a bed. They feed me," I defend. "I already skipped out on most of today. I should probably head back soon." I didn't even ask about taking off this afternoon, I just left. Though the look on Chiara's face proved she didn't mind.

He turns to face me again. "I'm just saying, this is your summer. Isn't that the whole reason you skipped out on Florence? To *see* Italy. To make your own rules?"

"Good point."

Darren stands and stuffs the bag of leftover grapes into his backpack. "Well, how about for today, you go back to work so you don't feel guilty, and I'll see if I can catch up with Tate and Nina on their gelato hunt?"

I stand too, brushing off the back of my shorts. "That works."

Darren shoves his hands deep into the pockets of his shorts and I take a long drink from my bottled water. The air is thick with the humidity of yesterday's storm and the strong aroma of seafood.

"So, tomorrow?" Darren asks before he makes the turn back to Manarola. "After your lunch shift?" He grins and I nearly melt into a puddle.

How can I say no? "Where to?"

"Have you been to the beach in Monterosso yet?"

The beach. Darren in swim trunks. Don't smile, don't smile. "The beach sounds like a great idea."

CHAPTER TWENTY-NINE

The beach is dotted with colored umbrellas and lounging bodies—thankfully, none of them completely nude. Several teens kick soccer balls to one another, and a child near the water flies a kite. I didn't bring my camera—hello, sand—but the scene is so vivid, it makes me wish I at least had a little point-and-shoot.

Darren spreads out the beach mats and drops his backpack on top of one. As soon as he crosses his arms and grips the hem of his shirt with both hands, I know what's about to happen. I should look away but I can't. Abs reveal themselves. One. At. A time. His chest isn't exactly lacking for hair, but given the amount on his face and head, I expected that. Not that I actively thought of what his chest might look like.

Not often, anyway.

As he wads up his shirt to stow under his backpack, he

glances at me, but I cast my gaze down, suddenly finding the sand-to-pebble ratio of the beach fascinating.

"Don't you have your suit on?" he asks, pulling off his shoes.

I nod and wait for him to get distracted again before shedding layers, turning my back on him as I pull out my sunscreen and work the cool lotion into my face, down my arms, stomach and legs. A grunt escapes my mouth, the hard to reach spot on my back mocking me.

No. The cliché *Can you rub this on my back?* is most definitely not happening.

Assuming the plan is to soak up some rays and chat, I lie down on my back, hiding the vulnerable strip of unprotected skin, determined not to ask for help. His eyes are on me. I can feel it.

I suck in, flattening out my stomach as much as possible, before turning my head and squinting at him. I was right. He's staring.

"What?" I ask.

"Do you want me to get your back for you?"

Cringe. "No, I'm fine."

"Okay, then could you get mine? I don't really want the striped look you're going for. A little too trendy for me." He laughs, snapping the lid shut on his sunscreen bottle. He shakes it hard to force the lotion to the end, every muscle in his body tensing, releasing, tensing, releasing.

My jaw goes slack. He asked me a question. What was it? The cliché come to life? I hesitantly sit up and he's already on his knees on the end of my mat, back to me.

"Oh. Okay, sure." I take the bottle from him and smear the

lotion on the middle of his back as fast as I can. Why isn't it rubbing in? Too much, I took too much.

His body is solid under my fingertips. And tan. And solid. And sweaty. Overstimulation. Accelerated heart rate. Bad thoughts, Pippa. Stop.

The lotion finally blends into his skin and I wipe my hands on my towel.

"That wasn't so terrible, was it?" Darren twists around and winks. "Now are you going to be stubborn or do you want me to finish your back for you?"

I give in for lack of a reasonable excuse and toss him my higher SPF. He kneels behind me and gently rubs even the places I know he saw me reach myself. When he nears the small of my back, I sit up straight as a board, goose bumps racing down my arms and legs, pulse loud in my ears.

I need a distraction, fast.

A green-and-yellow Hacky Sack lands on Darren's mat just next to me, and a girl about my age in a string bikini—emphasis on string—prances over to pick it up. She studies me with narrowed eyes, then smiles at Darren.

"Sorry, cutie."

Darren doesn't respond. I watch her thighs jiggle their way back to her group until an old man wanders into my line of sight, dripping wet. His little gray swim bottoms are probably smaller than mine, potbelly hanging over the top of them.

I lean toward Darren and whisper, "Take a picture of that. Five euros."

We both look back at the man just as he sheds his bottoms, revealing, well, everything.

"Oh, sick *out*," I screech, shrinking down and looking for something to hide under. I've seen a few sets of breasts on the beach so far—which is a little uncomfortable, though Darren does a good job pretending he doesn't see—but this is completely different.

I grab a towel and throw it over my head, laughing uncontrollably. Darren sits down cross-legged, our knees touching, and adjusts the towel to cover both of us. His lips fight back a smile.

"I can't believe you're hiding from that fine specimen of a man," he says. "I'm sure he'd love it if you helped him reapply his sunscreen."

"Thanks for that visual nightmare!" I'm laughing so hard, I'm crying. I just saw some dude's thing. Just hanging out there. Morgan is going to die when she hears about this. "Did he put it away yet?" I ask.

Darren peeks out from under the towel. "He's still changing into his clothes."

I meet his eyes as I recover, catching my breath. We're too close. Our lungs-are-sharing-the-same-moist-air close. The thick towel blocks most of the sunlight from overhead, but it reflects off the sand, illuminating our faces from underneath. We sit perfectly still, holding the gaze. This could be it. The moment Darren kisses me. He raises a hand and I hold my breath . . . but all he does is lift the edge of the towel to look out.

"He's done now. Aren't you disappointed?" His laugh is soft and gravelly as he folds the towel back up and lays it on his mat. "I think I may cool off in the water for a few minutes. Do you want to come?" He stands and brushes the sand off his knees.

Darren wet? Yes, please.

I smile and pop right up. "*Andiamo.*"

ASSIGNMENT NUMERO OTTO: FEEL YOUR FEELINGS

Write down the first thing that comes into your mind. Short and sweet. No pondering! Just WRITE IT DOWN!

Chiara was right. I like the nice boys. I like Darren.

CHAPTER THIRTY

~~Swim in the Mediterranean Sea~~

"Where's Bruno been?" I ask Chiara after we close up and head home for the night. Matilde stays behind to do the pesky end-of-day chores like counting her money. "I haven't seen him all evening."

"I am not sure," she says, though the scowl that appears on her face for an instant tells me otherwise.

"You don't know, or you just don't want to tell me?"

We power up the steep, poorly lit hill to the apartment, a climb I'm beginning to wonder if I'll ever get used to. I slow down and pant when we reach the gate, but Chiara keeps trucking along.

"I do not think Bruno would want you to know where he is all the time," she calls back to me.

"So he's with a girl." By her silence I guess she either thinks it would bother me to know, or she just wants me to *think* he's with a girl so I'll get mad and forget about him.

But I don't really feel mad. Should I? I probably would have a few days ago, but now . . . And I even kissed him just yesterday. Ugh, I am so messed up.

My hand flies to my temple and I rub it.

Chiara stops on the stairs ahead and turns to face me, arms crossed. "What—"

"Never mind," I manage to say, shaking my head. "Let's just go to bed." I pass her up, skipping every other step.

"*Aspetta!*" she calls out, so I obey and wait. "You have not told me about your date with Darren."

I rush to spit out, "It wasn't a date."

"Whatever you say," Chiara says through one of her wicked smiles, which makes me smile too.

The apartment's empty—Luca must have gone out too—so we take turns getting ready for bed, and soon I can hear Chiara's breath slow and deep from her top bunk. I pull the sheet up to my neck and close my eyes. Not comfortable. I roll onto my left side. Still awake. I try my right side and my nightshirt gets twisted tight around my stomach. I groan and sit up to straighten it out. I'm completely wired. My brain won't shut up.

I made out with an Italian. In his boat. And he's probably with some other girl right now, doing the same thing. I'm going on a trip with Darren. He rubbed sunscreen on my back. He bit my finger. The crooked pinkie I got from Mom, and she got from Gram.

I miss Gram so much, it hurts. Talking to her on the phone

almost made not seeing her every day even harder. Nevertheless, I'm looking forward to our next call. I can't believe she's letting me stay here. For some reason, I feel guilty. She thinks Mom won't be able to "punish" her, and sure, it won't be the same as my punishment, but Mom has the ability to make you miserable if she wants to.

Ugh. Too much to process. I'll never get to sleep at this rate.

I pull my computer out from under the bed—still connected to the Internet since I seem to be the only one using it much lately—boot her up, and sign in to my e-mail. Nine new messages. Two from Mom, the rest from Morgan.

I start with the subject lines from Morgan's oldest e-mails. The first few are just replies to the same thread, but the newer ones get increasingly desperate.

Open me; I have news; PIPPAAAAA; Where R U?; I'M GOING TO TELL YOUR MOTHER YOUR SECRET; I'M NOT KIDDING

I roll my eyes at her drama and click to compose a new message to Gram first.

To: Lorelei Mead <lorelei@prestonartsource.com>
From: Pippa Preston <pippers26@gmail.com>
Subject: Gram!

How are you? It was so great getting to talk to you and hear your voice. I'm going to try to call you tomorrow, but I can't sleep, so I'm reaching out to you the only way I can right now. I need your advice. You always know what to do.

There's this guy. I think he likes me. Maybe. How can I tell?

And I just realized I'm going to miss your birthday. I'm so sorry!

I love you,

Pippers

Skype chirps from my program dock and I rush to mute the volume. Chiara doesn't stir. The little box pops up on my screen. Morgan's calling me from her pumpkin-colored room, the sun streaming in from her window.

Her mouth moves, but since I've got her muted, I hear nothing. I put my finger to my lips, then mouth, "Just a minute!" I slip into a pair of flip-flops and carefully tiptoe my way through the living room, directing the long cord behind me. I steal a peek at the couch-bed. Neither of the boys are there. I climb the little spiral staircase up to the terrace, squeeze the cord under the door, and sprawl out on one of the lawn chairs.

When I glance back at the screen, Morgan's not the only one I see. My mother is next to her. Shock kicks through my whole body. I turn up the volume.

"Mom? What are you doing at Morgan's house?"

"Nice to see you too, Pippa." She smiles, but it doesn't reach her eyes. Something's off. Maybe I hurt her feelings? I didn't really think that was possible.

"I'm sorry," I say, smoothing back my hair. "Hi."

"Mrs. Arrant and I are hosting a tea," she says, waving her hand dismissively like I should have known. "How are you?" She leans in close to the monitor. Her eyes are on my image on the screen, not on the camera above, so it doesn't even really feel like she's talking to me. "Are you well? Enjoying yourself?"

Enjoying myself? How am I supposed to answer that? She knows I hated the idea of going to that summer program, but she'll want to hear that I like it better than I expected to. That I'm making an effort to actually learn something. She can't know that I'm having the time of my life somewhere else.

My inner moral compass urges me to tell as much of the truth as I can. "It's getting easier," I say. A breeze catches a few strands of my hair and it falls in front of my eyes.

"Are you outside?" Mom asks.

"Yes, ma'am," I say, instantly regretting such a formal tone. She'll suspect I'm hiding something if I suck up to her too much. "I didn't want to wake my roommate. It's pretty late over here."

Mom points to the face of her watch and counts ahead seven hours. "Oh, I'm sorry. You should get to sleep."

"Probably," I say, though I'm dying to talk to Morgan.

"But first, tell me about your roommate." Mom actually sounds interested. Though my paranoid brain wonders if she's just trying to make me slip up. Maybe she suspects? "What's her name?"

"Claire," I blurt out in a hurry, miraculously recalling that Claire is the English version of Chiara. I have no idea if Italians go to the program I'm supposed to be in, so I can't take any chances.

"Do you get along?" Morgan chimes in. "What's she like?"

"Oh yeah. She's great! Very . . . straightforward. Definitely not afraid to tell you like it is." Or how she sees it, anyway.

"Well, isn't that nice," my mother says as a statement. "I'd better run back downstairs and let you two girls catch up before you go to bed. Pippa, I'm so glad we finally got to talk face-to-face." She's still looking at the screen and not the camera.

"I'm sorry." I shake my head and stifle a laugh at her inexperience with this type of technology. "Things are really busy around here, and it's hard to find the time. I'll try to be better about it."

"Okay. As long as we know you're safe." She blows a kiss to the screen and disappears.

Morgan stares at the webcam with wide eyes and mouths, "I'm SO sorry." Her door clicks and she fires off a mile a minute. "I didn't know what else to do! She asked if I could try to get ahold of you and I never dreamed you'd have your computer on at this exact moment!" She leans in and whispers, "She's sort of pushy."

I snort. "Ya think?"

"I've been needing to talk to you so bad!"

"So your subject lines said. I haven't opened them yet though. What's going on?"

Her cheeks turn pink. "I have a boyfriend."

"What?" I gasp, clutching my chest. "Who?"

"Who do you think?"

I search my brain for the answer to this loaded question. All the boys love her, so it's hard telling who won her attentions this month. Though I do remember her sneaking out in the middle of the night with . . . "Jeremy Cable?"

"Yes!" she squeals, clapping her hands. "He actually asked me out, like, in person. It was the cutest thing ever!"

"Ahhh! Morgan! Is there kissing?" I prod, hoping to live vicariously through her potentially normal relationship.

"That's private information!" she exclaims, pretending to zip her lips.

I try to raise an eyebrow and she laughs. "You expect me to believe he didn't try to kiss you? You're hot, he's hot. The kissing needs to be hot!"

She tilts her head and pulls up a shoulder toward her ear, innocently. "The kissing is totes hot."

"Wow, this is crazy, Morgs." I can't believe I'm not there to jump up and down with her. We've never been this far away from each other. "I didn't even know you looked at him like that."

"Well, things feel more forbidden when you keep them secret, don't they, *Pippa*?"

I laugh and roll my eyes.

"What other secrets do you have these days?" She leans in super close to her computer with a devious smile. "Do you have an Italian lover I should know about? Or *lovers*?"

"What?" My cheeks flame.

"There is someone!" Morgan slaps her palm on the desk. "What's his name? Wait! Is it that Bruno guy? The one who kissed you? What aren't you telling me?"

"Settle," I say, turning down the volume to keep her shrill voice from waking up the whole building. "Uh, Bruno's . . . well . . ."

"Yes?" She moves her hand in a small circle, urging me to continue.

"There's this other guy, he's American. But there hasn't—"

"American?" She scrunches her nose. "We have those over here."

"Morgan!"

"I'm just kidding! How cute is he?"

Darren's insane hair curls around my heart and I warm all over. "He's really cute."

"Has he kissed you? What's he like?"

"No kissing," I say with a shake of my head, "but he, like, saved me. I hurt my ankle and he *carried* me."

Her eyes widen more than I remember ever seeing them. "That's how you met? Did you die? I would have *died*! That's so romantic!"

"It didn't feel romantic at the time." I laugh. "And no, that's not how we met."

"So, why's he in Italy? Where's he from? Where does he live? Is he in college? Details!"

I try to gather everything I know about him, but it's really not that much. I don't know where he's from, where he lives, where he's going to college in the fall. What if he lives in California? Or Alaska? How could I do a long-distance relationship, assuming it even goes that far?

Because it feels like it *could* go that far. Everything about Darren feels different. Real. Like not seeing him anymore would hurt.

What am I doing? What are *we* doing, spending all this time together?

This can't go anywhere.

The realization hits me like a crushing blow between the eyes. And I've forgotten to breathe.

"Pippa? What's wrong?"

I sit up straight when I hear yelling echo from the street below. "Hang on," I tell her.

Setting the computer down on the chair, I lean over the ledge of the balcony. Two guys stumble near the gate to our building. Rather, one of them stumbles and the other one holds him up, yelling at him. I recognize Luca's voice. It's Bruno he's supporting upright.

I run back to my computer. "Morgan, I have to go, but it was so good to see you. I miss you!"

We rush through sappy good-byes and I slam my computer closed, carrying it down to my room before opening the front door and leaning against the wall. I cross and uncross my arms a hundred times before they make it to the top. Luca looks up at me in surprise, then motions for me to help with Bruno's other side. I don't see anything physically wrong with him, but when I position myself under his arm, I fight back a cough. He reeks of cigarette smoke and alcohol.

We haul him over to the foldout bed and Luca lets him drop onto his stomach.

"*Uffa!*" The pillow thankfully muffles his outburst. He lazily rolls over and locks eyes with me. The dark circles are back, worse now. He rattles off something in Italian, too mumbled for me to piece together.

I look at Luca. "What did he say?" I ask. He hesitates but I insist. "Just tell me."

"He said you do not belong here." Luca shrugs and exhales, clearly exhausted. He mopes to the bathroom and closes the door behind him.

I clench my teeth and force my eyes back to Bruno. After everything he said to me yesterday. What changed between then and now? My top lip curls up in disgust as I look at his pathetic form passed out on the mattress. I wish I were leaving for Pompeii with Darren tomorrow.

I swallow down the tightness in my throat. "You're right," I say. "I don't."

CHAPTER THIRTY-ONE

Chicago honors a saint: Patrick. But unlike the San Giovanni Festival honoring John the Baptist, St. Patrick's Day is less about the saint, and more about dyeing everything green—hair, beer, the Chicago River—watching the parade take over the city, and getting wasted. You even get physically assaulted if you don't wear something green the entire day. You're supposed to just get pinched, but some of the guys at school take it a little too far. And if you forget to wear green, you can't get by with the excuse that your underwear is green, because they're not shy about asking for proof.

But they don't do anything that flashy here in the little fishing villages of Cinque Terre. Families gather for feasts of roasted pork, or *porchetta*, wine drinking, and what I'm sure will be a tasteful parade through the heart of town after the sun sets tonight.

Chiara flits around me during our lunch shift. The rush is over and we actually have time to chat while we wipe down tables.

"What will you pack *per domani*?" she asks, spritzing disinfectant on the vinyl tablecloths.

I straighten, my hand only going through the motion of cleaning. "I haven't even thought about packing. But I'm already living out of a suitcase, so I guess I'll just zip it back up."

She stops wiping the table and snaps her head up, crestfallen. "You are not coming back?"

I stop wiping too. I assumed I was coming back, but I guess I don't have to. There's plenty more of Italy to see. And I probably have enough money since I haven't been spending any of it. But there are still almost two months left, and I shudder to think about traveling alone now that I have friends here. A home base.

"Yes, I'm coming back."

Arms reach around my waist and pull me against a strong body.

"Pippas will come back," Bruno breathes into my ear.

I break free from his hold, fixing him with a glare. "This from the same guy who said that I don't belong here?"

He laughs. "*Cosa?*"

"Don't remember, huh? I guess you were too drunk."

Bruno's jaw hangs loose as the realization washes over him. "No, *cara mia. Per favore*, I was, as you say, drunk. Angry."

"At who? *Me*? Why?" I snort. "I don't know what I did between our boat ride and when you had to be dragged to bed by your little brother, but I do want to thank you for opening my eyes the rest of the way."

I glance at Chiara who's beaming at me like a proud parent.

"Pippas." Bruno waits for me to catch his eye before dramatically placing both of his palms over his chest. His brows wrinkle together above his nose. "You must not take what I said as true. You must say you forgive me."

"Bruno." I sigh. "You ca—"

Cutting me off, he plants a swift kiss along my jawbone and disappears back inside. Chiara's mouth twists into the closest thing to a snarl I've ever seen.

My own expression isn't far off. "Don't worry," I say, wiping my cheek with the back of my hand. "I know without a doubt now that he doesn't mean anything by it."

She harrumphs and goes back to cleaning. "It is what he does mean by it that you should be concerned with."

"Look, Chiara. You don't have to worry about him and me. I promise." In my mind, Darren smiles at me. I work at a stubborn sticky patch of the tablecloth. "I've got bigger problems than a flirtatious Italian."

This morning, residents scattered bright flower petals along the edges of the main street, and now, as the sun sinks into the horizon, they light the candles among them in preparation for the parade.

Chiara and I place candles in the center of each table at the trattoria and pass out candlesticks with protective cups to the customers who want one. It's not something every establishment does, but Matilde likes to think of it as a time of reflection and prayer for her husband.

All along Via Colombo, balconies—some draped with strings of lights—are crammed with spectators. Those of us on street level stand just behind the flower petals, passing the flame from our candles down from one person to the next. The walls echo the slow music of drums and horned instruments from the band following behind a procession of men clothed in white-and-black robes, some hoisting banners high. One man carries a golden statue of Jesus on the cross.

The crowd quiets as the main procession passes. I glance down my row at Chiara, then to Luca standing next to his mother, their faces marked with odd shadows from their candles. Even in the darkness, I can see that Matilde's expression is pained. Bruno ran off who knows where an hour ago, an angry Matilde spitting on his heels as he left, and he hasn't come back. It seems to me like he should be here with his family. What could possibly be so important?

"I thought you'd be here," calls a rough voice over my left shoulder.

I turn to find Darren only inches away, holding an unlit candle.

"Hey," I say with a smile much too large. "I was wondering if I'd see you today."

"Tate and I have been busy getting everything organized for our trip." He returns a smile. Something looks different . . . something with his hair.

I hold my candle higher and lean toward him, both to get a better look and to whisper, "Are you wearing a headband?"

His hand shoots to the black band of fabric pulled tight above his forehead, curls redirected up and over it. "I was sort of hoping you wouldn't notice it in the dark. I usually only wear them on dig sites to keep my hair from flying in my face."

"At least it's not pink," I tease. "Although I'm sure I have one of those you could borrow. It may even have flowers on it."

"Oh, could I, please?" He laughs, his hand still fiddling with it. "Seriously, should I lose it?"

I shrug. "It's practical. I get it."

He yanks it off and shoves it into the pocket of his shorts. A shake of his head lands everything where it belongs.

"Here," I say, angling my candle toward him.

"I already took care of the headband. Fire really isn't necessary, is it?"

I motion toward the unlit candle at his side. He smiles and raises it to mine. As he watches his wick ignite, I stare at the hundreds of tiny whisker-shadows dancing on his face and the contrast of the smooth, illuminated apples of his cheeks. He looks from his candle to me, his eyes glossy in the orange candlelight.

"I was just kidding, you know. About your hair," I say, reaching to adjust a stray curl. "But this is better."

Darren clutches my wrist and lowers my arm slowly, my eyes forced to meet his. The drums from the parade combine with the thump, thump, thump of my heart in my ears. Our smiles fade and my mouth is suddenly a desert. His fingers slide down my wrist until my hand rests loosely in his.

A *boom* from a drum as it passes causes us both to jump. I exhale and take the opportunity to pull away and redirect my attention. Nearly the whole town joins the parade behind the band, some carrying candles, some walking arm in arm. Some holding hands.

Did Darren really just try to hold *my* hand?

The parade has moved on up the hill and the onlookers go back to eating and drinking. Chiara and her family—still minus Bruno—busy themselves serving their customers.

"Well, I just wanted to say hi." Darren blows out his candle and tosses it behind us into the box with the rest of them. "I should head back and finish getting everything together for tomorrow. Are you all ready to go?"

"Nearly," I lie.

He grins. "Our first train leaves here around 7:30 in the morning, so I'll meet you at the mouth of the tunnel," he says, pointing toward the bottom of the hill, "around ten after. Sound good?"

I nod. "Guess I'll see you in the morning then."

We shift forward slightly, unsure if we're supposed to hug or go our separate ways. Darren opens his arms and pulls me against him, patting my back several times. I do the same, his sweat-dampened shirt warm to the touch.

"*A domani*," he says as his cheek brushes across my ear.

I watch him start down the street, and wave when he's about twenty steps away.

"Don't forget your camera!" he calls back to me.

I wave again and smile.

"And the battery charger!" he calls, feet moving him backward down the hill.

Laughter escapes my mouth as I continue to wave good-bye.

"And memory cards!"

I lose sight of him in the darkness, but the smile he brought to my face stays put.

Still gripping my candle, burned down to half its original size, I gaze into the flame's blue core. My vision blurs until I see nothing more than a glowing, pulsing orb. My thoughts slip into the past, and I know it's not the first time I've recalled this particular memory since I've been away.

Gram and I sat by the pool, watching floating candles brave the ripples. I fought back tears over learning my parents were sending me to Italy alone.

"Remember that she loves you," she said about my mother. "In her own way."

If that's true, will she still love me when she finds out what I've done? How I've lied to her? Our relationship is already screwed up enough as it is. What sort of irreparable damage am I causing now?

"It's better to have loved and lost," she said, "than to never have loved at all. Give Darren a chance."

What? No. She didn't say that.

Hot wax drips onto my finger, sending a shock up my arm and pulling me out of my daydream. A frustrated sigh whooshes through my lips. I ache for Gram's ability to calm me down and rationalize my situation. Maybe she'd say I need to be guarded because I'm still very young, prone to googly eyes and lust. That if it seems too good to be true, it probably is. That she doesn't want to see me get hurt.

But then she might also point out that you never know what could happen unless you try. That each of our choices, no matter how small, has the potential to change the course of the rest of our life. And that trying and failing is better than not trying at all. Which . . . is basically saying it's better to have loved and lost.

I just don't know if I can believe that. It sounds like unnecessary suffering. Suffering that can be prevented if you're strong enough to thwart attachment in the first place.

I stare back into the flame, wishing for my heart's sake that I had the strength to change my mind about going tomorrow. But I don't. Not even close.

CHAPTER THIRTY-TWO

Since I'll only be gone a couple of days, Chiara lets me borrow her big backpack and helps me pick which outfits to bring along. I count out my money and set aside a few hundred euros to bring with me, tucking the rest away deep inside my bag. Determined to worry about only one expensive gadget on this little excursion, I secure my computer between the layers of clothing in my rolling bag and stow everything I'm leaving behind out of the way in the boys' closet.

With the backpack crammed full and my camera bag slung over my shoulder, Chiara and I head to the trattoria to meet up with her family and say our good-byes.

Matilde swallows me in her pudgy arms. Then Luca offers a quick, awkward side hug, and disappears inside after his mother.

Chiara places a hand on each of my shoulders. "You," she says sternly, "must let yourself have a good time."

"Of course I'll have a good time. I'm going to Pompeii!"

She releases me and rolls her eyes. "That is not what I mean and you know it."

"Chiara—"

"You might not allow yourself to see clearly, but I do." She wraps her arms around me and squeezes. "And you will soon enough."

"Whatever you say." I dismiss her words with a wave of my hand, trying to ignore the fact that Chiara's been right about everything before. I look back at the door as Luca emerges with a tray of juices and coffee cups, and the smile on my face fades. For a second I thought he was Bruno.

"He did not come home last night," Chiara says, guessing my thoughts.

"What?" I'd assumed he came and went while I was sleeping. "Where is he? I mean, should we be worried?"

"No," she answers sharply before forcing a smile. "It is not uncommon for him. Do not think on it anymore. He will be here when you get back."

I thought he'd at least come say good-bye. I scan the surrounding area one more time, then straighten my posture, determined not to take offense at his absence. It doesn't matter.

"*Ciao*, Pippa." Chiara gives me one more hug.

I reposition my camera bag onto the other shoulder when I reach our meeting place a few minutes early. My stomach is in knots with that twisty, sick feeling you get when you know something's about to change.

While I'm observing the faces of people exiting the tunnel,

running footsteps and heavy breathing rush up behind me. I turn, prepared to step aside, but a hand clutches my elbow.

"Bruno!" I say as I notice his skin has been ripped open just below his left eye. His eyelid is deep purple and twice its normal size, and there's a bruise on his chin that seems to be spreading. I take a step closer.

"What happened?" My pulse quickens and my hand hovers near his face, but I'm too afraid to touch anything. I settle for smoothing back his ruffled hair.

"I wanted to see you before it was too late," he manages between pants. "Pippas—"

"Tell me what happened," I demand. A thought occurs to me and I whisper, "Does this have to do with that Mauro guy?" I take a cautious look around us as if Mauro might pop out from a hiding place and start beating me up too.

He studies me as he catches his breath. "Why would you think that?" he asks, then ignores his own question. "Pippas, I am sorry for what I say to you. You come here and make my mind, ah . . . you make me go—" He waves his hands close to his face and widens his eyes.

"I make you turn into a crazy person?"

"Yes!" he nearly shouts, pointing at me. Then his face falls and he grunts. "No. *Sono confuso.*" He tugs at his hair, messing up what little order I'd just brought to it.

"You're confused?" I quickly glance at the people near us—still no sign of Darren—and speak low. "Bruno, what—"

"You make me want better things. To *be* better. But I do not know how. I want you to stay but I want you to go. Too much but not enough. *Capisce?*"

"No, I don't understand you. You're ranting, like . . . well, like a crazy person." Unable to stop myself, I reach up to the cut near his eye again. The blood that's stained the skin around it is dry. "What happened?"

He pushes my concern away and grabs both of my hands, eyes cast down to our feet. "I do not want you to leave."

My stomach clenches even more and I take a step back. I need to get out of here. I should just meet them at the train.

"I'm coming back," I say to appease him so I can make my escape. I twist my upper body to show him the backpack. "Look, I'm not even bringing all my stuff. It's just a few days."

"Why do you like this Darren so? He is not *Italiano*. It is what you wanted."

My eyes narrow. "I never said that . . ." *out loud*. "You *did* read my journal!" There might as well be flames coming out my nose. "You told me you didn't!"

His expression is stern. "You told me to say—"

"Why would you—you know what? It doesn't matter." I rub at my temples.

"It does." He places my hand on his chest and holds it there. "*Io sono un Italiano*. Not him."

Bruno looks past me, over my shoulder, and grins. Before I can turn around his hands are on my face, directing my lips to his. I push at his chest but he's stronger. I clench my teeth together and keep my lips from moving. He finally gets the idea and releases me, but not before tucking a stray piece of hair behind my ear and stroking my cheek with his thumb.

"Bruno, you can't just do that." I shake my head and take two steps backward, wiping my mouth. "This isn't right. You don't really mean any . . ." I trail off when I realize he's looking over my shoulder again, the corner of his mouth hitched up.

Paralyzed, I shut my eyes tight. I know who's behind me and exactly what he just saw.

I swallow more than once though the dryness nearly chokes me, and muster enough courage to open my eyes. Bruno's gone, of course. I should have punched him.

I slowly rotate on my toes and want to disappear when I see it's not Darren staring me down.

It's Darren, Tate, *and* Nina, framed overhead by the arched opening to the tunnel. It would have been the first picture to document our trip. But I've ruined it, forcing a silence that makes me want to run back to the apartment, lock myself on the balcony, and eat a lot of pasta.

Darren's face is blank, completely unreadable. Tate's eyebrows are in the middle of his forehead, and Nina's fanning herself with a train schedule and studying my feet so intently, I look down to make sure my shoes match.

Someone needs to say something before I make a break for the carb therapy.

"Are you coming or staying?" Darren asks, voice tight.

"Coming," I say quickly, hooking my thumbs in my backpack straps. "Why wouldn't I?"

He narrows his eyes. "You tell me."

Nothing. I've got nothing. I'm staring into his honey eyes and I'm frozen.

Tate clears his throat and speaks with forced pep. "We don't want to miss our train!"

Darren's the first to turn his back to me, and we all follow into the tunnel, me a few steps behind. A child's laughter and the whir of the wheels from Nina's rolling bag echo against the mosaics and bounce above our heads. I look up as if the sounds are visible, but all that's there is the curved plastic ceiling, a blindingly bright blue. The sea, all around me, on top of me. Echoes morph into the rush of roaring waves, crashing down. I'm drowning, I must be. The icy blues leech into my skin and I shudder.

We make it out of the tunnel and up to the platform. I lift my chin and shut my eyes, willing the sun's rays to revive me. No one says anything to me. Do they not want me to go now? Just because of that? That wasn't even my fault. What could I say right now that wouldn't make things more pathetic?

The train arrives, the doors slide open, and we cram inside the already crowded car. Nina and I squeeze together in an open space, and the boys stand closer to the door. I catch eyes with Darren, but he looks out the window in a hurry, leaving me to stare at his profile. His stubble still has control of half of his face. He's opted against the headband, though a part of it sticks out of his pocket and I can't help but smile.

If only I could go back to last night, when he held my hand for the briefest moment. I'd hold on to it longer and not flinch when the drums bang around us. I'd start today all over again, saying a simple good-bye to Bruno and leaving before he had a chance to ruin everything.

My smile disappears and my heart races as I get what could be my stupidest idea ever. What if Bruno didn't actually ruin anything? There's not a good ending written for me and Darren, so this could be exactly what needs to happen. A nudge, some sort of kick to force detachment into action.

Bruno's kick was swift and unexpected. I guess I should be thankful. I should be relieved.

So why do I feel like I just broke something?

In La Spezia, we settle into our seats on the train that will bring us all the way to Naples. Nina and I take the window seats facing each other across a tiny table. Tate, of course, sits next to Nina, which puts Darren next to me. Before the train even leaves the station, the three of them pull out their iPods and press the earbuds into their ears.

You've got to be kidding me.

When both Nina's and Tate's eyes are closed, I yank on the cord to Darren's earbud. He startles and his eyes fly open as if I've woken him.

"Are you really not going to talk to me?" I ask, keeping my voice low.

He rubs his ear like I hurt him. "Of course I'm going to talk to you. I just . . . don't know what to say this exact minute."

I cross my arms over my chest. My head feels marshmallowy just thinking about taking this conversation further, but I don't have anything to lose at this point. I can't go the whole trip with him ignoring me.

"Just come out with it," I say, bracing myself for who knows what.

His eyebrows pull together and his nostrils flare as he inhales. "I don't like him."

"Don't like who?"

He shifts in his seat to face me head-on. "That Italian kid who just mauled you. He's Chiara's cousin, right?"

"Bruno."

"Bruno? That's his name? Seriously?" he snorts.

"I don't remember any of us naming ourselves," I defend.

"Sorry. I just figured someone like him would be named Fabio or something."

I want to be angry, I really do, but I can't resist laughing. "That's what I thought the first time I met him," I admit.

Darren actually cracks a smile, and hope blooms inside my chest for an instant before it fizzles. I'm itching to tell Darren that he's the one I want. But I don't know how, or if I should. Keeping Darren at an emotionally safe distance might be the only way I make it through this summer unscathed. If that's even possible at this point.

"Well, whatever his name is. I still don't like him." His voice is rough and his bright brown eyes pierce straight through me.

Tell me why you don't like him. Tell me it's because you're jealous he kissed me and you haven't. Tell me you want to. Want me.

"Gag," Nina says with a groan. "Would you two just kiss and be done with it already?"

Darren and I gape at her. Fire creeps up my neck, and I press my body against the window, as far from Darren as possible.

"I thought you were asleep," Darren says to her.

"With the both of you whining like children? Please," she huffs. "I'm going to the little girl's room." She stands and her long legs step over Tate's without waking him. "Fix this or we're all going to be miserable," she whispers to Darren loud enough for me to hear.

I face the window, but my eyes focus on Darren's reflection. He scratches the top of his head through his curls, then slides his hand down, pressing his thumb and fingers over his eyelids. I've lost my nerve to bring up Bruno again.

"Pippa." He sighs. "I don't want to argue with you."

I reach to grip the armrest between us but his hand is already taking up half of it. I'm caught off guard and I can't decide if it's more awkward to jerk my hand away or leave it there. Electricity runs up my arm when he hooks my pinkie with his.

"Still crooked," he says.

"I'm lucky it's still there, actually."

"Oh yeah?"

"Yeah, some guy tried to bite it off once."

He releases my pinkie and tugs at a loose string on his shorts. "He sounds like a real winner."

I pick at a ripple in the fabric of the armrest. "He's all right."

"I'm sorry," he says.

I'm surprised by the tightness in my throat. This week is going to kill me.

"It's just the little finger," I deflect. "I'm sure I'd have survived."

"That's not what I meant."

I swallow down the lump. "I know. It's fine."

We sit in silence a moment before he points his pinkie at me and wiggles it closer and closer to my face. We erupt into laughter and Tate jolts awake, giving us the stink eye, which makes us laugh even harder. I'm clutching my stomach when Nina plops back down in her seat.

She appraises us with wide eyes until a smirk plays at the corners of her mouth.

"Now," she says, "that's more like it."

CHAPTER THIRTY-THREE

It takes a change of trains in Naples and a bus ride from Sorrento to get to our home base of Positano on the Amalfi coast, but we make it before dark. I wish I could say all the weirdness is gone, but I can tell Darren's holding back. When he smiles, I can't see his twisty tooth.

For dinner, we inhale sandwiches from a street-side cart and Tate navigates our way to the hotel. I expected them to want to save money and crash in a youth hostel, but thankfully Nina put her foot down. She's scared of bed bugs.

The hotel is small, much smaller than the one I stayed at in Rome. The four of us cram into the little hallway, waiting for the big brass key to click in the lock.

"I don't think this is the right key," Tate says. "Why's it so clunky, anyway?"

"Because this hotel is ancient. You have to have finesse," Darren says, irritated. "Here, let me do it."

As soon as he takes over, the door swings open and we enter a musty room crammed with bulky furniture that uses up most of the floor space. There's just enough room to walk between the foot of the beds and the desk, the armoire housing the television, and a taller piece I'm guessing serves as the closet. A row of narrow windows just below the ceiling allow in muted natural light.

"Well, that's cozy." Nina giggles. "I get the one by the bathroom."

We push the rest of the way into the room and I see there are four twin beds, as requested, but with maybe an inch of space between each one.

"Then I guess this one's mine," Tate says, dropping his backpack on the floor and throwing himself down next to Nina. He bear hugs the pillow and yawns. "Wake me up when it's time for breakfast."

Wordlessly, Darren sits at the edge of the next bed, which leaves the one between him and the wall for me. I'm going to have to sleep next to Darren. For THREE nights. What if I dream about him? What if I say something during those dreams? What if he says something in *his* sleep? What if I roll over and bump into him?

I set my camera and backpack down on the desk, dig out a pink tank top, matching pajama shorts, and my toiletry pouch, and get ready for bed in the bathroom. When I come back out, Darren's sitting at the desk, elbow propped on it, head supported in his hand. He's already changed into a pair of red-and-white plaid pants and a black T-shirt. For some reason, the sight of him in his PJs gives me a little thrill.

He motions toward the beds. "They're passed out."

I glance at the fully clothed spooning figures and look away before my cheeks get the better of me. The clock on the desk shows that it's only 8:25. I know traveling wears you out but I feel completely wired.

"Are you ready to go to bed or . . . ?" I let my voice trail off and swallow. I don't know why I'm so nervous about sleeping one bed over from him.

"You want to go for a walk?"

I pinch the fabric of my shorts as if to say, *In these?* and frown.

He looks down at my bare legs, then meets my eyes. "Just throw on your sneakers."

There's a flutter in my chest, but I imagine myself squashing the little winged creatures. No butterflies allowed. I can do this.

Positano reminds me of the villages of Cinque Terre, but I notice right away how much larger this town is. The hills are steeper so there's basically one street that snakes through the town, running in zigzag fashion, and the buildings—similar in colors and style—are broader so they appear even more stacked on top of one another.

We stroll the winding street just as the sun slips behind a mountain, ducking under unruly branches of red and purple flowers and dodging locals speeding by on bicycles. Darren hasn't said anything, but I take the opportunity to control the conversation before he does. To keep it in the safe zone.

"So tell me about yourself," I say, mentally rolling my eyes for sounding like an interviewer. "Where'd you grow up? What's your favorite color? Biggest fear? All the basics."

He laughs, kicking at a cluster of broken flower petals on the ground. "I'd hardly put my biggest fear in the basics category."

"You know what I mean. I feel like I don't know that much about you, in the broad scheme of things."

"Well, in the broad scheme," he begins, "I grew up all over the world, my favorite color changes every day, and I'm terrified of green eyes."

I raise my brows and imagine my eyes shooting him with green laser beams. "That's—" I stop myself from saying *weird.* "Why?"

"It's just this feeling I have."

"My eyes are sort of greenish," I say through a nervous laugh. "Am I that scary?"

He looks at me and we both slow to a stop. A Vespa shoots past, swirling our hair in the wind. He doesn't speak, doesn't blink, so I don't either. I get the impression he's trying to subliminally relay his answer to me. That I'm supposed to know what he's thinking. I don't.

Suddenly he brushes my hair off my shoulder before continuing up the street.

"I mostly grew up in New Mexico," he says. "Arizona and Nevada too, with brief stints in Italy, Ireland, and a few countries in South America. Now we're in Texas."

"Oh." That sounds very, very, very far away from home.

"My parents both work at Texas A&M. So that's where Tate and Nina go, and where I'll start in the fall."

"And you're studying the same thing, following in their footsteps," I say. "Do you want to be a professor too?"

He shrugs. "Maybe one day. I'd like to travel more first though, work on dig sites in places like Greece or Central America. Ancient civilizations are buried everywhere. It's, like, no matter where you walk, you never know what could be under your feet. I want a job that lets me see all the things I want to see before I get stuck behind a desk."

"I know what you mean. I can't wait to see the world and document it, photojournalist style." An image of the two of us traveling together pops into my mind: him digging up the world and me taking pictures of it. I squash those butterflies too.

"Yeah?" he asks, his smile finally revealing teeth. "I can see you doing that, like for *National Geographic* or something."

"You haven't even seen any of my pictures," I scoff. "Besides, can you imagine how competitive a job that would be? Those photographers are incredible. They have years of experience under their belts. I'm not even eighteen years old yet."

"Doesn't matter. You've got time," he says. "You know what someone said to me once? Figure out what you love doing, then figure out how to make money doing it."

I turn the thought over in my head. "I like that."

He smiles, plunging his hands into his pockets. "So tell me about you. Who is Pippa, in the broad scheme of things?" He winks.

I return the smile. "Well, I'm an only child, born and raised in Chicago—"

"Ah, Chicago. That's the accent."

"I told you before, I don't have an accent."

"To *your* ears you don't." He laughs. "But it's definitely there to the rest of us."

"Is that a bad thing?"

"No," he says. "It's cute."

Oh, I might die. A boy used the word "cute." And when describing something about me. I can't look at him.

"Well, I can't really hear your accent," I say.

"That's what happens when you move all the time. I can sound like I'm from wherever I want."

"Prove it. Let's hear a British accent."

"I think technically it's called an *English* accent, and no. I don't work on demand."

I give Darren a little shove. "Come on, pansy. Just a wee little sampling," I say, attempting the accent myself.

He bites back a laugh. "That was . . . rubbish. And Scottish, if we're being picky."

"Hey!" I say, shoving him harder like I'm twelve.

He pokes my shoulder with his pointer finger and I rock back. I reach for him again, but he slides out of the way then takes off down the street in a run. Without hesitation I chase after him, hanging on to my camera to keep it from banging against my chest. He disappears between two buildings and when I round the corner after him, I'm met with a steep wall of concrete steps. A single light illuminates the way from the top. Darren's already a quarter of the way up, taking two at a time.

"Where are you going?" I call to him.

He grips the rusty handrail, gasping for breath. "I have no idea!"

The narrow space feels private and secluded, forbidden

even. I search for a NO TRESPASSING sign and when I turn back to the base of the steps, Darren's standing in front of me, hand outstretched.

"What?" I ask, staring at a thick callous on his palm.

Without a word, he snatches my hand and tugs me up the steps, our winded laughter echoing against the walls. At the top, he leads me over an iron railing to a vacant balcony and we look out to the darkening sea far below. Wispy clouds are just visible overhead, hints of pink from the setting sun fading fast.

"It's beautiful here," I say. "Reminds me of Cinque Terre."

Darren grips the railing and leans back, arms locked. "Would you rather have stayed there?"

"You're not seriously asking me that," I snort, narrowing my eyes at him.

All the muscles in his face are relaxed as he meets my gaze. "I'm serious," he says quietly. "Would you rather be there? With him?" He doesn't look away. "I hope you didn't feel like you *had* to come or something. Just because we asked you."

I blink and shudder as the memory of Bruno's last kiss plays out in my mind. I really wish I would have punched him now.

"I'm sorry," he says, finally breaking eye contact. "It's none of my business."

"No."

He meets my eyes again. "No to which part?"

"No, I wouldn't rather be with him," I rush to spit out.

"Really? Because that's not the impression I got before we left."

"That didn't mean anything. Not to me." I suck in a nervous breath. "And not to him either. That's just what he does."

"What else does he do?" His tone is harsh.

I clench my teeth together before saying, "Nothing, *Dad*."

He forces a half smile and his eyelids drift closed. "I'm sorry. I just have a weird feeling about the guy."

Tell me about it. The dude read my *journal*. He knew I wanted to fall for an Italian all along. He thought he could *be* that Italian. Was it a game to him? Was anything he ever said real?

"You really didn't see me trying to push him away?"

"You did?" Darren scratches along his jawline. "I guess I was too angry to notice that."

"You were?" So it was more than awkwardness. He was angry. The butterflies are back, flapping their stupid little wings in my chest.

He nods and looks away from me, eyes focused past me to the sky as it wanes into a deep-blue blanket dotted with pulsing stars. Bells from a church ring out in the distance.

"I'm glad you chose to come with us," he says, still looking out over the black sea.

With a sigh, I grasp the railing and follow his gaze. "Me too."

CHAPTER THIRTY-FOUR

ASSIGNMENT NUMERO NOVE: THE PERFECT MAN

We talk about boys a lot. Especially who's hot, who's not, and why. But if the movie actors of old have taught us anything, it's that good looks go away. The perfect man needs more than a cute face and big biceps, because even those muscles will one day shrivel. But good character, hopefully, will not.

List five attributes of the perfect man:

1. loyal
2. trustworthy
3. smart
4. funny
5. real

* * *

I don't want to accidentally find myself on Darren's pillow in the morning, so I curl up on my bed, back pressed against the wall. The room is dark, but as my eyes adjust to the outside light coming in through the small windows, I can see Darren sprawled out on his stomach across the entire twin bed. Half of his face disappears into the pillow, mouth slightly open, his sheeted figure slowly rising and falling.

I remind myself that I've been living in the same apartment as Bruno, and he's actually made a move, but I'm a mess of nerves. This feels nearly scandalous, practically sharing a bed with Darren. I turn over to face the wall instead. I can't look at him. If I don't look, he's not really there.

Just as my mind swirls with near-sleep, someone's breathing evolves into a soft snore. I concentrate on the gentle rhythm across the room and identify the offender as Nina. I roll onto my back and stare at the ceiling. I mentally count my toes, telling each one to fall asleep, working up to my ankles, shins, and knees, but it just makes me aware of the soreness of my calves and then I can't stop fidgeting.

Quietly as possible, I unzip my backpack at the foot of my bed and feel around for my journal and the tiny book light. Keeping on my stomach and facing the end of my bed, I clip the light onto the cover of the journal and turn to my next assignment.

In my periphery I see Darren's feet move. I quickly press the button on my book light, straining to listen as he wrestles with his sheets, presumably to get comfy.

"What are you doing?" he whispers, so close his breath causes a stray hair to tickle my cheek.

I startle, leaning away and curling the wisps behind my ear.

"Are you writing in your diary?" Even through the whisper I can tell he's laughing.

"No." I feel in the dark for my backpack and cram the journal inside.

"Please. Just admit you were drawing hearts around someone's name."

"I didn't even do that in junior high," I say, my high-pitched whisper threatening to break into full voice.

"Like I believe that." He whisper-laughs again.

A mattress spring creaks and I can hear movement near the head of his bed. A second later I can just make out Darren's outline as he folds a pillow in half and lies on his side, facing me. I grab my own pillow and mirror him. Nina's snoring deepens and Tate rolls over. I hold my head perfectly still and sense Darren do the same. It feels like we're about to get caught breaking some kind of rule, lying on our beds the wrong direction.

We're quiet for so long, I'm sure Darren's fallen back to sleep. I let my eyes close and start counting my toes again.

"I keep a journal too." His whisper seems much closer than I expected.

In the soft light from above, I can see the glisten of his eyes looking right at me.

I swallow and my throat makes an embarrassingly loud gurgling noise. "Is it full of hearts?" I manage to ask.

The corner of his mouth pulls up. "That's pretty much all I put in there. Hearts and flowers and more hearts."

My bed shakes from the chuckle I'm containing. "Hey, as long as it's not poetry."

"What's wrong with poetry?"

"Nothing." I bite my lip, worried I offended him. "You write poems?"

"Sure. I've won awards for it."

"Oh. Wow. That's . . . cool," I manage, reluctant to admit that poetry's one of those things I don't understand. At all. And people who do "get" it enough to write their own make me nervous with their intellectual prowess.

"Kiddiiiiing," he draws out in a gravelly breath.

"Make up your mind," I tease, secretly hoping he really is kidding. "Do you or don't you?"

Eyes completely adjusted now, I can see him raise his hand and cross his fingers. "Don't. Scout's honor."

"Funny," I say, snatching his hand and yanking it down. "Did you already forget how to promise?" I worm my pinkie around his and squeeze.

He squeezes back and lowers our joined hands to the bed. My heartbeat is strong in my ears. Do I pull away first? Do I wait for him to? What if he doesn't? What if we fall asleep like this?

"I promise I don't write mushy, girly stuff," he says. "I just like to keep track of what's going on, you know? The places I go, the things I find. The people I meet."

I could be imagining it, but the hold on my hand seems to be tighter.

"I know one day I'll want to look back," he continues, "and I don't trust my memory alone to remember everything. What's important to me right now might not be later, but that doesn't mean I want to forget it." He yawns and his eyes get watery, tired.

I fight the temptation to yawn myself. "I think you've just made an excellent case for diaries. Maybe I'll start keeping one."

He yawns again and his grip on my pinkie loosens, but we're still mostly hooked together. "It looked like you already were," he says in a fading whisper. His eyes drift closed.

I stare at his relaxed face, pale in the dim light. Nearly asleep, he looks vulnerable. Like I could tell him anything I wanted and he wouldn't remember it in the morning.

When I first met him, I thought he was attractive but not in an omg-he's-the-most-gorgeous-thing-I've-ever-seen way. But somehow, now that I know him, how his light brown eyes can sear right through me, how the corner of his mouth turns up when he laughs, how he blushes when he's caught wearing a headband, I can see that he really is beautiful.

His hand twitches and his breathing slows, deep and heavy. In an instant he's fallen asleep, and I've fallen even harder for him.

And I have no idea what to do about it.

The Roman Forum near the Colosseum is rubble, the layout hardly discernible to the untrained eye. But Pompeii is a preserved city. Colorful mosaics and frescoes, even some artwork on ceilings remain intact, protected for centuries by the very ash that killed everyone in its path.

Darren's in his element, dragging me from one point of interest to the next, leaving Tate and Nina in our dust. We reach a clear enclosure protecting thirteen body castings. Darren explains that the archaeologists who discovered the hollow cavities in the ash filled them with plaster, let them dry, then chiseled the pumice around them to reveal exactly how the bodies lay when they died. A few of them are small, obviously children, and all of them are on their sides or facedown except for one man in the corner who's halfway sitting, as if he gave one last vain effort to escape.

I snap a picture, then let my camera hang around my neck. It feels almost disrespectful to take pictures of these figures that were living people once upon a time.

Warily I gaze back at the looming Mt. Vesuvius only five miles away. Could it go up right now?

"Don't worry," Darren leans in and whispers, reading my mind. "It's an active volcano, but they're monitoring it."

"They better be." I eye it one more time before facing him. "Where to next?"

He studies the visitor guide and points in the direction we came from. "Let's go see the Great Theater."

"There's a theater?" I ask, instantly brightening.

"You're surprised they had a theater, or that it survived?"

"Well, that they had one at all, I guess."

We walk a few streets over, the afternoon summer sun beating down hard on my shoulders. Darren leads me through an arched tunnel that opens to a dirt U-shaped area where the orchestra pit would be in a modern theater. The slope of a grassy hill wraps around us, tiered with stone steps and remnants of seats, evidence that this theater held thousands of spectators once upon a time.

When the crowd thins a little, I rotate in a circle, taking a

360-degree panoramic. Darren ducks out of my way, so I make him pose for me to get a shot of him alone with the brick ruins in the background.

I preview it on the little screen. His hair is magically controlled today, every curl falling perfectly in place around his head, though his facial hair is the scruffiest I've seen yet. His smile is more of a smirk, mischievous. Like he knows I have every intention of making this the background picture on my computer.

A smile pinches my cheeks and I raise the camera to my eye, taking pictures of everything around me a second time just to hide.

"When did the volcano blow?" I ask.

"It's erupted quite a few times, but the one that did all this was in AD 79."

My eyes scan the perimeter of the theater. "Did it ever have a roof?"

"I think they used big canvas awnings." He tugs at the collar of his shirt. "Which we could use right now."

I lead us closer to the stone seats to get a better look at them. "It sort of makes it hit closer to home. I mean, when you imagine life back then, you think of the primitive parts: building things, growing food, trying not to get stabbed by someone's sword. You forget they might have had time for other stuff, like putting on plays."

"Oh, I know," he says. "I think about that too, how people were still people. They looked out of their eyes and lived inside their heads just like you and I do. Think of how differently their eyes saw this place."

I smile. "And you said you don't write poetry."

He laughs and palms the back of his neck. "Really though, you have to wonder how different we are. Minus electricity and modern medicine, I think things operated about the same. They went to work, came home to their families, ate meals together. The rich had the power, the poor did what they could to survive." His eyes travel up an ancient aisle of steps. "But people have always wanted to be entertained. These days we just have fancier methods."

I think of how cities now have separate venues for different types of entertainment. Concert halls for orchestras and operas, grand theaters for traveling productions, small clubs for lesser-known musicians. Even each type of sports team has its own place to play. But this broken-down pit was where the locals came for political speeches, concerts, plays, and festivals. All here in one place, right where we're standing.

"Too bad it was buried before Shakespeare," Darren continues. "This stage never saw the likes of Romeo or Macbeth."

I whirl around to face him in horror. "No no no no no, don't say the *M* word!"

"What *M* word? Macbeth?"

" 'Angels and ministers of grace defend us,' " I mutter, turning from him and heading for the exit.

"Pippa, what are you doing?" he asks, right on my heels.

I stop inside the tunnel and he bumps into me, clutching my elbows to steady me.

"I'm sorry," I say, shaking my head as embarrassed laughter overtakes me. "Theater background. Superstitious bunch."

"You're superstitious?" His rough voice echoes above our heads, so he leans in closer and says, "I didn't really see that coming."

"I'm usually not, but I guess that got ingrained. Everyone in my circle knows not to say that inside a theater."

"Bad luck, I take it?" he asks. I nod and he observes the place one more time before following me out. "Not to be insensitive to our surroundings or anything, but I think bad luck's already done its business here."

"Old habits . . . blow up in your face." I adjust my ponytail and try to concentrate on what's around us, but from the corner of my eyes I see Darren bite his lip. I'm not sure if he finds this new information about me endearing or insane.

He follows me quietly for a few minutes before speaking again. "So theater, huh? Not sure I saw that one coming either."

"Why?" My cheeks are warm, but I keep in front of him and look anywhere but his direction.

"The theater kids back at my high school were . . . a lot different than you."

I laugh a little louder than necessary. "There are definitely some characters in drama club. As far as style or individuality goes, I'm not much of a standout at school."

"You would have stood out to me."

"I don't need any tall-girl jokes from you, thanks."

He shrugs. "That's not what I meant."

Must. Look. Away. What else can I take a picture of? I point the camera to my feet and snap a few.

"You're taking pictures of your feet?" His tone is equal parts curious and amused.

"Oh yeah," I say, turning the camera on his sneakers. "I'll call it, 'Standing in Pompeii.' "

"How original."

Great. I've just made myself a certifiable nutcase.

"There you two are," Nina calls.

She offers a smile almost identical to Chiara's when she's up to something. Nina drops Tate's hand and presses the power button on her point-and-shoot camera. She motions for Darren and me to get closer together, but we're like rocks.

"Come on, I want a picture," she prompts.

Darren doesn't move, so I walk over to him and leave a few inches between us. Nina huffs and reaches for Darren's arm, wrapping it behind my head and resting his hand on my shoulder. My bare shoulder!

"Nina—" Darren starts to gripe.

"Shut up, I'm giving you direction. You two are pathetic." She stands by Tate again and takes a picture of us. "Smiling won't kill you, doll."

"I *am* smiling," I say through gritted teeth, Darren's hand burning into my skin.

She puts a fist on her hip and shifts her weight impatiently. "Not you. Him."

I turn to look at Darren, but he's still holding on to me and my body sort of melts into his. He turns his face to mine too and I bite back a nervous laugh, which makes him crack a smile.

"Finally," Nina says as she takes a couple more pictures.

My smile stretches ear to ear and I'm completely lost in Darren's deep eyes. Nina's still chattering on, probably asking us to change poses, but I don't hear any of it and Darren doesn't seem to either. It's just us. Me and the boy I watched fall asleep last night. The same cute face I stared at until my eyes burned with heaviness and forced me to close them. The hand on my bare shoulder is the same one that still held a loose grip on mine this morning when I woke up.

My head is light and my fingers shake, but I can't stop smiling. He's so close. All he has to do is lean—

"Where's the mistletoe when you need it?" Nina's voice cuts through my thoughts.

His eyes dart to my lips for an instant and his smile falls. "I think you got enough pictures, Nina," Darren says, dropping his arm and turning from me to Tate who looks as confused as I am.

Nina sighs and slips her arm through mine. "Are you hungry? I'm starving. Let's go find some food."

We follow the boys down the black stone street, heat radiating from it in waves. I glare at Darren's sweat-spotted back, a good twenty feet ahead of us already.

What. Just. Happened?

CHAPTER THIRTY-FIVE

~~See Pompeii~~

The view of the Amalfi coast on the boat ride from Positano to the island of Capri is the biggest reason the guys selected Positano as our home base. As the vessel pulls away from the marina, I'm able to take in the whole cliff-side town for the first time, the colorful buildings spilling from the mountains toward the turquoise sea. Houses become sparse, dotting the lush green vineyards tiered up the slopes reaching high into the mist of early morning.

I take way too many pictures of the coast, zooming in on buildings that look like castles along the shore, a giant cave on the side of a cliff, and boats we zip past that are much smaller than our ferry. Nina poses for a few with Tate at the railing of the deck with Positano in the background. They hang all over each other, grinning like fools and pecking each other on the cheek. If I wasn't so jealous of their relationship, I might be annoyed.

Okay, so maybe I'm jealous *and* annoyed.

"What should we do first?" Tate asks when we get off the boat at the Marina Grande.

Nina leans into him and points to a map of the island. "The chair lift to the top of Monte Solaro. Or we could check out la Grotta Azzurra."

Tate looks to me, then Darren. "All in favor with the queen?"

I nod but Darren pipes up. "No. It's overcast, so the Blue Grotto isn't going to look too spectacular. Plus it's a total tourist trap. The guys who row the boats in there just wear you down until you give them a tip."

"Of course they want tips. They have to row people's fat, rich tourist asses all day long. I'd say they deserve it." Nina frowns at him. "What's got your tighty-whities so tight today?"

He rolls his eyes like she's a child. "I wanted to check out the ruins of Tiberius. The Villa Jovis."

"It's always ruins with you," Nina snaps. "I need a break from all the history lessons, Darren. Plus that little excursion will take three hours minimum. There's too much other stuff to do here . . . like shopping." She links arms with Tate to show that he's not going either.

Darren crosses his arms and cocks his head to the side. "Fine," he says through an exhale. "Monte Solaro, then."

"Perfect!" Tate says, obviously trying to keep the peace. He pulls Nina toward the buses and Darren stalks behind them.

The tension is thicker than the humidity. I did not sign up for all the bickering.

"Wait," I call to Tate and Nina before they get too far. "How about you two go on ahead to your Blue whatever, and I'll go with Darren to see the ruins."

Darren's jaw slacks as he stares at me, which is the most attention I've gotten from him since he put up a wall yesterday.

"Are you sure?" Tate asks.

"Just let them go," Nina urges, shooting me a sinister smirk like this was her plan all along. "We'll meet you guys back here before our return ferry."

Once upon a time, the ruins of the Roman Emperor Tiberius were a multiple-level villa built on the slope of the land just along the edge of a cliff, for maximum protection. It has that same ancient historic feel, but after Rome and Pompeii, this place is sort of a letdown.

Nevertheless, Darren is completely engrossed in every part of it, and I find myself content watching him marvel at everything from the seemingly modern ideas the architect had to the breathtaking view of the island and the sea in the distance.

"Thanks for offering to come here with me," Darren says as we approach a vacant bench at a cliff-side lookout point. "I don't know why I didn't think about splitting up."

"Ah, that's because I'm smarter than you." I adjust the strap around my neck, putting an arm through it so the camera rests low near my hip. "The female mind develops faster, you know."

He lets out a gravelly laugh and my shoulders feel lighter. I didn't realize before how much I loved the sound of it.

"Well, I'm older than you," he points out. "So maybe we should be about even?"

"Hmm." I scratch my chin as I sit on the end of the bench to lean on the armrest. "You're not that much older, so my sources say no."

He chuckles again and sits, keeping a couple of inches between us.

"So, I have to ask something," I muster the courage to say. "You were kind of harsh back there with Nina. What's going on with you guys? I thought you liked her."

He inhales and absently plays with the part in his hair. "I do like her. She's just been getting under my skin lately."

I think of when Nina took pictures of Darren and me together. That seemed to be when his switch flipped.

"Why?"

"She's been butting into things that aren't her business."

"Then what was it this morning? I don't get what she said that pushed your buttons."

Darren crosses his arms. "I feel bad about that now. I think I was still irritated from yesterday's mistletoe comment. I'm sorry if you thought my attitude had anything to do with you." He looks at his feet, the slightest hint of color appearing on his cheeks. "She doesn't understand that things other people are going through might not be so simple."

I nod as if I have a clue what he's talking about.

"Plus she thinks she knows everything, so that doesn't help," he says, uncrossing his arms and cramming his hands into his pockets. He fidgets so much, it's making me edgy.

"Well, she's older than you are, right?" I nudge him in an effort to lighten things. "She's got the advanced model of brain, even better than mine."

He catches my eye and grins. "Nah. You've got her beat by miles."

I return the smile and take a drink of water. "How long have they been together? Tate and Nina. They seem pretty serious."

"Two years. I think."

"Wow. My longest relationship has been, like, two months. If that."

"Well, it's different when you're out of high school," he says.

I frown. That's right. I'm still a baby. Is that what he meant about things not being so simple?

"Thanks for the reminder," I mutter.

"I didn't mean it to sound condescending, Pippa. I *just* graduated, remember? I'm just saying—" He stops himself and sighs. "Look. Think about the relationships people have at your school. That your friends are in, or maybe even that you've been in. Isn't it just a bunch of drama? Fighting and whining and jealousy?"

I scrunch up my nose, but he's right. "Basically."

"It's ridiculous. People end up making mistakes when they're swept up in someone else, and they can't even see that the person they're with isn't right." He kicks at a loose pebble and it skitters off underneath the guardrail.

"You say this from experience?"

"I wouldn't go through high school again if someone paid me a million dollars." He snorts. It's a joke, but his tone is laced with pain. We're getting dangerously close to hitting a nerve. Maybe the same one Nina keeps tempting.

"A million, no," I say. "You'd still need a job with only one mil. What if it were two?"

His smile looks forced. "Not even for two."

I swallow, staring at his eyes though he's not looking at me. "Must have been some wicked girl. What did she do?"

He considers this for a moment, then shakes his head. "Nothing."

"You can tell me, you know," I push, for equal parts curiosity and because he might really need to talk about it. "I won't judge."

"No, she did nothing, that's just it. She didn't love me."

Whoa. Wasn't expecting the *L* word.

"And you . . . loved her?" A lump forms in my throat. Whoever she is, I want to punch her.

"Felt like it at the time." He finally turns to look at me. "Now I'm not so sure."

The lump in my throat turns into a gripping fist and I forget to breathe.

"What about you?" he asks. "Ever been in love?" He looks away as if he's embarrassed.

"Well, there was one guy about a year ago, and I thought maybe I was. But he turned out to be a major tool, so I sort of can't even remember that feeling I had."

Darren makes a grunting noise.

"What?"

He sucks on his bottom lip as if selecting his words carefully. "This just proves my point that most high school relationships are worthless. A waste of time."

I guess if you consider making out with the most popular

guy in school a waste of time. Everything I know in the department of French kissing I owe to that idiot. It may have been a crappy relationship, but I refuse to believe it was all for nothing.

"So what you're saying is that I've still got another year or so until I'm going to find anything worthwhile, seeing as how I'm still in high school and all." My words have a little more bite than I intended, but his signals are too conflicting. He flirts with me and a minute later he gets mad at Nina for hinting that we should kiss. How did he go from being just Darren to being such a guy?

"Yes. Maybe. I don't know," he says, deflated.

"You don't know enough about me to say that." My throat and my eyes both burn. Why am I getting so worked up over this?

Because I like him and I feel like he's telling me, in code, that I'm not worth his time. That starting something with me would be a mistake. I'm officially giving up being logical about this. He should too. I already know it's going to suck saying good-bye, so he should kiss me and at least give me a tingly memory to take back with me.

"I might be different." I clench my teeth when I realize I said that out loud, keeping myself from saying any more.

"Pippa." He breathes a sigh, eyes looking everywhere but at me. "You *are* different."

I slowly turn toward him on the bench, pleading with my eyes for him to look at me.

Footsteps crunching gravel behind me rob me of my daydream, and an older couple approaches the metal railing near the cliff edge. The tired-looking woman glances back at the bench with longing.

"You can sit here," Darren says to her. He clasps my hand, sending a current up my arm to my chest. "We were just leaving."

He leads me back down the path and for the brief moment he keeps hold of my hand, it's the only thing anchoring me to the ground.

The chairlift up Mt. Solaro seats only one person per chair, which terrifies me. I play it cool until I get on, then press myself back as far as I can and grip the seat with both hands as I rise into the air. It doesn't go nearly as high as a ski lift, maybe between ten and twenty feet, so after a few minutes I'm able to relax and actually enjoy the view.

Below me are manicured gardens, children playing in their backyards, women tending to potted plants, none of them paying attention to the human birds flying overhead.

Halfway through the ride I get brave and cling to the safety bar, twisting to look back at Darren in the chair behind me. When I meet his gaze, he offers a half smile, his thoughts clearly holding him back. I face forward again, heavy with the feeling that I'm to blame for that.

At the top of the lift, I mutter a "*grazie*" to the attendant that helps guide me off. I follow the little red arrows painted on the ground to get out of the way so fast that I nearly bump into the lady who got off in front of me.

I turn around just as Darren hops out of his chair like a pro. He holds his half smile steady as he leads me up to the lookout.

"Look how high we are," I say in both wonder and anxiety, standing so close to the edge of the highest point on the entire island. I clutch the railing with both hands and peer over. "We can see everything from here."

"What do you think?" he asks after a few moments.

"It's beautiful."

"Pippa . . ."

I can tell he's staring at me, waiting for me to look him in the eye. But I pick at the chipping paint on the top of the railing, fighting to appear interested only in the turquoise of the Gulf of Naples, the clusters of white buildings along the shore, the countless boats circling the island. Maybe Nina and Tate are on one of them, returning from the Blue Grotto.

"About earlier—"

My attention shifts behind Darren to a little blond boy in overalls trying to push his head between the rods of the railing.

Darren turns to see what I'm looking at and laughs. "You're gonna get stuck."

The boy looks up at him in confusion and yells something in another language. His mother rushes over and snatches his hand, giving both Darren and me the evil eye as she drags him away.

"Kids." Darren shrugs. "Do you want any?"

"Kids?" I choke. "Uh, I don't know. Probably. Someday. Not anytime soon, so don't get any ideas tonight back at the hotel." My cheeks flame from the shock of my own words and I conjure up a laugh to play it cool. Inappropriate jokes are Morgan's forte, not mine.

"Noted." Darren does a cough-laugh combo and rubs one of his ears. "What was I saying before?"

I can't let him get back to that train of thought, wherever it was headed.

"You were about to tell me your favorite color today."

"Huh?" He squints, studying me.

"You said it changes every day. So which is your favorite today?" I hold his gaze and try to convey that I'm not kidding. I'd rather hear his favorite color than another version of how I'm still in high school.

"Yellow," he finally says. "Let's go look on the other side."

I follow, catching a glimpse of my tank top as I adjust my camera strap. It's yellow. I bite back a smile.

"What's yours?"

"Right now," I say, pointing to the sea along the coast where it's the brightest aqua I've ever seen, "that."

He nods in approval. "Favorite childhood memory?"

I frown involuntarily. Thinking of my childhood makes me think about my parents, which makes me think about my rapidly approaching and inescapable punishment.

"When I was ten," I say, "Gram came to stay with us for Christmas and she taught me how to knit."

"Like with yarn?"

"Yes, that's what knitting is." I laugh. "I made a scarf. Which is still really the only thing I can make."

"Did you wear it?"

"No. I gave it to my mom Christmas morning."

"I'm sure she loved that. My mom always valued the homemade stuff most."

I take a seat on the low stone wall. The sun hides again behind a cloud and the muscles in my face are able to relax.

"She put it on right then, when she opened it. But I haven't seen it since, now that I think of it. Maybe she didn't wear it because it was hot pink." I try to laugh, but my throat shuts tight.

Darren sits so close to me that our thighs touch. "I'm sure she put it somewhere safe."

I'd like to think she did, but I have no idea. What happened to all the drawings and crafts I brought home from school that never made it to the fridge because magnets weren't allowed?

"Hard telling. She doesn't exactly have the motherly instincts most moms do."

"She probably has more than you think." His words float between us as I try to believe them.

"What about you?" I ask, anxious to steer the conversation away from me. "What's your favorite childhood memory?"

He sits up a little straighter and angles toward me. "When I was around eight, we lived in Arizona. We didn't really have any grass, so my parents buried all sorts of things in the backyard. They worked on it for weeks while Tate and I were at school or friends' houses. We had no idea they were doing this. Then on Tate's birthday, they gave us access to their shovels, picks, brushes, all of it. The real stuff they actually used in the field."

"Miniature archaeologists," I say with a tight-lipped smile, envious of the love and time his parents poured into creating such a memory for their boys. "What did they bury for you to find?"

"What *didn't* they bury?" He laughs, stretching his legs out and crossing his feet. "Some of our old forgotten toys, some new ones, plastic dinosaurs, matchbox cars—those were nearly impossible to get clean. They said they buried bones from dinner but some animal got to those first."

"Is that when you knew that's what you wanted to do?"

"Well, it definitely sparked something, but what eight-year-old wouldn't like digging in the dirt?"

I timidly raise my hand.

"You didn't play in the dirt?"

"I never really had any to play in. I guess I—"

"Hello. Sandbox?"

I shake my head. "I was prissy as a child. No dirt under these fingernails."

"You were prissy? I don't believe it."

"If you knew my mother, it wouldn't surprise you." I raise both of my hands in surrender. "But I've grown up. I'm not afraid to get dirty anymore."

A lone eyebrow skyrockets and color creeps up his neck. "Is that right?"

I drop my face into my hands and bump against his shoulder. "I didn't mean it like that."

His laughter is warm on the nape of my neck. "Don't worry. I know."

We stand to leave and I soak up the view one more time, taking a dozen more pictures before heading for the lift to go down. It's all going too fast. The sun's already descending on our last day. I'm not ready to go back.

CHAPTER THIRTY-SIX

Our south Italy excursion drawing to a close, we work our way back to Naples to catch the bigger train that will drop Darren, Tate, and Nina off in Florence—closest to their new dig site in Tuscany—leaving me to ride the rest of the way to Cinque Terre alone.

We settle into our seats around lunchtime, and after snacking on bread and fruit, it doesn't take long for Nina to curl up against Tate, whispering something in his ear. They're both asleep within minutes. What is it about traveling that makes everyone want to sleep all the time?

I suppress a yawn myself and look at Darren next to me, his head lolling over to the side and popping back up. A sigh escapes my lips. This is not how I wanted to spend my last couple of hours with him.

He sinks down farther into his seat and his head slams

against my shoulder, bobs back up for a second, and falls again. His dark curls brush against my cheek.

Do I move him? Do I wake him up so I can talk to him? I'm not particularly tired, but I'd be lying if I said I wasn't tempted to rest my head on top of his. It would fit perfectly if I just . . . leaned down a little. . . .

His hair is soft as any pillow, and I breathe deeper, memorizing his clean scent. Citrus and maybe a hint of rosemary. Probably whatever shampoo the hotel had.

Darren shifts and I freeze. He adjusts the placement on my shoulder and stills again, his breathing evening out to a slow rhythm. I let myself relax against him, enjoying the unconscious affection. It might be all I ever get, so I'll take it.

My eyes flutter open at the sound of rolling luggage wheels. Through my jeans I feel a light pressure on my thigh and look down to find Darren's hand resting near my knee. My face is still buried in his hair. I can't help smiling.

But my smile fades as soon as I piece together the noises I'm hearing with the people I can see walking outside the window. We've stopped.

I place my hand on Darren's shoulder to prop him up. "Darren. Wake up." I shake him.

"Hmm?" He licks his lips and slowly sits up on his own, opening his eyes cautiously as if the daylight is too much.

"We're at a train station," I say in a mild panic. "I'm not sure which one."

"What?" Nina jumps out of her seat, causing Tate to slump over before he jolts awake.

"What's going on?" Tate mumbles.

A few people board the train and stow their luggage. Darren looks out the window and frowns.

"We're in Florence." He looks at Tate and Nina with wide eyes. "We have to go. Now!"

They all scramble to gather their things, and I move to stand in the aisle. Tate's ready first and he gives me the one-armed side-hug thing, but he closes us in with his hand on my other shoulder, tapping it a few times.

"I'm glad you came with us. It's been fun," he says.

"Thanks for inviting me. It was good getting to know you guys."

Tate steps aside and Nina gives me a quick squeeze. "You're sweet, Pippa. I'm sure I'll see you again sometime." She pulls away and winks at me before following Tate off the train.

Darren holds the handle to his backpack on the seat. My heart is in my ears, my throat, exploding out of my chest, like waking up from a nightmare.

I force a smile. "I'm glad you asked me to come along. Well, Nina asked, technically, but—"

"It was my idea," he says. "To ask you to come. I wanted you to."

My face warms.

"Pippa, I—"

"Darren," Tate calls from the door behind me, "this train is about to leave."

Darren looks over my shoulder and nods, eyebrows tense, before he opens his arms and I walk into his embrace. Our chins sit on each other's shoulders, my cheek against his warm, scruffy one.

I try to ignore the sting in my eyes. I don't know how to say good-bye. I don't know what to say at all.

"Seriously," Tate calls again. "We've gotta go, bro."

We break apart and he's about to slip his arms through the straps to his backpack when he digs in the front pouch and pulls out a paper sack.

"I almost forgot," he says, handing it to me. "For you."

"What is it?"

"Just some things I found here and there." Darren smiles and I turn to mush. "I'll see you soon," he says as we change places in the aisle and he backs toward the door.

I manage a smile. "Promise?"

He flashes his twisted tooth in a wide grin. "I promise. Bye, Pippa."

I raise my hand to wave at the same time he does, and he hops down the steps to the platform.

I rush to my seat and watch the three of them through the window as they wave, then disappear into the crowded station. I reach into the little bag and pull out three refrigerator magnets: Pompeii, Positano, and Capri.

"Pippa!" Chiara excuses herself from the table she's waiting on and flings her arms around me. "You are back!"

"Chiara! I missed you."

She screws up her face like she doesn't believe me before letting a smile take over. "I missed *you*! Come, I want to hear everything."

Matilde fires up a couple of pizzas for us to take back to the apartment, and Chiara and I light a few candles out on the terrace.

Since I didn't eat much today, I inhale the mushroom half of mine at breakneck speed.

"Impressive eating," Chiara teases. "Did you forget to eat while you were away?"

"Just today," I say, picking up another piece and taking a bite. I'm determined to eat the whole thing and cross that goal off my list for Morgan. It's the easiest one. Not *impossible* like falling in love with an Italian and bringing him home with me to live happily ever after.

"How was it?" she asks.

"It's delicious. Chicago has nothing on this." I dab my mouth with a napkin.

"No." She laughs, facing me. "How was your trip south? With Darren?"

My heart sinks a little. Morgan's always had first dibs on boy talk. I miss being able to call her whenever I want.

"We had fun. I got some great pictures too. We stayed in Positano and took day trips from there to Pompeii and Capri. It was amazing. Did you know they had theaters even two thousand years ago? Of course you do, you live here, right in the middle of all this ancient history. I'm sure you already know everything about—"

"Pippa!" Chiara says, snapping her fingers in front of my face. "Ah, but you are a master at avoiding."

"What are you talking about? I'm not avoiding anything." I shove a huge piece of the last slice into my mouth, feeling sick but still determined.

"Why do you not want to talk about Darren? What happened?"

I force the bite down. "Nothing happened."

She crosses her arms and narrows her eyes.

"Well, he sort of held my hand for a few seconds, maybe." Her eyes brighten so I continue, "And he fell asleep with his head on my shoulder on the train today."

Her expression falls. "*Questo è tutto?*"

"Isn't that enough? I'm leaving in, like, a month and a half. It's better that nothing happened," I lie. One little kiss wouldn't have killed anyone.

"When will you see him again?"

My shoulders slump. "I don't know. He promised he'd see me soon, but we sort of . . . forgot to exchange info. I don't have a way to get in touch with him."

I realized it around the time I got to La Spezia to change trains. But I don't have a working phone here in Italy anyway, and I don't know if Darren has access to e-mail or not. It's just never come up. And maybe somewhere inside I was hoping he'd be the one to ask.

"He will be back," she says, relaxing into her lounge chair and gazing up at the dark sky.

I do the same, letting out a long sigh. *I hope so.*

When my eyes start to drift closed, I stretch and rise to my feet. "I think I'm going to get ready for bed."

Chiara gathers our trash and follows me downstairs. I head straight for my luggage in the closet of Bruno's room. Kneeling to unzip my bag, I'm puzzled to find my computer lying on top of my clothes. I could have sworn I'd stowed it between layers. I look around the rest of my bag and my stomach drops. Something's off. This isn't how I left it.

Chiara comes in and plops down on my bed. "I slept here

while you were gone, but I washed the sheets for you. I did not want to climb the ladder when I did not have to."

"I don't blame you," I say, distracted, digging for my money envelope.

Chiara falls onto her back. "I should tell you about Bruno before you see him."

I count through my euros. "Yeah, what's going on with him? He had a black eye when I left."

I'm six hundred short.

"Now it is his nose." I hear a noise that sounds like her fist slamming into the palm of her other hand.

"What happened to his nose? Is he a fighter or something?" I ask, half listening, though I can't help picturing Bruno bobbing and weaving in shiny little boxing shorts.

"Not a very good one, obviously," she mutters.

Anxiety floods through me as I count the money again. Could I have gotten the math wrong before I left on Monday?

"Does he fight with that Mauro guy?" I ask, trying not to let on that I'm in panic mode.

She rolls onto her side, propping her head up. Her voice is low, all humor gone. "It is not about fighting. He owes Mauro money. His latest installment was due yesterday."

I count the money a third time, and snap my head up to meet her eyes. "Let me guess. Six hundred euros?"

Her eyebrows pinch together above her nose. "How did you know that?"

"Because that's how much I'm missing."

CHAPTER THIRTY-SEVEN

Bruno bounds into the room. "*Pippas è qui?*"

"Oh, I'm here, all right," I mutter, tossing the envelope back into my suitcase.

Bruno's arms loop around my middle and he hoists me from the floor. He rotates me to face him and crushes his lips against mine right in front of Chiara. I can hear her draw in a breath as she rises to her feet.

I dig my knuckles into Bruno's shoulder before I slap him across the face, making sure to strike his injured nose.

"*Uffa! Che cosa?*" His hand flies to his face as a fresh bead of blood sneaks out of a nostril.

"Pippa!" Chiara shrieks, rushing to Bruno.

My palm stings but I shake it off. "That's for kissing me when I told you last time to stop! And for stealing money from me!"

"Pippas," Bruno pleads, hand still covering his nose. "I will explain."

Chiara's eyes widen and she glares at him. "Bruno? *È vero?*"

He ignores her and chases after me as I head to the door and cram my feet into my sneakers. "I will explain. Give me a chance, *per favore.* I did not steal. I, ah, ah—"

"You what?" My hand turns the knob. "*Borrowed* it without asking?"

"How could I ask? You were away."

I shake my head and take off down the stairs and through the gate to the street. My recently recovered ankle starts to burn so I'm forced to slow down.

"Pippas!" he calls after me, right on my heels. "I was to repay you—"

"With what, money you stole from someone else?" I ask without looking at him. I keep marching straight ahead toward the marina.

He doesn't answer, but I can hear him behind me, no doubt angry he got caught. He probably doesn't even know how to be remorseful.

Once we're at the marina, I climb over a railing to sit on the giant rocks protruding out to the sea. I'd seen an artist out here before, sketching with colored pencils, so I know it's not entirely off limits. It's dark out, but I aim my feet for the sections of rock reflecting light from the moon, avoiding the dark spaces for fear of disappearing into a cranny.

"Be careful, Pippa *mia.*" Bruno scrambles over the railing after me and snatches my hand, guiding me to a mostly flat rock and pulling me down to sit next to him.

For a few minutes we don't speak. I focus on the sounds of late evening. Someone stacks plates at one of the cafés up the hill behind us while someone else whistles on the other side of the boat slip. A woman's laughter echoes around us and drifts out to sea. All to the constant soundtrack of waves pulsing between the rocks below.

"I was not stealing," Bruno finally says. "I was to repay you before you returned. You were not to know."

I close my eyes and inhale deeply through my nose. "What's going on, Bruno?"

"It is nothing—"

"Nothing? I don't think nothing would give you a black eye and a busted nose within a week's time."

"Nothing for you to worry with," he finishes.

"You made it my concern when you used my cash to pay Mauro off."

"How do you—?"

"Chiara told me," I say, my patience for this conversation nonexistent. "What are you into? Drugs? Dog fights? What?"

He laughs, wrapping his arms around his bent knees. "I do not take drugs."

"Well, that's a relief."

"I made a bad bet or *due*."

"Gambling. Cards or sports or what?"

"Sports, that is all." He smiles as if I've forgiven him or something.

I take another long breath, letting the wave of oxygen course through my veins and clear my head. I imagine him rummaging through my clothing, my *underwear*. My computer is password protected so I doubt he did any damage there, but . . . .

I brace myself for the chance he took a memento. "Did you take anything else?"

He sits up straighter and covers my hand with his. "I did not!" His eyes, caramel even in the pale light, beg me to believe him.

I wriggle free from his grasp and shift my focus up to the stars instead. The stars I can believe. Not Bruno. Anything that existed between us before was only lust on my part. Lust and a freakish desire of snagging myself an Italian.

Gorgeous? Check. Italian? Check. Fall in love with and bring home to Mom and Dad? Not. Even. Close.

"Did you enjoy time with your friends?" Bruno forces my thoughts aside.

"Yes." My cheeks warm at the memory of falling asleep with Darren's hand on mine, but there's no risk of Bruno noticing. We both look like ghosts out here.

"With that Darren?" He spits out the name like it's gristle.

"You're impossible." I snort. "You know, Chiara warned me you were trouble before I even got here. Said you were wasting your potential. And when she saw me getting attached to you, she told me I should put a stop to it. That I didn't know who you really were."

He shifts uncomfortably on the rock, pulling a broken fragment from under his leg and tossing it into the water. "You know who I am."

"I know part of who you are, but she was right. I just didn't want to see it before."

He leans back, supporting his upper body on outstretched arms. "You have given up on us."

I twist my body to look at him. His expression is far from amused, jaw set in a hard line reflecting the bluish light from the moon.

"There was never an *us*, Bruno," I say. "I can't be with someone I can't trust."

He lies flat on his back and presses the heels of his hands over his eyes. A sigh of exhaustion mixed with laughter escapes my mouth and I rise to my feet. I just need to go to bed and start fresh in the morning.

Bruno peers up at me. "Why you leave so soon?"

"I wanted to get away from you so I could think."

"Pippas," he says, sitting up. "*Mi dispiace.* I walk with you."

"No," I say quickly. "I know my way home."

Without looking back, I leave him behind and stare at the street until my vision blurs. A dull ache settles in my chest when I realize tonight I have to go to sleep without Darren one bed over.

CHAPTER THIRTY-EIGHT

~~Eat a whole pizza in one sitting~~

The weekend arrives and I'm on edge, especially working at the trattoria. I'm hyper-aware of everyone around me, twitching at the sight of every youngish-looking guy with a full head of brown hair. The super curly heads are even fewer and farther between, but sightings of those nearly spark heart attacks. Only as the sun sets Sunday night do I let myself truly mope. I know they just started at a new dig site in Tuscany, and I can't expect Darren to come to Cinque Terre every weekend, but it still stings. I could smack myself on the head for not making sure we had a way to get in touch with each other. Forget about waiting for *him* to ask me, that's crap. I can be a take-control girl when I want to be, can't I?

I'm desperate to see his smile, and not just because it's his, but because moods are in major need of brightening around here. Considering Bruno stole quite a large amount of money from me, I haven't exactly been chatty with him, so that makes things nice and awkward. The only excitement comes from my phone call with Gram.

"I have a few things I need to talk to you about today, honey," she says. "First, I want an update on this guy you met."

I've made a point to keep it vague with her. She knows that I'm crushing on someone, but not that I went on a little trip with him. Or that he hasn't been back to see me since.

"I don't know, Gram." I sigh into the phone. "I don't think he's interested in me like that."

"Impossible!"

"I mean, I thought so, maybe. But I haven't seen him in, like, a week. I think I might need to just forget about it. I'm coming home soon anyway, right?"

"Well, that's very logical of you," she says. "All I can say is follow your heart, honey. Sometimes it's best to ignore your head."

"I think *I'm* the one being ignored, Gram."

"Your Papa used to say that whatever happens is the way it was always going to happen, so live your life. Regret nothing."

"Speaking of regrets," I say, desperately trying to change the subject. "I still regret that I'm going to miss your birthday."

She gasps. "Oh, that! That was the other thing we needed to discuss."

"Your birthday?"

"Your mother is trying to talk me into going to Italy to celebrate."

My stomach drops. "What?"

"And to surprise you."

I jump out of my seat and start pacing behind the bar. My mind whirls a million miles an hour as I picture myself packing up my clothes, catching a train to Florence, knocking on the school's door, and begging to be let in. This can't be happening.

"Gram, that's—"

"I told her I didn't want to go."

My back slides against the wall as I sink to the floor in relief. Chiara peeks her head curiously over the bar but I wave her away.

"And she believed you?"

"She didn't have a choice. I just refused to let her buy the tickets and informed her that friends from my book club were already planning something big. I guess I have to tell them now. But they won't mind. Any excuse to eat cake."

"So you're not coming?" I ask, my heart rate starting to slow to a normal pace. "And Mom's not coming?"

"Well, she's still thinking about visiting you for a couple of days. I'm not sure how to talk her out of that one. I thought about faking an illness or something. But then she'd drag me to the doctor . . . and then I really would get sick."

I'm pacing again. Chiara is still watching me with concern, but I ignore her.

"This is so not good, Gram. Why does she want to come all the way over here to see me? I've lived with her for almost eighteen years!"

Gram clears her throat. "She talked rather enthusiastically about going to all the galleries in Florence with you."

I close my eyes and let my forehead smack against the wall

as I lean on it. "Of course. Galleries. That's what she really wants to see." She probably doesn't miss me at all.

As if reading my mind, Gram says, "She misses you more than you think."

"Right."

"She does. She's been talking about how fast time goes by, and how soon you'll be going to college. I think it scares her."

I have no idea how to respond to this. I thought I was supposed to be the one scared about going to college.

"I wouldn't worry too much about it, Pippa. She's been extremely busy with clients, and of course the preparations for the gallery opening. If it turns into more than talk, I'll let you know right away."

Whatever happens is the way it was always going to happen.

"Thanks, Gram," I say, and then a thought occurs to me. "But . . . if you want to spend your birthday in Italy, don't let my lie stop you. I really can face her when you get here." Somehow.

She laughs. "Oh, honey, I love you."

"I love you too," I take the opportunity to say.

"You know I don't get around that well these days. All that traveling makes me tired just thinking about it."

"I miss you. I'll be home soon."

When we hang up, I catch eyes with Chiara.

"What was that about?" she asks, brows together and arms crossed.

I let out a long exhale. "A very, very, very close call."

Two weekends later—with thankfully no word from Gram about a surprise visit from Mom—there's still no sign of Darren, Tate, or Nina. I've got myself convinced I'm ready to go home and face the music. July's nearly over, the heat is lung crushing, and I miss Gram and Morgan something fierce. And with Luca's birthday celebration tonight at the trattoria, seeing his friends and family love on one another is sure to put a stake right through me.

I sit at an empty table after the lunch rush and turn to the last assignment in my journal. This one's the worst yet. The page is blank except for the instructions:

DRAW YOUR SELF-PORTRAIT.

Obviously, she ran out of ideas. She knows I can't draw worth a flip, and she especially knows I don't like it when this kind of art is pushed on me. A self-portrait is an interpretation. It's not the truth—not a real image. It's going to look nothing like me.

I open my makeup compact and set it on the table next to the vase of flowers and let my mechanical pencil hover over the page. I adjust until I can see most of my face in the tiny mirror and start drawing an outline of the compact itself first. Seems easier than tackling an eye right off the bat.

"Drawing hearts in your diary again?"

I perk my head up, pulse racing. "Darren!"

Instinctively I stand and he rushes to me, opening his arms and pulling me close.

"I wasn't sure if I'd see you again before I had to leave," I say, out of breath even though he's the one that just trekked up the hill.

His eyes widen. "Are you leaving soon?"

"Well, my flight's scheduled in a couple of weeks when the

summer program I'm supposedly going to is over. Gotta keep up appearances."

He laughs and my smile spreads. It seems like it's been forever since I heard that sound.

"I'm glad I caught you then. When I woke up this morning . . . I just had to see you. It's been too long. I started getting antsy," he says, dimples appearing in his cheeks. "Things at the new site are intense. It's really not even a completely free weekend, so I don't have that much time. I need to leave tomorrow around noon."

It hits me that our little jaunt south was the last solid chunk of time I'd get to spend with him, possibly ever.

"At the train station in Florence, as soon as we walked out to the cab station I realized I didn't get your number," he says. "Again."

"My cell phone doesn't work here." I lift my shoulders toward my ears. "I meant to get your e-mail address, but I forgot to ask you for it."

"I didn't bring my laptop to Italy. Didn't want to have to worry about it, you know?"

I picture Bruno rifling through my luggage while I was gone. "Totally."

"Were you spying on someone?" Darren asks, finally sitting in the chair next to me and pointing at the open compact on the table.

"What? Oh, no." I laugh, snapping it shut and pulling it and the journal closer to me. "It's nothing."

"You're awfully secretive with your diary." He says the word *diary* with a childish tone to it, as if the cover of mine has a picture of Hello Kitty emblazoned on it. "What are you hiding?" He reaches for it but I'm faster.

"It's just this project for my friend," I say, hoping he'll leave it at that yet knowing he has the power to make me say anything he wants.

He stares at me and waves his hand for me to continue.

"My best friend, Morgan, gave this to me at the airport when she dropped me off. She had me write a list of goals for the summer, and she also cooked up assignments for me to do."

He raises an eyebrow. "She added schoolwork to your schoolwork?"

I laugh his joke away. "It's sweet. They're just silly things mostly, like writing a haiku, getting on a vessel of the public transportation system and getting off at a random stop to explore—which is the one I was working on when I saw you the second time, by the way."

"I guess I should thank this Morgan girl."

"But I didn't even talk to you then. It was just a wave and POOF. Gone."

"Even so. It was a memorable wave." He leans back in his chair and crosses his legs, resting an ankle on one knee and grabbing on to the other with laced hands. "So what about these goals?"

"Oh, they're lame. And I only have a few left now, so—"

"What are they? Can I help you finish them?" He shakes the foot near his knee super fast like he's eager to get up and do something.

I bite my lip. "Well, I already got Morgan a real souvenir, but I was planning to find something off the wall for her."

"Oh, shopping!" He sits up straight and claps the tips of his fingers together. "I mean"—he clears his throat and lowers his voice—"let's do this."

We laugh together and I cram my journal and compact back into my tote bag.

"Speaking of shopping," he says, reaching into his backpack and producing yet another small paper sack.

"Another magnet?" I snatch the bag from him and find a rectangular magnet with the red-roofed cityscape of Florence. I can't believe I haven't even been there, the place I was supposed to be living all summer.

"Thank you." I trail a finger across the glossy surface. "For *all* my magnets. I love them."

"Even though you have nowhere to put them," he says with a wink.

I beam at him. "I'm sure I'll come up with something."

We decide on shopping and swimming in Monterosso. Since it's the village best suited to tourism, they're sure to have something bizarre I can get for Morgan.

It doesn't take long before Darren spots a shelf packed with handmade figurines. "What *are* these things?" he whispers.

I study the squat, white ceramic creatures with holes for eyes and colored noses and ears, trying to figure them out. "I think they're cats. No, that one's an owl. Owls and cats. Oh, I think you've found it. A nonsensical owl from Italy. I'm buying it." I carefully pick up a smaller one. "You know you want one of the cats," I add, nudging him with my elbow.

"Funny." He smiles and nudges me back. "What exactly is your friend supposed to do with it?"

"That's the point. A souvenir without function that she's obligated to keep. She'll love it."

With that goal checked off my list, I can relax and shop for myself too. A few carts down, we find the most luscious scarves I've ever seen. Darren helps me pick one that manages to make my eyes an intense shade of green, and we find some for Morgan, Gram, and my mother because it would be a nice gesture. She might actually wear this one too, because it's not hot pink and it was made by professionals.

Darren keeps eyeing the fedoras until I make him try one on.

"I don't wear hats," he protests.

"I saw you drooling over it; just try it." I pick out a dark-gray one with thin white stripes and settle it on his head. "You have too much hair. I'll bet if you chopped it you would rock this hat."

He takes it off without even looking in the mirror.

I match his frown. "What's wrong?"

He lets out a sigh. "There's a reason I stopped wearing hats."

"Besides your hair?" I say, attempting and failing to get him to smile.

He coughs into the back of his hand. "Remember that girl I told you about?"

"Yes. But you never told me her name."

"She liked it when I wore hats. She said so all the time."

"Oh," I say. "Well, did you wear them before you got together?"

He cocks his head to the side. "Yeah . . . ?"

“Then she stole it from you. When she broke your heart, she took part of who you are with her.”

“Part of who I am?”

“You’re a hat guy,” I explain. “If you like them, wear them. Who cares if they remind you of her, you’re done with her. You’ve moved on to better things.”

His mouth fights back a smile. “You think so?” He places the hat on his head and looks in the little mirror hanging from the cart. “You’re right, though. Too much hair.”

“So . . . maybe you can be a hat person again when you’re not a hair person anymore.”

We laugh and he returns the hat to the hook before picking up a tan-colored newsboy cap with a dark flower off to the side just above the brim. “Put this one on right now,” he says, switching back into exaggerated, giddy-girl mode.

“You better cut that out or you’re going to have me thinking things about you that you probably don’t want me to.” I giggle and tug the hat down on my head.

Darren adjusts it for me, off-centering the brim from my forehead. He takes me by the shoulders and turns me to the mirror, moving sections of my hair from behind so it lies on my chest. My eyes take in the hat—which I secretly think I adore and must have—before they meet his gaze.

Keeping his hands on my shoulders and his eyes locked on mine in the mirror, he tilts his head, leaning closer until his lips nearly brush against my ear. “What kind of things?”

My whole body quivers as I close my eyes, unable to look at him looking at me that way if he’s not going to do anything about it. I’m so far gone now, there’s no turning back.

CHAPTER THIRTY-NINE

We claim an empty spot on the beach and drop our bags onto a towel. The water is warm yet refreshing enough, especially when we find a cool pocket. Darren's been quiet since we stripped down to our bathing suits and waded into the water, like his mind is somewhere else. I make small talk, but he gives a lot of halfhearted, one-word answers.

"Is something wrong?" I finally ask.

Darren cups a hand and repeatedly scoops at the water, letting it leak out between his fingers. "What do you see happening a few weeks from now?"

I try to meet his eyes, but he's focused on the water. "What do you mean?"

"I mean at the end of summer, when you have to leave. What happens after that?"

I open my mouth to speak, but not a sound comes out. I want

to say a million things. I want to say that watching him walk off that train, then realizing I had no way to get in touch with him, nearly killed me. That I can't believe I'm expected to say good-bye to him again. That I think about him. A lot.

What comes out instead is, "I finish high school and you start college."

"Right . . . right." He nods and exhales, sinking into the water up to his neck and running a dripping hand through his still-dry hair.

Follow your heart, not your head. Regret nothing.

"Darren," I begin, swallowing the lump in my throat and forcing myself to keep eye contact. I need answers. I can't go back home without knowing exactly what there was or is between us. "Why did you come back here?"

No response.

"Why did you ask me to go to Pompeii with you guys? Why did you get so upset you couldn't even talk to me when you saw Bruno kiss me good-bye? Why did you completely freak when Nina took our picture together? Why did you come back here? I need—" I groan and ball my hands into fists at my sides. "I need you to tell me what you want me to think, Darren. What am I supposed to take away from all this?"

"I don't know, Pippa, okay?" He yanks at his hair. "I . . . needed to see you again. When I'm not with you, all I think about is you and your shy little smile and the two freckles on your right cheek. Your terrifying green eyes."

He stands again and my eyes dart to the ribbons of water streaming down his chest. He takes a step toward me and raises a hand to my cheek, stroking it with his thumb. My eyelids drop involuntarily and I melt into his touch.

“I just—” He stops himself.

His lips gently press against mine and I pull in a sharp breath before I lean my face into his palm even more. Just as I fear my legs might not hold me up any longer, his other hand snakes around to the small of my back, supporting and pulling me against him.

After a moment he drifts a few inches away, keeping his hands in place, nervously meeting my eyes to gauge a reaction. Everything around me except for his face is a blue blur as I stare back at him.

Darren just kissed me.

As many times as I’ve imagined him kissing me, the shock of it as a reality sends a quake through my entire body.

“I don’t believe it.” I straighten and stare at his chin, his cheeks, his sharp jawline.

He almost gets knocked over by a wave that slams him in the chest. “What?”

“You shaved! How did I not see that earlier?”

“Finally she notices!” He laughs. “I went through great pains to smooth out this face for you. Even cut myself.” He juts out his chin and points to a spot so small I can hardly see it.

“Aww, poor baby,” I tease and give it a swift peck, still in shock that I’m suddenly allowed to get this close to him. To touch him with my lips. “You knew this was going to happen, didn’t you?”

He smirks, resting his hands on my waist. “Hoped.”

My cheeks ache from smiling, but I don’t care. I don’t care about anything but Darren and him kissing me again. I trace the smooth skin around his mouth.

“You better be careful,” he says, kissing the tip of my finger with each word. “I’ve been known to bite.”

We laugh and he tightens his hold at my waist and pulls me against him, pressing our lips together. I rake my fingers through his hair and grab a fistful, tugging him closer and deepening the kiss. Electricity courses through me from my chest to hips and back again. His warm, wet hands explore my bare back, setting every inch of my skin on fire. His shoulder muscles tense and release in synchronization with his hands all over me.

He takes my face in his palms and slows the kiss down, our breathing still heavy. I've never been so dizzy in my whole life. My head, my body, are part of the sea, ebbing and flowing with the tides.

I get it now. This is what kissing is really supposed to be. Any others before were merely run-throughs with understudies. Darren is a leading man.

Our foreheads rest together and the pads of his fingers slowly trail up and down my arms.

"What do we do now?" he asks.

I inhale deeply, trying to clear my mind, to be struck with a brilliant solution. "I have no idea."

He plays with the wet ends of my hair. "I think we just made saying good-bye the next time exponentially more difficult."

"Infinitely more difficult."

But I'll worry about that tomorrow.

We lace our fingers together as we trudge through the shallow water to our spot on the beach to dry off.

"The sun's starting to go down," I point out, brushing the tiny rocks off the bottoms of my feet and sliding into my flip-flops. "I should probably head back for Luca's birthday dinner.

They want me to lead the 'Happy Birthday' song to him in English for some reason."

"Oh, right. Yeah, it's getting late." He lets go of my hand and reaches for his T-shirt.

I watch his abs disappear, then pull my tank top over my head. "I'm sure you could come if you want."

He frowns. "Won't Bruno be there?"

"It's his brother, he'd better be."

"Uh, I'll pass."

I grab his shirt near the hem and tug him toward me. "Even though I'll be there?" I bat my eyelashes intentionally fast.

"Tempting." He leans in for a kiss, letting it linger. "But I can't crash a birthday party for a kid I've never met. And I don't feel much like getting into a fight with a ripped-up Italian tonight. You go ahead, have fun. I'll see you in the morning, right? Before I leave?"

"That," I say, pecking his lips again, "is a necessity."

We catch the train that makes stops in every village, sitting as close to each other as possible, freely kissing whenever we feel like it. I'm torn between wishing we hadn't waited so long to get to this point and almost wishing it never had happened at all. Now I really know what I'm going to be missing.

The motion of the train conflicts with all the crap in my head and I panic. I lay my head against Darren's chest and wrap my arms around his middle. He puts both of his arms around me, hugging me tight. I can feel him sigh. Is he thinking through everything like I am?

"We'll figure it out," he says in my ear before he kisses the top of my head. "I promise."

I squeeze him tighter and memorize the rhythm of his heartbeat.

We decide to meet at the trattoria for breakfast first thing tomorrow and spend the whole morning together before he has to leave. I already can't wait to kiss him again, but I don't look forward to figuring out the logistics of a long-distance relationship, if that's what he even wants. If it's what I want.

Our lips touch until the last possible moment when the doors of the train threaten to close at his stop in Manarola.

"I'll see you tomorrow," he says, a smile stretching ear to ear.

"Tomorrow," I reply, beaming back at him. "Good night."

"Good night, Pippa."

He hops down onto the platform and the doors slap together. I look at him through the grimy window, reminded of the time I saw him across the metro station in Rome, when I didn't know if I'd ever see him again. Now I know I will for sure.

And I also know there will be kissing.

CHAPTER FORTY

~~Find random souvenir for Morgan~~

The sky is a fading orange-pink by the time I emerge from the tunnel and begin the trek up Via Columbo to the trattoria. As I approach the outdoor section, I hear Luca's rowdy friends swarming around one of the tables piled high with food. The savory aroma makes my mouth water and my legs move faster.

Chiara speaks to a man whose back is to me, his arms waving madly. Her face is scrunched in concern and for a moment I wonder if this has anything to do with Bruno's gambling problem—he swears he's done with all that—but then I recognize the man's stance. His posture. His hand gestures.

Chiara spots me coming up behind him and points at me. The man turns around, and I might throw up. My feet refuse to take me any farther.

"Dad? Wha—"

"Pippa!" Dad closes the distance between us in three hurried steps and wraps me in his arms, murmuring into my hair, "Oh, thank God."

There's so much swimming through my head, I don't even know where to start. *How did you find me? What are you doing here? Am I grounded until I'm thirty?*

After what feels like a lifetime of making up for lost affection, he releases me, keeping a hand on my shoulder, and looks me over.

"Dad," I say slowly, still in shock. "How are you here? What—?" I stop myself and study the bags under his eyes, the frown lines. The troubled, glassy eyes. "What happened?"

He takes his time inhaling the longest breath in the history of breathing. "Can we sit somewhere and talk?"

"Just tell me."

Dad's broad shoulders slump and his hand slips down to mine, squeezing it tight. "It's Gram."

My heart plummets and my knees start to shake. "What about her?"

"She fell a few days ago. We thought everything was fine, but—"

"She *fell*? She's going to be okay, right?"

"I don't know, Pippa."

Chiara rushes to my side to put her arm around my waist and I lean on her, suddenly unable to support my own weight.

"We should go inside and sit," she says, leading us inside the restaurant where it's quiet. I see Bruno sneak in with us, but he stands off to the side.

"Look at me," Dad says once we're seated at a table. My hand is numb from his grasp. "She's still alive. I just talked to your mother. But we need to go home right away."

My eyes spill over with tears, thankful to hear she's alive but terrified that he used the word "still." *Still alive*. It sounds so . . . temporary.

"What do you mean by 'she fell' exactly?" I ask. "Like, down the stairs or . . . ?"

"When she got out of bed one morning, her leg was still asleep but she didn't realize it. She fell and hit her head against the wall."

I release the breath I was holding. "That doesn't sound so awful."

"She made a dent in the sheetrock."

I rub my temples, closing my eyes so tight, a fresh stream of tears makes its way down my cheek.

"She seemed fine at first, just a bit bruised. More embarrassed than anything. But after the first twenty-four hours she stopped talking and . . . she's in a coma now."

"A coma?" My insides disintegrate, my mind a jumble of confusion, hurt. Anger. "And you just *left*? You spent all this time coming out here to get me when I could be there already?"

"Pippa," he says, somehow staying calm despite my near hysteria. "This isn't exactly news for you to hear over the phone. And do you really think you'd even be able to think clearly enough to get yourself to an airport and on a plane?"

"You don't think I could have handled it? I've done a lot more—"

"I couldn't just sit at the hospital and worry about you too."

His voice cracks and he wipes beads of sweat off his forehead with the back of his hand. "When I finally got the whole story that you weren't at school, I just reacted. I had to *do* something. Find you. Make sure you were okay."

If I weren't so shocked by this whole situation, I'd be a lot more irritated by the uncharacteristic babying. But the truth is, I'm glad to see him. I don't resist when he pulls me close again. There's really no one else I could stand to hear this news from. Dad's always been on my side.

I break away and swipe my eyes before I completely lose it. "So even when we do get home, we can't talk to her?"

"I just want you to be prepared for the worst." Dad rests his hand on mine. "We need to go. Let's get your stuff packed."

I nod, swallowing the lump in my throat, and Bruno helps me up.

"This way, *signore*," he says to my father as he leads me to the door. "She stays with my family."

Eyes wide and unfocused, I take the flights of stairs so slowly that I'm not even winded once we get inside. Luca and Matilde beat us there, Matilde already having collected my things scattered throughout the apartment.

Luca stands in the corner with a few of his friends, their celebration interrupted by my drama.

"Luca, I'm so sorry," I say, bottom lip quivering so much, it's hard to form the words. "You should go back to your party."

"Do not worry for me," he says, offering a hesitant smile.

"I almost forgot." I dash into my room and come back with a roll of twenty euros tied with a green ribbon. "For you. Happy birthday."

I don't wait for a reaction or a thank-you, but instead jump right into packing. I hastily throw everything into my suitcase and backpack, suddenly frantic to get back to Chicago. I can hear the murmur of voices from the other room, Dad's standing out the most. It's so bizarre to have him here, like he's trespassing in a part of my life he was never meant to see.

"You are really leaving tonight," Chiara says behind me. "I am not ready. I thought we had more time."

I zip up my suitcase and turn to hug her. "I can't tell you how much I'm going to miss you. Thank you for everything, Chiara. This summer has been—I'll never forget it," I whisper.

"Nor will I," she says, squeezing me tight.

"I'm sorry I have to go so quick like this. But it's important. It's Gram." I choke on my words and pull in a few shaky breaths. "I can't believe this is happening."

"I am so very sorry, Pippa. Please let me know how she gets on."

She reaches into one of her bags and pulls out a little pad of paper and a pen, scribbling her e-mail address and phone number for me. I write down every available way for her to contact me, even giving her Morgan's e-mail address if for some reason she can't reach me.

"We will stay in touch, do not worry," Chiara says.

We hug one more time and I realize Bruno's leaning in the doorway. Chiara excuses herself to give us a moment.

"Pippas," he says, "I am sorry. *Per tua nonna.* And for the money I took."

I shake my head. "If stealing my money helped keep you

from getting beat up beyond recognition or worse, I'm glad you found it."

He laughs, hesitantly. "I do not think it would have come to that. But Pippas," he says, taking both of my hands in his, forcing me to look at him. "You helped keep my family from more heartache. I now see that I have been . . ." His voice trails off and he shakes his head. "Mamma does not need that. I am trying."

I so want to believe him. But he's got such a long way to go. All I can do is nod and return the squeeze of his hands. He pulls me into a quick hug and I take one last scan of the room to make sure I haven't forgotten anything, and to commit it to memory. It was a short while, but this was my home.

Nestled among cliffs,
my temporary home lies.
Time pulls me away.

Matilde wraps me in her soft arms, muttering something in Italian about loving me and for death to stay away. She gives my dad a bagful of food for us to eat on the way to the airport, though I'm not sure I'm ever going to be able to eat again.

"Wait," I say, digging into my camera bag. "I want a picture with all of you. Us. Together."

Dad takes the camera from me and I stand in the middle of everyone. Nestled under Chiara's and Matilde's arms, I find it easier to smile than I expect. I'm surrounded by people who care for me, and who I care for, all because I wanted a chocolate pastry for breakfast in Rome.

The shutter clicks and I pry myself from their embrace. At the door I turn and look at each face once more, knowing that this will likely be the last time I'll see most of them. Matilde, who welcomed me, an American stranger, into her home, even kicking her own children out of their room. Luca, a quiet boy with a good heart. I have confidence he'll be ten times the man his brother's been. Bruno, the gorgeous smooth talker. If my dad had a clue about what's gone on between us this summer, he'd have him beat up all over again.

Chiara. One of my very best friends who I didn't even know existed a few months ago. All-knowing, beautiful Chiara.

Throat tight, eyes blurred with tears, I wave to them all one last time and turn to Dad, his hand on the doorknob. "I'm ready. Let's go home."

On the plane, I keep internally repeating that Gram's going to be okay, miraculously maintaining composure. That is, until I see Darren's face in my mind.

I bolt upright and snatch Dad's hand from his armrest, checking the time on his watch. I count out the time difference. It's seven-thirty in the morning in Italy. The exact time I was supposed to meet Darren.

Darren.

My chest constricts and my face flushes. I recline in my seat and tap a rhythm on my thighs to a made-up song in my head, flirting with a full-on meltdown.

"We still have a long way to go," Dad says. "Try to relax."

I shake my head, not about to tell him what's really on my mind. Right this very second I'd have my arms tight around Darren, unwilling to let go. He'd lean in for a kiss and we wouldn't stop until he had to catch his train. We'd figure out when we'd see each other again. We'd have a plan. But now we have nothing.

How trivial, how selfish. How dare I be upset about missing Darren when Gram is on her deathbed? I'm a horrible person. A horrible daughter for lying to my parents. A horrible granddaughter for thinking about a boy I kissed and regretting that I can't be with him right now.

I deserve the worst kind of punishment my parents could ever dream up.

"So," I muster the courage to say, eyes still closed, "how much trouble am I in?"

"Oh, good. You want to talk about *that*," he says, abandoning his book and stowing it in the bag near his feet. "It might take us a while to come up with just the right punishment for this situation. I never expected you to completely lose your mind."

"When did you find out I didn't go to the program?" I ask.

"Yesterday, I think. It's all turning into a big, ugly blur." He looks at his watch. "Gram's consciousness was sort of slipping and she kept saying something about you not going to school, and that she needed to call some woman named Matilde."

Tears prick my eyes and my throat is officially on fire.

"Morgan filled in the blanks for us."

I refrain from pointing out that more involved parents would have noticed right away that their daughter wasn't where she was supposed to be. Maybe in the back of my mind I wanted them to figure it out all along. To worry about me. And now that I know they didn't, that they were content with me out of their way and getting groomed so they could get their work done . . .

Just another crack in my heart next to the one with Gram's name on it. Next to the one with Darren's name.

Unable to stop fidgeting, I sweep my tangles into a sloppy pile on top of my head and secure it with a band. The ends are crunchy from the salt water, but I push the happy memory with Darren aside.

"Pippa." Dad sighs for the millionth time since we sat down. I can feel his eyes burning holes through me as he waits for me to look at him before continuing. "Do you have any idea how scared we were? To find out that you'd been lying to us for two months? That we didn't know exactly where you were? If you were safe?"

"Morgan knew where I was. And it's not like I didn't keep in touch with you guys. I e-mailed Mom all the time. I even Skyped with her," I say, but my confidence is waning. "And I talked to Gram every week, sometimes more. She was fine with it."

He ignores me. "You are a young, beautiful girl gallivanting alone across a foreign country during high tourist season. You could ha—"

"And whose fault was that?" I say, raising my voice.

He leans closer and keeps his tone down. "You're completely oblivious, aren't you? At how lucky you are. Lucky you didn't get killed, or worse. Do you know how many young girls get kidnapped and sold into sex slavery?" He squeezes my hand tighter. "How could you just . . . not *think*? I don't understand you. I know we raised you better than that. You've completely disrespected us."

"I did think. I saw all the money you gave me and I thought, wow, I can do whatever I want now that I'm here and no one's dictating me anymore."

"Oh, the money. That's great. Your mom will love to know it's my fault. I suppose I practically told you to skip town."

"No one told me to skip town, that's the point. I made my own decision for, like, the first time in my life. I did what *I* wanted."

He rubs his temples. "You're almost eighteen and I'm sure you'll try to find a college as far away from us as possible." He shifts in his seat, the leather squeaking underneath him. "Soon we won't be able to tell you what to do anymore. But I want you to think for just one minute how dangerous that was. And lying to—"

"I get it, I lied. It was wrong. I was horrible. What do you want me to say, I'm sorry? Okay, I'm sorry."

"Are you?"

"I'm sorry I lied. I'm sorry I didn't think about how dangerous it was."

But I can't be sorry I met Darren, even if I die a little every time his face pops into my mind. Although if I hadn't even gone, his face wouldn't come to mind at all, and I wouldn't know what I was missing. And Gram . . .

"If I hadn't gone," I manage to say despite my quivering chin, "Gram might not be in a coma."

"Don't play that game, Pippa," he warns, his angry tone matching mine.

"What game?"

"The 'what if' game." He reclines the seat and closes his eyes. "You won't win."

CHAPTER FORTY-ONE

She was supposed to wait for me. At least until I was able to say good-bye while her heart was still beating. But she died before my plane even landed.

They call it Talk and Die. She hit her head on the wall as she fell and everything checked out fine when they examined her. She even made jokes, they said. But the next day, her brain began to bleed, weakened from the impact. By the time they realized what was happening, she'd slipped into a coma and it was too late to do anything.

Dad takes care of the paperwork right away so Mom doesn't have to think about it. The rest of us zombies are ushered into a private waiting room.

"Why didn't she hang on so everyone had a chance to say good-bye?" I ask softly, the shock of knowing I will never hear Gram's voice again slowly taking hold of my body. "They always hang on—"

"This is real life, Philippa, not one of your movies," my mother says, her tone even, flat. Beyond a fierce hug when Dad and I arrived at the hospital this evening, she's hardly looked at me.

Morgan's in the chair next to me, her fingers running absently through the sections of my hair that fell out of the band. I don't like people playing with my hair, but I don't tell her to stop. She needs to comfort me, so I let her.

I glance at my mom sitting across from us, her glassed-over eyes staring at the floor. She traces the diamond pattern on the carpet with the tip of her shoe. I know she's hurting, but I'm jealous she was here for Gram. I wasn't. And that's Mom's fault.

"I should have been here," I say, an edge to my voice that I don't try to hide. "You shouldn't have made me go to that school. You knew I didn't want to."

Mom's eyes bore through me. Morgan goes so still, I wonder if she's breathing.

"You didn't even *go* to the program so don't give me that."

I raise my voice and sit taller. "If I'd been here with her, it probably wouldn't have happened, don't you get that? I would have spent time with her—"

"Yelling at me because you're angry isn't going to bring her back."

I shrink in my seat and stare at my hands. I've picked at my hangnails so much in the past twenty-four hours, a few of them are bleeding. But I welcome the pain. It's so hard to believe that someone can be talking and laughing one minute, in a coma the next, and then dead. She's dead. Gone. There's a scarf for her in my luggage that she'll never get to wear. It can't be real. My greatest ally. The only person in my life who actually knew how to love, who never made me doubt she loved me for even a second. Gone.

I risk a glance at Mom and she's still staring at me, eyes bugged and watery. Her bottom lip is trembling. I've never ever seen her get emotional about anything in my life.

I pull in a shaky breath. "Mom?"

She looks at the floor as a single tear slips down her flushed cheek. "Was I really so terrible to you?" Her voice is so quiet, I strain to hear, watching her lips form the words.

"What are y—"

"I just don't understand." She pauses, swallowing. "What did I do to make you want to run away?"

"That's what you think I did?"

"What was I supposed to think? You just take off and do your own thing, tricking us all into believing you're safe."

"I *was* sa—"

"I didn't know I was going to have to hold your hand and march you into that school myself," she mutters.

I visualize that nightmare and inwardly cringe.

"So what was it?" When I don't respond, she prompts, "What made you do it? What made you lie to us?"

I shake my head. "Gram knew where I was."

Mom winces. "We're not talking about her right now, we're talking about you and me. She wasn't your mother. I am."

She wasn't your mother. Wasn't—past tense.

As I bite back the lump in my throat, I slide my eyes to Morgan who looks just as terrified as I feel. This is it. My chance to tell Mom exactly how I feel. Everything I've been holding in for years. She's actually *asking*. She wants to know.

"You never listen to me," I begin slowly, carefully. "If you did, you would have realized that I had no interest in going to Italy by myself to study art."

"But I—"

"Please, Mom, you're doing it even now. Just listen." I wait a beat before continuing. "I understand you want so much for me, I get it. But it's always what you want. I want you to want what *I* want for me."

Morgan shifts in her seat, and I shoot her a look that I hope says, *Don't you dare leave me.*

"You pressure me and push me toward things I don't see in my future. You don't support me in the things I love to do." I'm on a roll now, heart racing. "Gram bought me my camera because even she knew what it meant to me. She saw I had the talent to do something with it, and she encouraged me. Dad comes to my plays, but you hardly ever make the effort. I take vacations with Morgan's family because we never go anywhere together. We never do *anything* together. We don't even eat dinner in the same room."

I have to stop to catch my breath. My chin quivers and my fingers are shaking. I think I'm about to lose it. Mom doesn't look like she's too far behind me either.

"Why didn't you just talk to me?" she manages. "Told me how you felt before?"

"Oh, I stopped trying to get through to you years ago. It never did any good. I made one last-ditch effort before Italy, but you were set."

"And that's what made you run away once you got there . . ."

"Mom. I didn't run away." I rest my elbows on my knees and lean forward. "I just took the opportunity to stand on my own, you know? To have a couple of months where I could breathe."

More tears sneak down her face. "When I found out you weren't at the school, I—" She covers her eyes with her hands and I can tell she's holding back a sob. "I was so scared I was going to lose you too."

I see Morgan swipe at her eyes, and I do the same. "I'm sorry. I know what I did was wrong. I just . . . wish you'd be more, I don't know, *there*. For me. I don't want us to end up like—" I can't believe what I was about to say. It might kill her.

"Like me and my mom," she finishes for me, eyes locked on mine.

All I can do is nod. We both know their relationship was crap. They went years without speaking, and even when Gram came to live with us, things were tense.

"I never knew how to be a good mother," she says. "That magic power people seem to get when they have a child never came to me."

I don't bring up the fact that Gram was amazing, so she should have known something. Why didn't she just follow Gram's example in the same way I'm learning from my mom what *not* to do with my own kids one day?

"I thought I was doing the best I could." A sob breaks free but she quickly regains control. "I hope you know how much I love you. I really do. I hate that you might not know that. I'm so scared it's too late. I don't want it to be too late for us, Pippa."

My eyes sting and my vision blurs. Hope blooms deep inside me. "Me neither."

Her chest heaves and she buckles over. She leans forward so far, she begins to slide off the chair. Morgan and I both rush to catch her. She grips my arms and I fall with her, the three of us a weeping heap on the floor.

"My mom's gone," she says, burying her head in the crook of my neck, her entire body shaking. She mumbles, "I'm sorry. So, so sorry."

The regret in her voice is thick. My heart finishes the break, completely shattering. All that time they spent arguing is lost. It's too late to mend fences, they've all been torn down.

With my mother in my arms, completely broken and vulnerable, I feel her desperation transfer to me. We have to fix this. Us. Me and her. We can't go through the rest of our lives like she did with her mother, because some day it's going to be too late.

We had Gram's funeral on the first of August, the day before her birthday. She lived a long time, nearly seventy-eight years. Not as long as some, but longer than others. It's what you do with your years, not the number of them, that matters most. Sounds like something she'd say. And she was my biggest fan. She believed that I was capable of everything under the sun. I'm still not convinced, but the memory of her encouragement motivates me to not do anything halfway from now on. You only live once. And she wouldn't want me to regret anything.

Punishment for my behavior is imminent, but to help with the grieving, Morgan's been allowed to spend every available moment in what's left of our summer with me. When she's not with the boyfriend, that is. Most of the time we sprawl out on my bed, her nose in a book, mine in Photoshop, slowly working through my Italy photos.

Sorting the Pompeii pictures into their own folder on my computer, my stomach drops when I find the picture of Darren standing in the Great Theater, that sly grin still daring me to make the image my background picture.

"Morgan," I say preparing to turn the screen toward her. "I need to tell you about someone."

"Darren?" she asks, brightening. She rolls onto her side and closes her book.

"How—?"

"The journal," she says. "You wrote 'I like Darren,' remember? I was wondering when I'd get to hear the story."

I laugh. "You could have asked."

"Well, I wasn't sure what happened, and with Gram and everything . . . I was just letting you deal." She props her head up in her hand. "Now spill."

I show her the picture.

"Pippa!" Her hand flies up to her mouth, eyes wide, and she sits up to get a closer look. "He's adorable! Man, look at all that hair."

I've been home two weeks and I miss him more every day. What went through his mind when I wasn't there to meet him? I'd hoped Chiara saw him and explained everything, but when I talked to her a few days after I got back, she said she didn't work that morning. Of course, had she known Darren was supposed to meet me, she would have told him what happened. If only I'd thought to tell her in the chaos of that night. But I can't go back. And even if I could, the only thing on my mind at that point still would have been Gram.

My eyes sting as I fight back tears.

"Oh, Pippers." Morgan leans over to put a hand on my shoulder. "Tell me."

We lie back on my bed, staring at the ceiling, and I start at the beginning, telling her every detail. Running into him in Rome, when I hurt my ankle in Cinque Terre and had to piggyback. How he was always popping up on weekends. When he asked me to go south with him, Tate, and Nina. The kissing.

"He gave me these," I say, pulling the paper sack full of magnets from my desk drawer and spreading them out on my bed.

"You've been to all these places?"

"Everywhere except Florence, the one place I was supposed to be all summer." I laugh. "He thought it was funny that Mom never allowed magnets on the fridge, so he bought me one everywhere we went."

Morgan smiles. "How romantic!"

I attempt to raise one eyebrow. "Is it?"

"It's precious." She bites her lip and jumps to her feet, stacking all the magnets together. "You know what you have to do, right?"

I suddenly feel very possessive. Why is she handling my magnets? "What?"

She starts for the door. "We're putting them on your fridge."

We pad our way downstairs to the kitchen. Mom's sitting on

a stool at the bar staring at an untouched piece of toast, hands wrapped around a coffee mug. Small piles of mail surround her on the counter. Her head perks when we enter the kitchen and go straight for the fridge to arrange the magnets. We keep them as organized as possible, knowing we're already breaking a rule so it better at least look presentable. I hold my breath as the last magnet snaps into place, and Morgan and I turn to face my mom.

She opens her mouth and I'm sure she's about to say "Get those off my fridge this instant." Instead she simply says, "Those look nice."

Mom and I share a smile. This is progress. We're going to be okay.

"Something came for you in the mail," she says, sliding a small envelope across the counter. "From Italy."

I snatch it and study the handwriting. It's not Chiara's.

Pulse pounding in my ears, Morgan and I race back upstairs and shut the door to my bedroom.

"Open it, open it!" Morgan chants. "Who's it from?"

"I have no idea." I tear at the thin envelope and pull out a 4x6 photo. It's me, my profile. Eyes wide in wonder, lips slightly parted in awe. "Get. Out. This was the moment I first saw the Colosseum."

"What?" She looks at the photo. "Who took that?"

There's nothing else inside the envelope. I turn the photo over and we read the note on the back written in small, careful handwriting.

I miss you, Pipperoni.
—Darren

I swallow the lump in my throat and look up at Morgan. We both have tears in our eyes.

"Why are *you* crying?" I ask, laughing.

"Because this is the single most romantic thing I've ever heard!" she says, swiping at the corner of her eye. "How did he get your address? I thought you never exchanged info."

"We didn't." I sit down on my bed and invent scenarios. "Maybe Chiara really did see him. Maybe she didn't want me to know, so this could be a surprise?"

"Oh, I would die to have something this epic happen to me," Morgan squeals. She falls onto the bed with the back of her hand against her forehead as if she's fainted.

I log into my e-mail and compose a letter to Chiara, telling her to call me right away. Then I stare at Darren's note some more, especially the "I miss you" part. And the "Darren" part. Which is basically the whole thing.

Darren misses me.

Goals update:

* ~~Don't get arrested~~
* Don't make a fool out of myself in public—FAILED
* ~~Get my picture taken at the Colosseum~~
* ~~Find random souvenir for Morgan~~
* ~~Get a makeover~~
* ~~See Pompeii~~
* ~~Swim in the Mediterranean Sea~~
* Have a conversation with someone in only Italian—FAILED

* ~~Eat a whole pizza in one sitting~~
* Fall in love with an Italian—FAILED

A few more days pass and Mom finally dives headfirst back into work, arranging for the gallery to be opened sooner than they originally planned. Dad's in California meeting with some photographer about displaying his work. Apparently I inspired them to support more than one type of art. I'm even preparing some of my Italy images for display. There just might be perks to working in the family gallery after all.

I lounge alone on the deck surrounding the pool. I like the chair that Gram always sat in. It makes me feel closer to her somehow, more connected, to touch things she touched. To sit where she sat.

The morning sun warms my skin more than I expected, and I'm just about to jump in the pool when my phone buzzes on the little table next to my chair, a sound I'm still getting used to after not hearing it all summer. Chiara's name illuminates the screen.

"Chiara!"

"*Ciao, Pippa! Come stai?*"

"Oh, it's so good to hear Italian, I can't even tell you." I sigh. "I'm okay. It's been tough."

"I am still so very sorry. I feel as though I should be there with you. For you."

"I wish you were here too," I say, fighting to keep the emotions under control. "How are you? Are you in New York yet?"

"Yes! I arrived early this morning and this is the soonest I could call you. We are in the same country once again!"

We laugh together. "Are you so excited to start school?" I ask.

"*Sì!* But I must tell you, it is hotter here than it was back home. Truly miserable."

"It's warm here too, but the wind helps." I adjust the phone on my sweaty ear. "Hey, Chiara?"

"*Cosa?*"

"I thought you said you didn't see Darren after I left."

"I did not see him. I am sorry—"

"But I got a note in the mail from him. On the back of a picture he took of me in Rome."

"*È vero?* What did it say?"

"Only that he missed me."

"That is sweet," she says. "But how—you gave him your address somehow?"

"No . . ." My eyebrows press together. She's not breaking.

My phone beeps in my ear that I've got another call coming through. It's a number I don't recognize so I let it go to voice mail.

"Chiara, if you're keeping this a secret for him or something, I think it's safe to tell me now."

"I promise to you. I did not know what you had planned. I only wish I had been there to meet him for you."

"Well, this is all too weird then," I conclude, truly stumped. Surely my home address isn't that easy to find on the Internet. I mean, I spent hours looking for Darren to no avail. Apparently he's not that into social networking.

"*Sì. Questo è strano.*" Chiara mutters something in rapid Italian to someone on her end, then says, "*Mi dispiace.* I must go now. Liana and I are going to shop in the city!"

"Okay, have fun! I miss you," I say.

"I miss you. *Addio,* Pippa."

We hang up, and I click on my voice mail button from the missed call.

"Wow, there's a voice I miss hearing. It's Darren. I really want to talk to you. You can call back this number. It's my cell. Hope to hear from you soon. Bye."

Holy. Crap. He has my number too!

I press CALL BACK and my pulse pounds in my ears. But it's a short ring. Straight to voice mail. No. This is not happening. I hang up and try again. It goes to voice mail even faster this time, but I let it run so I can hear his voice.

"Hey, this is Darren's cell. Leave a message and I maybe might possibly call you back. If you're lucky."

I clear my throat just before the beep. "Hi, Darren. It's Pippa. I was actually on the phone with Chiara when you called. I can't believe you have my number, but I'm so glad you do. I can't wait to talk to you. Call me. Bye."

I program his number into the contacts and listen to his message a few more times. Then I stare at my phone for ten minutes before I allow myself to get in the pool. Turning the ringer all the way up, I nestle it in the middle of a beach towel so I can reach it without getting out of the water. Just in case.

CHAPTER FORTY-TWO

"Pippa!" Mom shouts to me from the back door. "Another letter from Italy."

In what feels like slow motion, I race through the water and up the ladder to meet her. She sets the envelope and a sandwich with carrot sticks on the table.

She studies me, looking me over from head to toe as I dry off. "You're so tan."

"Spent a lot of time outside," I say slowly, fingers crossed that she doesn't want to talk too much about my summer of lies.

"And I don't think I told you yet, but I like that dark hair on you." She grabs a carrot off the plate and crunches. "Your roots are coming in, though. Maybe next week I can take you to get it touched up? Maybe bring Morgan too? We could get mani-pedis." She finishes her carrot and smiles. The first smile I've seen from her in ages.

"That sounds great, Mom."

"Hey, Pippa! Mrs. Preston." Morgan appears from inside the house. "I rang the bell but no one answered, so I figured you were back here."

"Hi, Morgan," Mom says. "We were just talking about the three of us going to get makeovers next week. How does that sound?"

"Uh . . . great! I'm free!" She takes a seat across the table from me under the umbrella.

"Excellent, I'll make the arrangements." With a pointed look to me she adds, "But I don't want you to think I've forgotten all the trouble you're in. The coach always turns back into a pumpkin."

I crinkle my nose. A small part of me thought she might let it go. "I know."

She smiles, satisfied with her new parenting style, and heads for the house. "Would you like a sandwich too, Morgan?" she calls before opening the door.

"No, thanks. I already ate." She waits for Mom to disappear inside before shooting me a *Who is this woman and what did she do with your mother?* glance.

"I know. I keep waiting for her to slip back to her old ways."

"You think she will?"

"I guess we'll find out," I say, munching on a carrot and fingering the padded yellow mailer. "Bring your suit?"

"You know it." She flashes me a pink strap near her neck. "I've got a lot of catching up to do. Your tan is amazing."

"Right? I hope it lasts. Hey," I say, investigating the penmanship on the address. "This isn't Darren's writing."

She leans onto the table. "You got another one?"

"Yeah, but this one's different."

I pull the tab and peek inside to find a smaller envelope. Inside that one is a stack of euros. I count it out. Six hundred.

A Post-it note is stuck to the last bill. It's written in Italian.

"Can you read that?" Morgan asks, on the edge of her seat.

I read it slowly, piecing together what I know with guesses at the words between.

"I think it says: 'Pippa, I'm sorry about everything and I want to thank you. You have helped me more than you can know. You have helped me become a better me. A thousand thanks. With love, Bruno.' "

"You can read Italian!" she squeals. "That's so unreal."

I read through the note again, gaining confidence in my interpretation.

"It's seriously pretty. Like from a board game," Morgan says, investigating the bright green bills. "Why did Bruno send you money, though?"

"I lent him some." I can't help but smile. There might be hope for him after all.

We swim for a little while, then lie out on the lawn chairs. Morgan's engrossed in some biography, and I bring out the red leather journal from my trip, opening it to the next blank page. I'd decided to write out the entire story of my summer, starting at the very beginning when my parents announced I'd be going. So far I've written up to the part where I see Darren in the metro.

My phone blares on the little table between us and we both jump. I hastily mute the ringer, then nearly drop it when I see the name.

I gasp. "It's Darren."

"WHAT?" She rotates in her chair to face me, throwing her book down. "Freaking answer it! What are you doing?"

I answer the call and swallow, talking myself into staying calm so as not to appear psycho. "Hey!" I say, excited yet relatively restrained, considering who's on the other end of the line.

"Hey, you." His familiar, rough voice melts my insides.

"How are you?" I ask, cheeks killing me from smiling so hard.

"I'm great now. You? How's your grandmother?"

"Oh," I say, my shoulders falling. I catch eyes with Morgan and her smile fades as she tries to read my face. "She passed away actually. Before I got home."

"Oh, Pippa. I'm so sorry."

My chest is tight. "But . . . how did you know something happened to her?"

"When I went to meet you, Bruno told me what was going on."

"Bruno did?" I ask, shocked. Morgan's eyes widen as she deciphers the other half of the conversation.

"Yeah, he brought me to the apartment and had me copy down your contact info since we're totally lame and never exchanged on our own."

"Totally lame," I agree. "I can't believe you guys actually conversed."

"Please, he's my new BFF." Darren cough-laughs. "So, what are you up to today?"

"Morgan and I are just hanging out by the pool."

"Oh yeah? Hey, pass the phone to her for a minute."

"To Morgan?"

"Yeah, I still need to thank her for making you that little journal thing."

"Okay . . . hang on."

I hold the phone out to her and she raises an eyebrow expertly. I mouth *he wants to talk to you* and she takes it from me.

"Hello? Yeah, I've heard a lot about you too. . . . Wha—Oh." She holds up a finger, wraps a towel around her waist and whispers, "I'll be right back," before scampering into the house.

"Do you have to take him with you?" I shout after her.

I grunt and return to my journal. I write a few lines but it's impossible to concentrate.

The back door opens again a few minutes later and I stand, fully prepared to wrestle the phone away from her. But Morgan's not standing in my backyard.

"Hey, you."

I blink. He's here. Dark-red T-shirt, brown fedora. I blink again. The corner of his mouth turns up and I take off in a sprint, fly down the stairs of the deck, and jump into his arms, which he wraps tight around me.

His hand cups the back of my head and repeatedly strokes my damp hair. Our bodies sway back and forth, and I slowly slide down until my feet touch the ground. I take a step back to study him.

"You're a hat guy again." I grin. "But, that means—" I gasp when I pull the hat off him. "Your hair! You cut it!" I reach up and rake my hand through his subdued curls, more like waves now.

"I cut it for you." His hands at my bare waist send shivers through my core.

"I liked the curls, you know."

"You thought I had a perm!" He leans his head back and laughs fully. "That's the very definition of not liking the curls."

I giggle and shrug. "They grew on me. But this can grow on me too."

I circle my arms around his middle and press my cheek against his baby-smooth face. "I'm so sorry I never got to meet you that morning." My body shudders.

"Hey," he whispers into my ear. "You don't have anything to apologize for."

"I was worried I might not see you again. And then when Gram died, I—" The threat of tears choke out my words.

"I'm so sorry." He strokes my hair again and presses his lips against my forehead.

"I can't believe you're here," I say, clasping his hand in mine. "Where were you when you left that voice mail earlier today?"

"Ah . . . I was waiting for my connection in Newark. I was supposed to fly home, but I changed my ticket for Chicago last minute. Like, seriously last minute. I was the last person on the plane before they closed the cabin door."

"Just like that?"

"Just like that," he says. "I had your address, so I crossed my fingers that you were home."

"Risky."

"Worth it, though. Here we are." He rubs his thumb along mine.

"Here we are."

We move to sit side by side on the deck and dangle our legs in the water.

"Hey," he says, waiting for me to look at him.

I smile as he leans in and presses his lips against mine. He palms the side of my face and I reach around the back of his neck, pulling him closer and hastily deepening the kiss, making up for lost time.

A little groan of relief escapes his throat. "I've been waiting for so long to do that."

"Me too."

"I missed your eyes," he says, killing me with his intense stare.

"About that. Why did you say you're afraid of green eyes?"

He chuckles. "I'm not afraid of all of them. Just yours."

"Why?"

He meets my gaze head-on and inhales deeply. "Because when you look at me, you really *look* at me, like you're actually listening and really care about what I have to say. From the first time I met you . . . I knew I was in trouble."

"I think I knew too." I lean against his shoulder, our legs entwined under the water.

"So, how did everything work out in the end? How did your parents deal with the subterfugery?" He looks behind us cautiously as if we're about to get caught breaking the rules.

"I'm pretty much grounded until further notice."

I steal a glance at the house and spot Morgan and Mom peeking through the window, but they back away as soon as I catch them. I'm surprised Mom is giving Darren and me so much time alone. *Thank you, Morgan.*

"Really? How bad could it be though, if Morgan's here?"

"Oh, well . . . they've been a little relaxed because of Gram's passing, but I've been assured once school starts my life will be all work and no play." I kick my feet under the water and watch the surface swirl.

"Well, we better take advantage." He pulls me in for another kiss and when we break apart, I'm overcome with laughter. This is *so* the opposite of how I saw my summer ending even just a few hours ago.

"You're really here. I can't get over it."

"When I called and heard your voice mail greeting this morning, something inside me just clicked. I had to see you. Today." He leans toward me until our foreheads press together, his fingertips trailing torturously slowly up and down each of my arms. "I tried all summer to talk myself out of liking you, to stay away from Cinque Terre once I knew you were there. Especially when I thought you might be with someone else. But I couldn't. I want to make this work, Pippa. I know we met for a reason." His breath is warm on my face as he whispers, "I can't *not* be with you."

I close my eyes and absorb his words. He wants to make this work. *I* want to make this work. It will. Somehow.

"You really like me that much?"

I hear him swallow. "I'm not sure *like* is a strong enough word."

I lift my chin until our lips meet in a sweet, gentle kiss. And then I ruin it when I surrender to another giggle fit.

He leans away to look at me, alarmed. "Why is that funny?"

"No no no, I'm not laughing at you." I stroke his wrist with my thumb. “It’s just . . . I actually brought a guy home from Italy. This is crazy.”

He relaxes a little. “What do you mean?”

“Remember when I told you about that list of goals Morgan had me write out at the beginning of my trip?”

“Yeah.”

“Ugh, this is going to seem so stupid to you.” I pause to get the last bit of laughter out, preparing myself for what I’m about to reveal to him. “One of my goals was to fall in love with an Italian.”

The dimples pop in his cheeks before he draws out, “Reaaally?”

“I was going to fall in love and bring him home with me when summer was over. But I just had to eat gelato *before* dinner, and there you were, throwing me off course on my first day in the country.”

Now he laughs. “So I foiled your master plan, huh?” he asks, and I nod with pouty lips. “Am I that hard to resist?” He straightens, smoothing out the front of his shirt.

“Well, you kept popping up everywhere! How was I supposed to fall in love with anyone else?” My hands are shaking so I slide them underneath me. “It was a silly game anyway.”

“I don’t—wait.” Color spreads through his cheeks to the tips of his ears. “Are you saying you’re in love with me?”

Is that was I was saying? Am I in love with him?

I’m mute. All I can do is stare at him, soak him up.

Darren gets a spacey look on his face as he pats at the surface of the water with his feet, mumbling something that sounds like, “Oh, my parents are gonna love this story.”

"What?"

He ignores me and looks behind us. "That's *the* journal on your chair, right?" He holds out a hand, demanding to see it. "Show me this list."

I grab it and turn directly to the page with the list.

He takes it from me and holds out his hand again. "Pen?"

I eye him curiously but he doesn't say anything, so I hand the pen over too.

He makes a humming sound in his throat as he studies my handwriting, then says, "*Ciao.*" When I don't respond, he says it again and holds out his hand for me to shake. "*Sono Darren.*"

My eyes widen when I realize what he's doing. "*Ciao. Sono Pippa.*"

He squeezes my hand. "*Che bel nome, Pippa.*"

I blush because I can't help myself. He thinks my name is pretty. And I forgot how hot it is when he speaks Italian. "*Grazie.*"

"*Arrivederci.*"

I wave as if we really are going to part ways. "*Arrivederci.*"

Darren clicks the pen into action and strikes through "Have a conversation with someone in only Italian." It wasn't exactly my original plan, and it's elementary at best, but it had a beginning, middle, and end. And summer's not over yet, so I'm counting it.

The pen touches the paper again at the bottom of the page and I freeze as he draws a slow, thick line through "Fall in love with an Italian."

I snatch the book from him and scan the list of my goals. "Why did you do that?"

He brings my face closer with a finger under my chin, diverting my attention to him, and gives me a swift but tender kiss.

"Because lucky for you," he says, lips still brushing against mine, "I was born in Rome."

I gasp and part my lips to respond, but he covers my mouth with his and slips his hands around my bare back. As I glide my hands into his thick hair, he pulls me up until I'm straddling his lap. He leans forward, holding me tight against him, and we crash into the pool, our lips never pulling apart.

Goals update:

* ~~Don't get arrested~~
* Don't make a fool out of myself in public—FAILED
* ~~Get my picture taken at the Colosseum~~
* ~~Find random souvenir for Morgan~~
* ~~Get a makeover~~
* ~~See Pompeii~~
* ~~Swim in the Mediterranean Sea~~
* ~~Have a conversation with someone in only Italian—~~ FAILED
* ~~Eat a whole pizza in one sitting~~
* ~~Fall in love with an Italian—FAILED~~

THANK YOU:

God, for filling my life with a variety of loving people and for this unshakable desire to create.

Josh, for your love, patience, support, and for dealing with my many whims. I love you more every day. Mom, for always encouraging my artsy side and all those trips to the library. Dad, for setting such a great example of hard work and generosity. To both parents for the insane amount of love and confidence. Grandma Rosie, for your eagerness to read more of my pages. You'll never know just how much your excitement kept me going. My husband's incredible family, Bill, Cindy, Jon, and Kelly, for welcoming and loving me. I couldn't have dreamed up a better family to marry into. Seth and Angela, for traveling to Italy with us on the adventure that inspired so much of this book. We can make it through anything after sharing a room with four twin beds crammed together.

Marietta Zacker, my amazing agent, for picking me out of the slush. Your enthusiasm for Pippa and your faith in me mean the world. I'm so thankful for you and all that you do!

My editor, Caroline Abbey, for taking a chance on me. Thank you for every heart and smiley face alongside your spot-on suggestions. I will never stop telling you how awesome you are!

The wonderful team at Bloomsbury. I'm thrilled to be part of this new line, If Only!

Katie M. Stout, for the countless hours of brainstorming, critiques, friendship, and squees. SU SU! Kristi Chestnutt, who can talk anyone off the ledge, you are an invaluable critique partner, encourager, and friend. Get *out*! Amy Sonnichsen, for the inspiration, direction, and friendship. Mari Ferrer, for our brainstorming/writing cupcake outings. Joy Preble, for all the writing dates, advice, and encouragement. Maria Cari Soto, for your beta reading expertise and our bookstore/movie escapades. Kim Franklin, for the fangirl rainbows!

So many others have influenced where I am at this exact moment in my writing life: Lindsay Arrant, Tanner Jones (*waves to Holly*), Amy Rose Thomas, Heather Dettmers, Sarah Ahiers, Colene Murphy, Abby Minard, Deana Barnhart, J. R. Johansson, Karen Akins, Kiki Hamilton, Amy Fellner Dominy, Lydia Kang, and my debut buddies in the Class of 2k14 (*waves to Lauren Magaziner*).

My muses: Mindy Gledhill, for your perfect album, *Anchor*. I like to think your music is in Pippa's head while she travels throughout Italy, as it was always in mine when I was writing her. Darren Criss, for your voice and your crazy curly hair. Michael Giacchino, for composing such moving and inspirational film scores. Switchfoot, my favorite band of all time, whose music has been there for me no matter the circumstance. "Love is the movement."

Kristin Rae was born and raised in Texas, though her accent would suggest otherwise. She started writing her first novel during her graduation ceremony from Texas A&M and realized too late she may have studied the wrong thing. A former figure-skating coach, LEGO merchandiser, and photographer, she's now happy to create stories while pretending to ignore the carton of gelato in the freezer. Kristin lives in Houston with her husband and their two boxers.

www.kristinrae.com

WANT MORE OF WHAT YOU CAN'T HAVE?

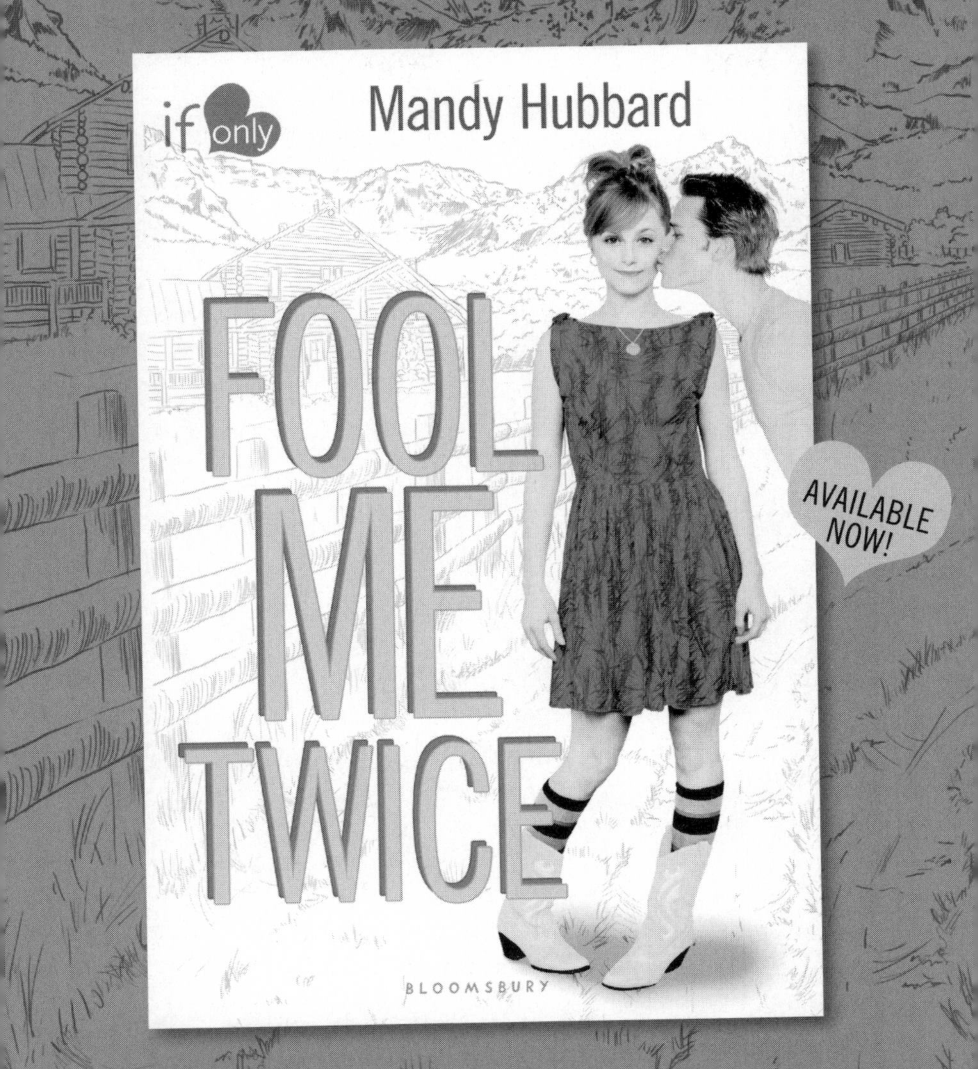

Read on for a glimpse at another romance filled with gorgeous cowboys, a touch of amnesia, and an epic revenge plot against an ex-boyfriend!

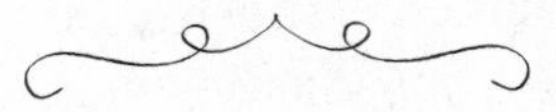

“I pledge allegiance, to the flag . . .”

I stiffen, my grip on the pitchfork, tightening so hard the wood bites into the still-developing calluses on my palms. The voice behind me is the very one I’ve waited to hear for the last week. . . . But he’s *mocking me.*

I slice a glare in Landon’s direction. He’s standing in the entry to the empty stall, his lanky, all-too-muscular body a silhouette against the fluorescent fixture hanging behind him. The dust kicked up by my work swirls in the light hugging his body.

I wish I could make out his expression, to figure out if it’s the same sneer he gave me that first day back at school last fall. When he broke my heart.

I smirk, saying, “Ha, ha, ha. You must think you’re super clever.”

"Actually, I do." He puts a hand to his heart. "You really wound my ego."

I roll my eyes. " 'No tears, please. It's a waste of good suffering.' "

He drops his hand back to his side. "Are you quoting *Hell-raiser*?"

I blink. "Um, no?" I turn back to the pitchfork, hoping he buys it, and toss another scoop into the overflowing wheelbarrow. I should have emptied it already, but this is the last stall.

"Since when do you like classic horror movies?" His voice has that old familiar drawl to it, that same twang I loved when he whispered to me, his breath hot on my ear. His family is from Texas. They moved to Washington State six years ago, but he's never let go of the accent.

"Since when do you care what I like?" I scoop at a pile of manure near his toes, daring him to stand still as it slides dangerously close to his battered Justin cowboy boots. He doesn't move. "I mean, I was *just* getting used to the silent treatment."

"Meh, I got bored," he says.

Bored. I scowl. "I'm sure there's a *real* flag somewhere in desperate need of your allegiance."

I scoop up another forkful of soiled bedding. Maybe he thought he'd get away with just waltzing up, that I'd somehow forget what he did, like I'd fall at his feet at the first sign of his interest.

When I look up at him again, he hasn't budged, he's just chewing on his lip. He licks his lip, and for a second I forget I'm staring, thinking about how it felt when we'd kissed, when he'd traced his tongue across *my* lips. When he grins, I realize he's caught me.

Ugh. I should not be thinking of how good he is at kissing. Actually, scratch that. I should be thinking of how good he is at kissing *other girls.* That made it pretty easy to stay angry. Like he did in the halls the first day of school last fall. I wore this adorable Zac Brown Band T-shirt because he said they were his favorite band, and I was practically bursting with excitement to see him after a few days apart . . . and then I saw him, but it didn't go the way I'd pictured.

He was leaning in to kiss *her,* while I stood there dumbfounded. He knew exactly what he was doing because midway through their steamy makeout session, he saw me staring, a strange gleam in his eyes as he watched the way I unraveled. It was like he enjoyed watching me shatter, just like little boys love burning ants with magnifying glasses.

And it sucks to be the ant. I am *so over* being the ant.

"Nah, you're a little more . . . lively."

I snort, shaking my head. Lively. Yeah, I could show him lively.

"What?" he asks, crossing his arms and leaning against the doorway. The effort makes his muscles bulge. He probably practices the move in his mirror in the hopes of using it to ensnare his next summer fling.

I toss the pitchfork onto the heaping wheelbarrow. "Just leave me alone, okay?" I grab the cart's handle and yank.

But he doesn't move, and I back right up into him, our bodies colliding. Instead of stepping aside, he grabs my elbows to keep me from knocking him completely over, and then actually removes me from the stall and slides me into the aisle, like I'm a kitten that's run into his path.

Then he turns and easily pulls the overladen cart over the bump, onto the smooth cement of the aisle. The stall door screeches as he rolls it shut.

"I still have to put pellets in there," I start.

"I'll get it."

I stare at him, unwilling to believe he'd volunteer to take on even a tiny portion of my workload without wanting something in return. "Well, you just go zero to sixty in about five seconds, don't you?"

He flashes me a wolfish smile, the one that makes him seem half-dangerous, half-sexy. But now I know what really lurks beneath all those muscles and cowboy swagger, and his smile is no longer so attractive.

"What's that supposed to mean?" he asks, tipping the rim of his cowboy hat back far enough that I can see into his intense brown eyes. He's . . . irritated.

Good.

I narrow my own eyes and match his look. "The silent treatment, to mockery, to doing me favors," I say, ticking them off on my fingers. "Before you turned on the roller coaster, you could have at least warned me to keep my hands and feet in the car at all times."

He huffs. "Can't a guy do a girl a favor?"

"No." I laugh, and not in a pretty way. "Not you, anyway."

Dang. I had wanted to be aloof. Unaffected. I'm screwing it up.

He shrugs, totally unbothered by my visceral response. "Fine then. Do it yourself," he says. But he doesn't move out of my way or open the stall door either. Instead, his eyes sweep over my now-dirty polo shirt, down my legs, and then back up again before he smirks. "What's with the getup?"

I grit my teeth and check out my outfit. I'm in my Serenity Ranch polo, as required, along with my jean shorts, but I have lime-green leggings underneath, and my cowboy boots don't match any of my clothes—they're powder blue. It's like my outfit is a mullet—business on the top, party on the bottom.

"Can't wear plain old shorts in a saddle, you know that," I say, like he's being stupid. "It pinches."

"Right. And regular jeans would just be too . . ."

"Boring?" I say, throwing his words back at him.

"Uh-huh, and being a freak show—"

My anger explodes. "What do you want, Landon? Hurting me last year wasn't enough and now you've gotta waltz in here and insult me?"

Crap. I wasn't planning to admit how much he hurt me. I'm ruining all of this. Bailey's going to laugh me out of our cabin later.

In response, he crosses his arms and waits as if he was the one to ask the question and he's expecting an answer, but I have nothing else to say. And then he just shrugs and walks away, whistling an all-too-familiar tune.

Oh say can you seeeeeeee.

Ugh.

EMMA

"*Celebrity Seeker* claims that I'm dating Troy again," I say as I skim the pages of the gossip magazine. Tabloids are scattered like fall leaves all over Rachel's bedroom, and I want to rake them up and stuff them into trash bags. "How stupid do they think I am?"

I haven't talked to Troy since he shattered my car window three months ago. Rachel doesn't know anything about that, though. No one does, and I have to keep it that way.

"I'd feel bad for you, Emma, but some of us don't have any guys to ignore." Rachel has her back to me, admiring the collection of men who cover her otherwise lavender walls. Most of the space is taken up by carefully cut out magazine pages featuring a male model she calls The Bod. "And worse, the only guy I'm dying to date doesn't know I exist. Literally."

"I doubt he's worth dying for," I say. "If a boy looks like he belongs in a museum, there's a pretty good chance his head is solid marble."

Rachel huffs at me, offended, as if she actually knows him. Or even his name.

I leave her bouncy desk chair—great for girls with energy to burn—to study a close-up of The Bod's face. "At the very least," I go on with a teasing tone, "those puffy lips are airbrushed."

Chancing a peek at Rachel, I find her bright-green eyes narrowed at me. "You know," she says, "for someone who's on *People* magazine's Most Beautiful Young Celebrities list, you're awfully critical of beautiful people."

I suppose being my best friend for over a decade gives her the right to call me out on things like this. And Rachel is all about straight talk and honesty, which is usually a good thing.

My life doesn't always feel genuine, even when cameras aren't rolling.

Whenever I return to my hometown in Fayetteville, Arkansas, I expect the world to somehow seem real again, but work still has a way of taking over. Today especially, because a full five minutes hasn't passed without me checking my e-mail. The final details for the new TV series I'm starting next month are being sent out today, including the casting choices.

The scent of coconut-and-lime body spray wafts toward me. Rachel snaps her fingers in front of my face. "Are you even listening?"

Yes and no. She's been going on about the endless charms of her paperweight soul mate. "All I'm saying is that guys who look like The Bod are usually the most overrated gimmicks on the planet," I tell her. "And crappy boyfriend material. Trust me."

I hear a screen door squeak open, and a canary-like chirp belonging to Rachel's mom instantly echoes in the house. Trina enters the room and says, "Oh, Emma honey, have *we* got a big surprise!"

For as long as I can remember, Trina has dressed like she's forty-going-on-sixteen. At the moment she's in black skinny jeans and a plum tee with a glittery fleur-de-lis stretched way too tight over her five-thousand-dollar chest. Trina's curly platinum hair matches her daughter's, but everything about Rachel's beauty is perfectly natural.

"You're just gonna die!" Trina adds.

My mother is right behind Trina and shoots her a *please stop* look, but I seem to be the only one who notices. Typical for her, Mom is wearing a white button-down shirt and gray tweed slacks, looking like she walked out of a Neiman Marcus window display. She wouldn't be caught dead in Trina's leopard print stilettos. But despite being polar opposites, they've been going out for regular lunches since Rachel and I first met in a community acting class.

I sometimes wonder if Mom only does it to stay on the good side of a careless gossip who might be too close to me. Or maybe Mom just wants to keep up on what's *really* going on in my personal life. She likely gets more from Trina, via Rachel, than she does from me.

Trina is still grinning so widely that every tooth in her mouth is showing, but my mom's smile seems fake, and her lashes are batting way too fast to be simple blinks. "I just heard from the studio," she says.

I only stare at her for a second. "But . . . why wasn't I on the e-mail list?"

"I'll forward you a copy, Emma. I always do."

That's not the point, and she knows it. I had asked her to tell the studio to put me on the direct list, and she obviously didn't. Like a lot of parents in this business, my mom became my manager when I landed my first big job, so *everything* goes through her. But now that I'm finally an official adult, I can hire a new management team if I want to, a team who would at least agree that I should know—before the rest of the world—what's going on in my career. Like me, Mom must realize this isn't working anymore, but she hasn't even mentioned the possibility of a new manager, like it isn't something I'd consider anyway.

As if she could never imagine me making a mature decision without her.

Mom tacks on a sigh. "We should head home so we can discuss this casting."

"I want to stay. Just tell me what the e-mail says."

"I'm dying to know too," Rachel adds. "We've been waiting all day."

Trina whispers something to Rachel, then Rachel looks at me with her mouth half open, her eyes bulging. "Holy crap, Emma! You're gonna FREAK!"

Perfect. Now even Rachel knows before I do.

"Can we borrow this room for a minute?" I ask.

Trina and Rachel appear disappointed by the request but finally step into the hallway, whispering again. My mom shuts the bedroom door and pulls out her phone. "I had hoped we were past this nonsense," she mutters, "but you won't believe who's playing—"

I snatch the phone from her hand, open the e-mail from the studio, and read out loud. "Executive Producer Steve McGregor will launch the production of *Coyote Hills* in Tucson, Arizona, the second week of July . . . table read . . . camera tests . . . I'll go back to that later . . . Okay, here it is: one male lead is still in negotiations." Ugh. This is practically code for *casting problems.* "The remaining cast is as follows: Eden will be played by Emma Taylor. The role of Kassidy will be played by Kimmi Weston." I have no idea who Kimmi is, so I glance at my mom before going on. She's never heard of her either. "And the role of Bryce will be played by Brett Crawford."

I drop the phone.

I want to stomp on it. Scream at it!

Or possibly hug it and jump up and down.

I'm not sure which yet.

"You see?" Mom says. "This is why I wanted to tell you privately."

My arms are as limp as overcooked fettuccini, but I manage to scoop up the phone. "Okay, yeah. Him," I say, going for indifference. "A bit of a shock, but whatever."

Mom puts a hand on her hip. *Here we go.* "Emma, you know how tired I am of dealing with high-publicity romances," she begins, in full-blown managerial mode. "The last two years have been ridiculous, putting out one tabloid fire after another. You're at a crossroads here and have a chance to prove yourself as a serious actress. Brett Crawford is the worst sort of boy for you to get involved with, so don't even consider dating him."

Does she really think *I* would want to go through all that crap again? On-set romances are usually total disasters, and not just for me. Until last spring I was on a primetime drama that, despite sky-high ratings, was cancelled due to conflict on the set. I played the president's daughter, but the actor playing the president was caught having a real-life relationship with the actress who played the first lady—and unfortunately, she also happened to be our executive producer's wife. It wasn't pretty.

And it eventually shut the entire show down.

That was when Steve McGregor, the do-it-all executive producer/creator/director of *Coyote Hills*, called my agent to ask if he could meet with me to discuss his new project. It was the very day the cancellation of *The First Family* was announced, and I haven't received a bigger compliment in the six years of my career.

McGregor is responsible for more hit dramas than any producer in television—his shows don't even require pilots. I think his methods are brilliant, but some people say he's a nutcase. For one thing, he's already slated to direct about one-third of the first season, which either means the guy really is insane or he plans to live with a caffeine drip attached to his arm. McGregor is also notoriously secretive about who he's considering for his cast or I would have already known about Brett. And he rarely takes time to screen-test a pair of actors—who he's already familiar with—for chemistry. But I've worked with enough cinematic geniuses to know there's no use questioning them. You just go along.

"Listen, Mom," I say, trying to hide the likelihood that the pizza I had for lunch is about to land on her Jimmy Choo pumps. "This isn't a big deal. I had a silly celebrity crush on Brett when I was, like, eight." Well, it started about then, and went on and on. But his growing reputation as a guy who never commits, just loves whoever he's with at the moment, has definitely dampened my enthusiasm. "That's ancient history. I'm totally over him."

Totally may be pushing it. I might still watch his movies, a lot, and rewind certain parts that I think he's especially amazing in. But is it so wrong that I think he's the best actor of my generation? Isn't it natural that I would be attracted to someone with so much talent?

Mom gives me a thin, cynical smile. "I noticed just this

morning that your laptop wallpaper is yet another picture of Brett Crawford."

Yeah, well, about that . . . I also just like to *look* at him.

"The only time it's been otherwise in the last ten years," Mom goes on, "is when you've been dating some other Hollywood hot-shot who thought nothing of dragging your name through the mud."

Why did she have to bring *them* into this? "It isn't my fault that they all cheated on me. *I* didn't do anything wrong."

Mom's icy expression melts a little, and I realize I rarely see this softer look on her face anymore. She has brown eyes, mine are blue, but we share the same dark hair and small-framed bodies. I've never felt like she's forced me into a life I don't want—I'm the one who got the lead in a first-grade play and begged her to let me become a real actress—but it feels as if she sometimes forgets that I'm not just a client.

It's all business, all the time.

"I know that," Mom says. "And your dad and your closest friends know that. But the majority of the world looks at a girl who dates this same type of guy over and over, as someone who has very poor judgment. It just can't happen again."

How could she possibly think I pick losers on purpose?

When I first met Troy, who was my costar during the last season of *The First Family*, he was always smiling, laughing, joking around with me, surprising me with flowers or a dinner overlooking the ocean. But it isn't exactly easy dating professional actors—guys who can fake their way through anything.

I look my mom square in the eyes and say, "I get it, okay? I'm totally done with Hollywood guys. Can we move on now?"

Someone sneezes. Rachel and Trina are just outside the door

and have probably been there this entire time, listening. Mom breathes a familiar sigh of irritation. "We'll talk more when you get home," she says. "And perhaps you can find a new wallpaper for your laptop?"

I nod and return her phone. "Don't worry. I'll be . . ." Fine is what I'd intended to say, but a vision of Brett Crawford sitting next to me in a cast chair—with his perfect surfer tan, blond hair that always falls in front of his eyes, and a smile that puts a hummingbird in my stomach—enters my mind, and I can't speak.

"You'll be *amazing*," Mom says with a squeeze of my shoulder. "Steve McGregor didn't even consider another actress for this part, and he always knows what he's doing. You just need to focus on your career, not boys."

Mom leaves the room, and Rachel soon takes her place. She shuts the door again and says, "Are you freaking out or what? *Brett Crawford?* This is fate!"

"It's *ill*-fated, you mean." I collapse into her bed pillows and throw one over my face. I've had several chances to meet Brett. A few times, I've even been in the same room as him. But besides the fact that he's more than two years older and would have only thought of me as a silly little girl before now, I've intentionally avoided Brett because I don't want to know the real him. "I have a perfectly happy relationship with my laptop wallpaper version of Brett Crawford, thank you very much."

As things are, we never fight, he never cheats on me, and he doesn't . . . scare me.

"Brett was in television for the first several years of his career, so why would he want to come back?" I add. "He's been doing *great* in big-budget movies. He should stay where he is."

Rachel plops into her desk chair. "Don't you keep up with anything? It's amazing how much more I know about your world than you do."

It's not such a bad thing that Rachel always knows more gossip than I do; Hollywood is practically her religion. When we met, Rachel had already been doing commercials since she was a baby in a Downy-soft blanket, so she was quick to make herself my mentor. But a few years later, when we were twelve, we both went to an open audition for what turned out to be an Oscar-winning film, and I got the part.

It was a lucky break. Right time, right place, right look.

Since then, I've done whatever I could to get Rachel auditions for other major projects, but nothing has worked out. And tension builds with every failed attempt. A few months ago she straight out told me, "How did this even happen? You have *everything* I want."

Why doesn't she get that I wish she had it all too?

No matter how different things sometimes feel between us, though, one thing stays the same: Rachel is the only friend I have who's been with me all along—the only friend who keeps my feet planted firmly in the dark, rich soil of Arkansas. Even when I'm dressed from head to toe in Prada, with red carpet beneath me and cameras flashing from every other direction, Rachel is a constant reminder of where I came from. Who I really am.

I blow the silver fringe from her pillow off my face. "Are you talking about Brett's girl issues?" I ask. "Because, crazy enough, being a player only seems to *help* a guy's career."

"But it's more than just that," Rachel says. "According to insiders, Brett's been a pain to work with on his last few films. He misses call times and keeps the cast and crew waiting for hours." Rachel sounds like a newscaster as she presents a tattered tabloid as evidence. "Critics say he's lost his passion for acting, that he'll be nothing but a washed-up child star if he doesn't do something quick to redeem himself. So his management team must think television is his best bet. It's worked for a ton of other actors."

I've read some of this, but not all. "Everyone knows what a great actor Brett is—he's been nominated for major awards since he was *five,*" I say. "He's probably just burned out, and McGregor is smart enough to realize he'll push through it."

"Yeah, I guess I can see that. But back to the girl issues," Rachel replies and tacks on a sly smile. "You know what Brett's problem is? He just hasn't dated the *right* girl yet."

I toss a pillow at her. "The last thing I want to be is Brett Crawford's next 'throwaway party favor,' so don't look at *me*," I say, then I make a silent promise to put soap in my mouth for quoting a tabloid. Reporters tell plenty of lies about my own life, so I question everything I read, but I've seen enough myself to know that every once in a while they're surprisingly dead-on. In their pursuit of a quick, juicy story to sell, however, gossipmongers often miss the details that could *really* damage someone. "It's just that this is all sort of sad," I go on. "Brett has always been someone safe for me to crush on, but now—"

Rachel cuts me off with laughter. "Oh, please! You *know* what's gonna happen. Brett will fall head over heels in love and change his whole life to be with you. So just flirt a little and see where things go."

"No way," I reply. She might understand if I told her how bad things got with Troy, but I can't take the chance of Rachel telling

Trina, who would go straight to my mom. Then Mom would freak out even more about me living on my own in Arizona, which is something I've had to fight for every day for the past few months. "I just need to get over Brett before we start working together. That's all. Or he'll be . . . well, a bit of a distraction."

"More like a tall, beautiful problem with a killer smile." Rachel turns back to her wall to swoon over The Bod in a western-themed cologne ad for Armani. "I can only imagine how distracted I'd be if I ever worked with *my* dream guy. Distracted by his perfectly toned arms, and his amazing green eyes, and his luscious mocha hair, and . . . gosh, I better not talk him up *too* much, or you'll want to start a collection of your own. But The Bod is all mine, got it?"

I probably sound just as ridiculous as Rachel does when I talk about Brett—I mean, when I *used* to talk about Brett—but I laugh anyway. "Yep, he's all yours," I reply. "Down to his last curly eyelash."

I have to agree with Rachel on one thing, though: The Bod, whoever he is, makes leather cowboy chaps look seriously hot.